Colin's Conundrum

Colin's Conundrum

The Victorians Book 3

Simone Beaudelaire

Thank you to Sandra Martinez, who has been there from the beginning. Muchas Gracias. And to my husband, Edwin Stark. Te amo, mi esposo. Thank you both for not letting me give up, no matter how the darkness falls on my heart. Without you both, I probably wouldn't still be here. Finally, thanks to the publication team at Next Chapter. We're in this together, and I'm glad of it.

Dedication

This book is dedicated to those who struggle out of darkness into light.

Prologue

"ENTLEMEN." Colin Butler, Viscount Gelroy, addressed the ragged band of farmers gathered around him.

Nods greeted him, but excessive displays of obeisance had long since collapsed.

"How goes it?" he asked, stomach jumping. *We're so close to disaster. Another month, Lord, please. And another idea. Any idea.*

A blond man in his early fifties, his hair streaked with silver, his face with dirt, scratched a cheek that seemed too hollow for his hearty frame and answered, "It could be worse, my lord. The red fescue is coming up nicely, along with clover and wildflowers. The fields look right pretty, and they have a chance to heal now."

Colin sighed. "Well, that's good, at least, Bullock. I appreciate how all of you agreed to this measure, despite the consequences of no money to pay the rents that go to taxes and the estate's debts. It won't be the first time, and at any point, the creditors may come after us."

"What choice did we have?" a small, rat-like man with a sharp nose and prominent front teeth piped in a voice too high for his age. "As depleted as everything is, it's not like we would have gotten any crops to speak of. We still have our animals and our gardens to sustain us. Are you sure, my lord, that you're willing to suffer the consequences of defaulting again?"

"What else can I do? If we plant, nothing will grow. No money will come of our labors, and the end will be the same. If the creditors come, if I'm taken to a debtors' gaol, you'll have to leave, to seek employment elsewhere. Our estate, our land, will be abandoned and we'll scatter. That's the likeliest outcome, yet I see no other choice. We cannot plant."

1

The others muttered, and Colin could see the despair and exhausted rebellion in their eyes.

He sighed. "I don't like to think that we shall finally fail, after all these years of toil."

"No one wants to," Bullock said. "Do you have any ideas, my lord, to create income without crops?"

Colin shook his head. "Not a one. I wish I did." *I also wish you'd stop calling me 'lord.' I hardly deserve it. Since inheriting the damned title, I've accomplished precious little to improve anything.* He lifted his gaze to meet those of his tenants. Gray, blue and brown eyes all met his with the same expression of dogged determination paired with far too little hope. *They're willing to die for this land, and they know they probably will. How many years has it taken from them, from me?* Already, though only thirty-two, silver-streaked his temples and threaded through the darkness of his hair. Worry creased the corners of his mouth and crinkled his eyes. *I could be a decade older.* "I would appreciate a suggestion even if it's idiotic. Can anyone think of anything?"

The men turned to look at one another. Shoulders lifted in defeated shrugs.

After a long, exhausted moment, Bullock spoke. "What about animals, my lord?"

"Animals?" Colin lowered his eyebrows and regarded his foreman.

"Aye. My daughter's ewe had twin lambs, and my old bull managed to produce a calf. Fescue ain't bad grazing, and the sheep love the clover."

The idea wended its way slowly through Colin's mind. "Animals. Hmmm. How many animals are there?"

"I have three goats, two sheep plus the lambs and a bull," Bullock said. "Mind you, he's a stringy old thing, but he's still potent, as Farrell's cow can attest." The weakly bawdy jest produced a round of tired chuckles. "But my paddocks are falling down, and I can't spare a single board to replace them. Not if I want to patch that hole in my wall."

And they'll have no money to buy supplies. The wall can only take so much mud patching before it's more patch than wall.

"My chickens have been breeding like mad," Billings volunteered. "I've made a hobby of them since my wife passed, and they're thriving."

"Don't forget," Jones piped up, "the ducks in the pond have so many ducklings, it's a trouble not to step on the poor things."

From the beleaguered crowd, a mad plan began to hatch.

"Are you suggesting," Colin asked at last, "that we turn the fallow fields into a huge grazing pasture?"

"Aye," Farrell said quickly. "The breeding season ain't over yet. Maybe we can sell critters at market. They'll help the land heal too, they will."

"Or," he said, speaking without thought, "we could take them to London. Country-bred animals command higher prices in the city."

A murmur greeted him.

"That might just do the trick," Bullock said thoughtfully. "If we can sell the chickens and ducks at midsummer and the lambs and geese in fall, it might not cover the entire cost of taxes and debts, but could it be enough?"

It won't, he thought, but then, a newspaper article flitted across Colin's mind. *Pesadilla is retiring from racing. Why did that stick with me? Something about his owner... about a favor I forgot to call in... Animals, hmmm.* "Perhaps. You pose an interesting notion, gentlemen. I think there's merit here. Maybe we won't lose our situation after all. I need to head to London one last time, to make a few arrangements, and then I'll be back. In the meanwhile, feel free to move your animals to the fields."

Nods and grins greeted his announcement. *We'll not see prosperity in our lifetimes, but maybe these men can leave their children more than mere survival.*

Chapter 1

 OLIN patted the neck of his ancient horse. "Poor Stormcloud," he murmured to the beast. "You're done in. We'll have to stop soon."

The horse snorted in response, shaking its silver mane.

"I know you've been a gray all your life, friend," he told the animal as they crunched side by side through the undergrowth. "You worked hard during my father's time and quite a bit of mine. Now, with that sway-backed gait and your sore feet, you look very much like the old man you are. Let's just take it easy, shall we? I know life is waiting for me, but surely nothing will go horribly wrong in my absence. Bullock is perfectly capable, and my tenants all know what they need to do. They're going to be fine. Meanwhile, I can enjoy these ancient woods one last time before I settle in to work hard for the rest of my life."

He frowned at the melancholy turn his thoughts never would stop taking.

"As for you, Stormcloud, this is your last journey as a beast of burden. My friend Christopher has promised to find a nice, quiet place for you to live out your remaining days, with better feed and more congenial company than me."

The horse turned to look at him with what appeared for all the world to be a sour expression.

"Sorry, friend," he said with a bitter chuckle. "I'm in a poor state today. Too much has gone wrong in my life, and I can't feign hope anymore. Bear with me. Your toil will soon be done."

Feeling ridiculous, he fell silent, listening to the calls of birds and the buzzing of insects. A breeze stirred the leaves of the ancient trees and set them all whispering.

His worn boots crunched softly in the leaf litter. The saddle creaked on the horse's back, though his small pack constituted its only load. *Everything I own is failing, and I can't replace anything,* he thought. As though in response, a cool breeze sprang up, blowing a puff of tree-scented air into his face. He inhaled deeply. *Fresh air is free. Friendship is free. Hard work is free. Life goes on, Colin. Never forget that.*

Squinting up through the trees, he took in the angle of the sun. *Keep heading east. Sun at your back. It's getting late. Maybe there will be a comfortable barn without angry dogs ahead. I hope so. It's sure I won't make London today.*

A sense of difference slowly registered on Colin. A soft rustling of leaves paired with quiet piping that did not sound like larks. *That's not birdsong. What is it?* Colin moved forward along the trail. The horse's hooves crunched in the dry leaf fragments, wafting a scent of last winter's decay to clash with the fresh leaves, grass and flowers. *Always something to bring a fellow back to reality,* he thought. *Spring may be a time of hope, but always winter waits just beyond the horizon, poised to sink claws and fangs into anyone who dares believe too much in those promises.*

"Goodness, you're moody," he told himself aloud. Up ahead, the soft piping stopped.

"Who goes there," a voice called, drawing Colin's attention upward into the impenetrable canopy of a sturdy oak. Though he could see nothing, the sound reminded him of a youth, perhaps a young boy poised on the brink of adolescence. *Even when I was so young, did I ever sound that carefree?*

"Are you going to ask me to stand and deliver?" he quipped back, amusement tugging the corner of his mouth. "I haven't much to offer, save a worn-out old horse and an empty leather pocket."

The leaves rustled and the branches shook. "I'm no highwayman," the disembodied voice replied. "Since when do they climb trees?"

He laughed at the youth's tone of irrefutable logic. "I have a friend whose wife is from India. She says leopards hide in trees and drop down on the unsuspecting prey below. If beasts can do it, why not highwaymen?"

A trilling laugh drew an answering tingle from Colin's insides. *But surely that's a...* His thought cut off as a voluptuous golden figure dropped from a low branch onto the path before him. The horse snorted at the unexpected appearance of this seeming apparition of spring, but being old and tired, he did not react in any other way.

Colin, on the other hand, experienced an immediate and visceral reaction that began in his guts and radiated outward and downward until his every hair stood erect and his manhood showed signs of following suit.

Dear Lord, what a beauty. From her disheveled golden hair to the tips of her bare toes, she burst on his senses like sunlight through forest branches, calling to mind the legends of the fair folk and the nature spirits said to haunt the wild places of England. Though his rational mind shut down his musing in an instant, his tongue uttered a bit of nonsense that seemed to fit the moment. "'How now, Spirit. Whither wander you?'"

The head tilted to one side, sending a shower of loose golden locks to pool and cascade over her shoulder. "'Either I mistake your shape and making quite,'" she quoted back at him, "'or else you are that shrewd and knavish sprite call'd Robin Goodfellow.'"

Her return of quote for quote left him blinking. He drew in air and his lungs fought the mundaneness of such an action. "'Thou speakst aright. I am that very wanderer of the night.'"

She beamed, showing white teeth that overlapped charmingly in the front. "Well, then, Puck," she continued, dropping the Shakespeare in favor of common speech, "what brings you to these parts? Oberon and Titania have no plans to revel in woods so close to our sleepy little village."

"Just a traveler passing through, sprite," Colin admitted, "and not a very interesting one. But tell me, what town is it?"

Her grin turned to a wry twisting of lips. "I do hope you're not lost. The path you were following is used more by deer than men." She turned and scanned the flattened undergrowth behind them, as though it would answer some question for her. "Well, if you continue this way, you'll end up reaching the pond." She gestured vaguely to the south before turning back his direction. "The mill is there, to be sure, and you can reach civilization that way, but if you'd rather be more direct, walk with me. The charming village of Loughton lies straight ahead, just through the trees. There is an inn there."

Slowly, Colin's senses were returning to him. "So you would consent to guide me then?" he asked, noting her archaically formal speech pattern and imitating it.

"I suppose I must," she said with a dramatic show of suffering. "Poor Puck. If I don't show you the way to town, the fairies will certainly carry you off to their revels, given you seem to know all their names. They'll transform you into a changeling and make you consort to a fairy princess."

You are the fairy princess, sweet, Colin thought, once more eyeing the vision of nature's loveliness brought to life. "Well, then, I would thank you for your assistance," he said, "but are you certain it's wise for you to be in the woods alone? Unless you're truly a fairy, you might be in some danger out here. I'm harmless, but what if some other fellow wandered into the wood and found you?"

"Far more danger in town than here," she muttered, her grin fading. Or at least, that's what Colin thought she said. Clearly, she didn't mean the comment for his interpretation. "Come along, Puck. I know I'm safe from you, mischievous spirit." She gestured forward and began walking in the direction she'd indicated, leaving the trail and crunching through the undergrowth.

Interesting. Sticks and leaves must be digging into her bare feet, but she shows no sign of discomfort. "Do you have a name, lass, or shall I call you Titania?" he asked her, tugging on the reins to urge the horse along. Stormcloud released a grumpy snort and began to step delicately onto the low groundcover, as though it feared soiling its iron shoes.

The girl gave an unladylike snort at his quip. "I would prefer Titania," she admitted, "but no one I know would allow me such a title. I'm actually called Daisy Granger."

"It's a pleasure to make your acquaintance," Colin told her.

"Likewise. It's rare to meet anyone who knows Shakespeare so well. And are you really called Robin Goodfellow?"

The absurdity of the exchange tickled Colin's sense of humor, and he couldn't help emitting a bark of rusty-sounding laughter. "Sorry, Miss Granger, no. Colin Butler at your service." He deliberately omitted his title—*Damned little good it's done me to have it*—and waited to see if she would react.

Miss Granger turned her head and shoulders to give him a quick and considering glance. "Mr. Butler, eh? Are you a butler? And here you were presenting yourself to be a fairy."

He chuckled. "No, ma'am. A butler in name only." *More's the pity. Honest work and far fewer impossible decisions.* He tugged the horse forward again, drawing along beside her in the spaces where the trees allowed such a movement, following closely behind when they did not. "It's a lovely day, isn't it?" he asked, then frowned at the banality of the comment.

"Indeed," the girl agreed. "Spring is my favorite time of year."

You look like spring brought to life. Damnation, my life is unfair. If I were a humbler man, I could court this lovely lass. If I had anything to spare, I could offer carte blanche, but I have nothing, save a few moments of conversation. Despair, always looming beneath his veneer of civilized stoicism, threatened to engulf him. Ruthlessly, he squashed it down. *Don't brood. A moment of lively conversation is a prize in itself. Enjoy it without ruminating.* "I've always appreciated spring," he murmured. "A season of hope and rebirth. A season of the promise of green and growing things to sustain us through the long winter."

She paused to consider him. "You sound more modern, suddenly. Like Wordsworth or one of his ilk. Do you enjoy poetry as well as Shakespearean plays?"

He shrugged. "I like to read. Because I'm essentially a farmer and live close to the land, Wordsworth makes sense to me. I've always found his writing appealing."

"Without farmers, there would be no food," Miss Granger commented as she resumed walking. "Food, far more than money, provides the nails that hold everything together. It makes sense to venerate the farm and what it provides, even in these days of industry."

Colin couldn't help but grin. "You're a natural philosopher, sprite. When next I see my friend, who is a great lover of industry, I'll have to tell him what you said."

Miss Granger giggled. "Will he be offended?"

"Far from it," Colin replied, adding his grin to hers. "When he's not weaving fabric and repairing looms, he's devouring poetry. He loves it. I think he might singlehandedly be sponsoring half the serious poets in Britain. And when he finds something, he's not shy to share." *I'll not be around to listen to the poetry Christopher discovers anymore,* Colin realized sadly. *Maybe he'll send me some of his best finds from time to time. Might break up the monotony of endless work.*

"Sounds like someone I would like to meet," she agreed. "I prefer plays to poetry, but I appreciate either one. Are you a particular poetry aficionado?"

"More or less," Colin agreed amicably, pushing away gloomy thoughts in favor of an enjoyable conversation. "My friend Christopher has become fanatically devoted to Robert Browning, and I have to admit, I find his work... thought-provoking, if somewhat ragged in style. Tennyson is my personal favorite of this particular crop. His elegant style and otherworldly topics fascinate me."

"The otherworldly is my specialty," she replied with a grin. "*A Midsummer Night's Dream, The Tempest*, even *Macbeth* make me happy." Her grin widened.

Colin bit his lip to stop his tongue hanging out of his mouth. *Lord, she's pretty. Like a summer's day. If only things were different.*

The wooded thicket opened up into a grassy meadow. A brook meandered through one corner. From the brook, a loud quacking revealed the presence of many ducks. On the far side of the meadow, a small collection of charming thatched-roofed cottages appeared; the town he hadn't realized he'd been seeking. They lay along either side of a comfortably broad central path, from which other paths wound and meandered at angles that in no way resembled a grid. A couple of plump children in sturdy garments laughed and chased one another among the houses. A dog snoozed in a patch of sunlight. A fat duck led a line of golden ducklings out of town toward a glimmer on the horizon that seemed to be a pond.

"Very nice," he commented idly, before mentally adding, *If my tenants ever looked like this, I would die a happy man.*

"I've always thought so," Miss Granger replied.

He glanced her direction and took in a soft smile that turned her face into a beam of living sunshine. *Goodness, she's pretty.*

"If you'd like," she added, "I can take you to the inn. It's growing late in the day to travel, and dinner is almost ready."

"I can't... er..." Colin colored. Trying to explain to this charming young woman that he had no money for a meal or a room and planned to munch on dry bread in the hedgerows. *Is it vain that I don't want to sound like a vagrant? Well, if so, perhaps I can be forgiven a small vanity.* "I have to move along. I have friends expecting me in London." *At least that's the truth, more or less.*

"You can't mean it!" Miss Granger exclaimed. "It's much too far. You'll be on the road all night!"

Colin sighed but did not respond. Not that she gave him a chance. Seizing his arm near the elbow, she hurried forward. Amused by her exuberance, Colin let himself be led past the cottages and children to a small side road, where they turned left, away from the pond. There, a wide two-story thatched structure lured passers-by with a tantalizing aroma of simmering stew and baking bread. "Come in," she urged.

Colin dropped the horse's reins, knowing an animal so tired as this one would rather nibble grass than wander, and stepped over the threshold into a wide, sunny room filled with comfortable-looking chairs that encircled simple round wooden tables. Custom wallpaper in an intense shade of green with stylized brown twigs enriched the walls. "Is this a tavern?" he asked stupidly, and then shook his head to realize he'd already been told it was an inn.

"More or less," Miss Granger replied. "While we do get plenty of overnight guests on their way to London, the locals prefer ale and stew."

Colin nodded. *And I can afford none of them. Now, what do I do?* The more he thought about disappointing this intriguing young woman with his inability to pay for her family's services, the hotter embarrassment burned in his guts, until he feared he might retch.

"Daisy!" a low-pitched voice bellowed from beyond an open door. "Did I hear you come in?"

"Yes, Father," Daisy replied. "I'm back."

"Good. The stew needs tending, and you know I don't know how."

The young woman rolled her hazel green eyes heavenward and then hurried toward the doorway muttering, "It's not difficult to stick a spoon in and stir it about. Silly man."

In spite of himself, Colin chuckled.

"Father," Miss Granger said just before she ducked out of earshot, "I've found someone to…" The door swung shut, cutting off her words.

Colin regarded the room again, admiring its simple, well-appointed tidiness. It occurred to Colin that he should probably duck out and make for the woods again. It would be his one opportunity to avoid explaining his unfortunate circumstances.

But he had already waited too long. The door swung open again, and this time, instead of a lovely young lass, a middle-aged man emerged.

Miss Granger's father, he guessed, noting the faint resemblance that lingered around the jaw and lips. Unlike his daughter's dainty features, her father resembled a bear, with small, sleepy eyes, round cheeks and a wild tangle of dark hair curling around his ears.

His face broke into a broad grin. "How do you do?" he asked, his accent surprisingly cultivated. "Peter Granger, at your service. Can I interest you in a hot meal and a comfortable bed?"

Colin approached cautiously, extending one hand. "I'm well enough, I suppose." He gulped. "I hate to disappoint you, but I've not a penny to my name, not enough for that fine-smelling stew." Honestly proved a far less palatable bellyful, and Colin swallowed hard to avoid choking on it.

The craggy face fell.

"Sorry to intrude. It was more than I could manage to disappoint such a spirited girl." He turned to leave.

"I hear you," the man said. "My Daisy is an impetuous lass but a well-intentioned one. She'll be sad if you don't at least taste her cooking. She's about to bubble over with excitement." Granger eyed him, his sleepy, ursine eyes seeming to see more than the simple sense allowed.

Colin ground his teeth. His pride would admit no hint of charity, though his rumbling stomach begged it to try.

"Tell you what," Granger continued, "have a meal with us. Maybe I can find something or other around here for you to do to make up the cost. You look like a sturdy fellow."

Pleased to be presented with a solution that provided dinner while sparing his pride and still allowing him to spend a few more precious moments with the intoxicating Miss Granger, Colin found himself nodding before he fully grasped the details. "I'd appreciate that, but one moment. I need to tend to my horse."

"Come on, man. Take a seat," Granger urged. "I saw the poor old fellow outside. I'll put him in the stable and feed him. You eat. We'll decide what's next later."

Suddenly weary, Colin dropped into a chair. He felt a strong urge to lay his head on the table, as though the cares of his existence weighed more than his spine could support. He felt fragile and tired.

How long he drifted in a sea of exhausted misery, or even if he had dozed for a moment, Colin couldn't be sure, but a heavy hand clapping his shoulder brought him upright again. Up close, Granger's ursine appearance intensified, with the addition of a broad, round belly and a dense darkness around his chin that, had he not shaved that morning, would quickly have transformed itself into a wooly beard.

Granger set a heaping dish of stew in front of Colin and walked away, allowing him to devour the repast with unmannerly eagerness.

After a few ravenous bites had sated the sharpest edge of his hunger, he sighed, settled back in his chair and began to savor the intense, wine-soaked flavors of lamb, herbs, and vegetables. It tasted like ambrosia.

"Care for a pint, sir?" The familiar female voice broke through his idle perusal of the zigzag pattern on the wallpaper.

He regarded his new acquaintance with interest, not sure how to answer. *Do I want a pint? Yes, very much. Whether I ought to have one is a different tale altogether.*

"Father said to offer it to you," she added. "He said something about chopping wood…"

Oho, so that's how this will go. "Very well, Miss Granger. I will happily accept your kind offer, and please express my sincerest thanks to your father."

The young woman smiled shyly and approached, setting the foam-capped tankard before him. Then, without warning, she plunked into a chair at the table, watching him closely.

Her scrutiny should have unnerved him, but for some reason, it didn't. He felt a bit of prolonged visual lingering might be just the thing. A bellyful of hot stew, the pungent aroma of a most welcome ale… What could complete the picture better than the lovely gray-green eyes of a woman who seemed as interested as he felt? *If only.*

Colin lowered his eyelids and took a sip of the ale. Savory, sharp sensations danced on his tongue. While his friends freely shared brandy and cognac, the homespun, humble brew perfectly suited the moment and his mood. "Talk to me, won't you, Miss Granger?" he urged.

"About what?" she asked.

He chewed a mouthful of tender lamb, swallowed, and said, "You know, I have no idea. But you're here, and you've gone to a bit of trouble to be sure I was here too, and so… here we are."

"Profound," she said solemnly hiding a dainty giggle behind one hand.

"Deep as the ocean," he replied and snorted. Belly full and, at least for the moment, at peace, everything seemed funnier than it should have.

Miss Granger's eyes sparkled. "This is a foolish conversation," she pointed out.

"So it is," he concurred. "Isn't it marvelous?"

"Without doubt." She lifted her hand again, fingers hesitating. Then, firming her resolve, reached forward and plucked a twig from his hair.

His scalp tingled. "My crown," he protested.

"Well, My Lord Oberon, we cannot have your identity revealed so callously."

Colin grinned. *I like this girl.* "After dinner, I suspect your father will have me earning my keep with many tasks."

"Oh, yes," Miss Granger agreed, eyes wide. "His friends have been urging him to take an evening away from the tavern to play cards with them, but he always refuses. While you're drawing water and chopping wood, he'll be drinking wine and playing whist."

"All that sounds tolerable," Colin replied. "I appreciate the opportunity, as a matter of fact." Then his face burned as he realized he had more or less admitted his penniless state to this intriguing woman. He met her eyes and blushed deeper at the expression of dawning awareness on her face. "Isn't he worried about your reputation?" he asked to take his mind off his usual gloomy ruminations.

She shrugged. "I don't know. There are plenty of people around, and with each of us having so much to do, who would have time to get into mischief? Um, you're not planning anything, are you?"

"Any mischief?" He twisted his lips to the side. "Not that you aren't tempting, sprite, but it would be poor thanks for your generosity. Not to mention, I'm not a despoiler of innocents."

She nodded, and with matching sighs, they both fell silent.

"Life isn't what we wish, is it?" he muttered.

She responded by turning up one corner of her mouth in a grim half-smile but said nothing.

"So, apart from making excellent stew, Miss Granger, what do you do around here?"

She raised her eyebrows at the abrupt change of topic but gamely answered the question. "Make up the beds, sweep the floors. Handle the money. Plan and change the décor. All the usual things, I suppose."

"Ah, I see." Colin also saw that their easy conversation had grown strained. He sipped his ale and ate another bite.

A hum of quiet conversation and the shuffling of boots signaled other diners entering the room. Daisy jumped up to serve them. Bowls and tankards thumped on wooden tables while Colin took another bite, chewing slowly. A few minutes later, Daisy returned with a dish of her own and sank into a seat beside him.

Despite the lull in conversation, Miss Granger proved a comfortable dinner companion. She sat by, not filling the silence with idle chatter, but her presence brought only awareness, not awkwardness. Again the idea that under different circumstances, meeting this woman might have felt like fate crept into Colin's mind. He pushed it away. No point in torturing himself. *It isn't fate and it can't be. No matter what different circumstances I might imagine, nothing would make her available to me. Not if I cared about her, which I do.*

The meal finished, she reached for her dishes, but he scooped them up himself. "A poor guest I'd be if I let such a generous lady as yourself clean up after me. I'm no stranger to washing and tidying."

She grinned. "If you insist. This way, Lord Oberon."

He chuckled at the ongoing joke and trailed after her through the door into a spacious kitchen. A stack of used dishes sat beside a washbasin, and he added his own, pushing up his sleeves and reaching for the first crusted plate.

"Now, that's going a bit far," Miss Granger protested. "My father will certainly ask you do to his chores tonight, but there's no need for you to do mine as well."

Colin shrugged. "If not for your timely intervention, I wouldn't be here. What's washing a few dishes in exchange?"

"I'll wash, you dry," she replied, her jaw set in stubborn lines.

Colin grinned at her serious demeanor. "As milady wishes." He reached for a length of rough toweling and stationed himself near her.

At this distance, he could smell her subtle fragrance. Sunshine and the outdoors, along with an alluring hint of womanly sweetness. He swallowed hard. That scent acted on his awareness like the most potent lure. *Not that I'll likely ever marry, but if I did, I hope my wife would smell just like this.*

Chapter 2

COLIN swung the ax over his head and brought it down, straight and true, into the heart of a section of log, neatly splitting it in half. No stranger to such a task, his calloused palms easily guided the heavy tool. In his younger days, he'd used times like this to think deep and powerful thoughts—or at least what his adolescent brain considered deep and powerful. *Probably pure tripe,* he acknowledged ruefully. But in the last few years, the burden of unanswerable questions left him unable to entertain more than the most fleeing rumination without agony, and so manual labor had become an opportunity to rest his mind. Except that today, thoughts kept creeping in.

Such a pretty lass, and so bright.

If I could take the time to get to know someone like her, life might not seem so bad. Why must it be that I have nothing to offer? I'm sure a humble existence wouldn't offend her, but even that is beyond me.

He swung the ax again and missed the wood, sinking the blade into the block, far too near his leg.

"Easy, lad," he urged himself under his breath. "Injuring yourself won't change your fate for the better."

"Looks like you have enough," Miss Granger commented, appearing around the front of the house.

"Well, I thought I might do a bit extra," he explained, "since your father fed and housed my horse as well."

"I noticed the poor beast in the barn. You don't actually ride him, do you?"

Colin shook his head, drops of sweat flying from the tips of his hair. "That would finish the old boy off for sure. No, he's only carrying my pack. I have a

15

friend who is willing to take him in and give him a comfortable, easy life for the rest of his days. I intend to accept that offer."

She grinned. "I like men who are kind to animals." Then her smile faded. "So many see them as slaves to exploit or tools to use up." She bit her lip and muttered, almost too softly for him to hear, "They usually see women the same way."

She has someone particular in mind, Colin realized, not that it was truly any of his business. "I hope no one is bothering you, Miss Granger. That would be a pity."

She shrugged, her lips curving into a smile of painful falseness. "All women are 'bothered' by a man at some time or another. It's sort of our fate."

Her words brought to mind Colin's best friend, Christopher, who had rescued his wife from the clutches of an abusive father. Christopher's brother Devon, had traveled to India to rescue his wife, whose meddlesome uncle had tried to send his bride-to-be away into prostitution. *Hell, even my mother lived half her life at the mercy of people who saw her as a means to an end, rather than a person in her own right. How difficult it must be, living a female life.* "Just because something is common does not mean it is right," he pointed out.

Miss Granger's grim grin turned real, her hazel eye lighting up. Behind her, the sun sank slowly toward the horizon, illuminating her lovely features with a scarlet glow. Her angelic appearance stopped his breath in his chest and set his heart pounding. "Be careful with that smile, Miss Granger," he urged. "I would hate to catch myself 'bothering' you as well."

A soft giggle escaped her. "I don't think it's possible you could, sir." Her cheeks glowed with their own internal luminescence at the admission. "I would rather fancy being bothered by you, I think. I mean, I don't know you well, but…"

Colin sighed. "My dear lady, I beg you not to say such things. It can never be… but the temptation appeals so much, it almost hurts."

She lowered her eyelids, shutting out the light of her eyes, and broke the spell holding Colin captive. "Are you sure it's impossible? Distance is a bother but surely not insurmountable, and we could write letters."

Colin swallowed hard, and the mouthful of disgusted regret nearly made him retch. "I mustn't. I am so sorry. Please, Miss Granger, don't tempt me any further." He closed his own eyes, shutting out the sight of her lovely, expressive face.

A strong, capable hand closed on his upper arm. "As you wish. But… will you remember me?"

He nodded without opening his eyes. "Every day of my life. I swear it."

A change in the quality of the ambiance told him he was alone. He opened his eyes to find her gone. "Why?" he choked in despair. "Why must my life be thus, that I cannot even agree to correspond with someone, let alone care for her? What sin did I commit to condemn me to a life so empty of joy?"

The setting sun touched the horizon, turning the sky before Colin into a copper plate, from which his anguished prayer rebounded, unheard.

"The iniquities of the father are visited upon the children," he paraphrased.

The sun set, and darkness shrouded the inn yard.

Chapter 3

 OLIN woke hungry. Nothing unusual in that, nor in the aches in his muscles from hard work. In contrast to his usual morning, however, he woke cradled in a comfortable mattress, not the lumpy reject he'd dragged from a forgotten corner of his crumbling home. An enticing smell wafting up the stairs set his mouth watering. *No thin gruel. No watery tea. Smells like heaven.* He stared up into the thatch of the attic bedroom's ceiling as rosy sunrise filtered through a small window and cast lights and shadows over him. For a long moment, he luxuriated in the unfamiliar comfort of a homey morning. *All over the world, people wake to this,* he contemplated. *No luxury or any expectation of it, only a day filled with toil and another day of the same, day after day, until life's journey comes to an end, and yet, they find contentment in hot, tasty meals, peaceful slumber, evenings spent with friends and nights with their own willing woman. Simple, family life. In a way, it's what Christopher and his brother have. They live at peace despite their labors.*

Middle-class life seemed a blessing he could only dream of. Nobility had provided precious few pleasures. *No less toil, but much fewer rewards, and the burden of worrying about my tenants.* Sitting up on the bed, he shook his head. *Inheritance be damned. What wouldn't I give to work in Chris's factory?*

Though such an option would never be available to him, he paused to imagine it for the briefest of minutes. Then, shaking off the dangerously appealing nonsense, he rose to his feet, dragged on his clothing, and washed his face and hands in an ewer of cool water, before descending the stairs, passing an entire floor of guest bedrooms, and arriving in the cozy kitchen.

Miss Granger stood before a cauldron suspended above a small fire, her back to the room. Colin allowed himself a moment to regard the womanly curve of her hip, where it flared below the string of her apron, before clearing his throat. "Good morning."

She turned and grinned at him. "Mister Butler. I hope you passed a pleasant night?"

His lips curved in an unfamiliar sensation: a genuine smile. "Marvelous. I can scarcely recall feeling so well-rested."

Her hazel eyes narrowed, and she seemed to search his face for a moment, reading his expression with discomfiting shrewdness.

Yes, my lady, my life is hard. Harder than I would like, and no sign of it ever easing. It's the reason I cannot pursue this luscious flirtation, no matter how my heart and soul long to.

Unearthly compassion set the green in her eyes welling. Had he been less hardened, he might have wept at it. Mercifully, when she spoke, it was of the mundane. "I'm glad to hear it. Let us cap off a comfortable night with a hearty breakfast."

"Sounds marvelous. What are we having?"

"Take a seat," she urged. "You worked hard yesterday. I'll bring you a plate."

Having someone bring him a meal seemed like such a luxury, Colin's knees went weak. He sank into a chair and without thought rested his forehead against the table.

A soft thump in front of him drew his awareness, but he didn't rise. The weariness of his soul far surpassed the weariness of his body. His eyes slid closed as he fought to keep all thought from forming.

A soft pressure on his shoulder transferred heat through the ragged sleeve of his shirt into his skin, where it seemed to take on a life of its own, a golden glow that radiated out from the touch to soothe him. Finally, he raised his head and his eyes met hers. Again, her empathy struck a deep chord with him.

"Are you a fairy in truth?" he demanded. "What is this magic you possess that makes hope seem possible again?"

She tilted her head slightly to one side and regarded him curiously. "Strange for such a young, handsome man with so much humor and kindness to be so sad. I know we've just met, but a burden shared is a burden eased. Can you let me help you?"

He shook his head. "I cannot. If I told you everything, you would draw back from me, fearing I would harm you. Let me remain a mystery, my lady. The truth is far too painful. Knowing it will harm me without helping you."

"I'm not highly in favor of mysteries," she admitted tartly, shuttering away her rejected vulnerability. "They often cause the harm they're intended to prevent. But at any rate, will you be running away today, or can you linger?"

"I dare not stay," Colin replied with regret. "I must go on. Too many people need me to complete my mission quickly. There is no time to spare."

"Let me walk with you," Miss Granger urged, "at least to the edge of the village. I wouldn't want to miss an opportunity to talk to you one last time."

Colin tried to refuse, he really did. Further association with the lady in question would do her no good and would infinitely extend his suffering. And yet, when he opened his mouth to refuse her, what emerged was, "I would like that."

Miss Granger beamed brighter than the sunshine pouring through the kitchen window.

"Then eat hearty, my friend," she urged. "You have a long journey ahead of you."

"More than you know," he muttered, unable to tear his eyes away from her beaming face. Time seemed to suspend itself between them, drawn thin and immobile as it connected heart to heart. It seemed the most natural thing in the world to lean in, and for some reason, Colin couldn't recall why it would be a good idea to resist.

"Good morning," a loud voice blustered, shattering the spell. Colin quickly shoveled a forkful of food into his mouth to cover his surprised embarrassment.

"Father," Miss Granger rasped.

"Seeing our guest on his way?" the craggy older man guessed.

His daughter replied with a curt nod.

"Good work yesterday, Butler," Granger added. "I must say, it was a welcome change from my usual routine. Don't suppose you'd consider moving to town and helping out permanently? I'm getting old for all this."

Colin snorted into his porridge. Though no youth, Granger retained masses of corded muscle that threatened the sleeves of his shirt. He had many years of strength left to him.

"No, sir," Colin replied with regret, wishing he had the freedom to accept such a humble position. *How wonderful would it be to have work that led directly to meals—a clear correlation between effort and reward?* "I must go. Vital duties await me in London, and at home. I simply cannot delay. I do appreciate your hospitality, both of you, more than I can say."

A huge hand clapped Colin on the back, but no further conversation on the topic appeared. Colin, grateful for the silence, continued filling his belly at a pace just shy of unmannerly while father and daughter turned to other topics of conversation.

"I ran into young John Orville this morning. He asked about you."

Colin watched in fascination as Miss Granger's face took on an expression of rage and humiliation. Bright color flared in her cheeks. Her eyes narrowed and her teeth clenched. "And what makes you think I care about that dirty blacksmith's apprentice?" she hissed.

To Colin's surprise, Granger threw back his head and roared with laughter. "Sheath your claws, kitten. I will never understand why such a fine young gentleman sends you into such a bother."

Miss Granger squeezed her eyes shut. "I've told you many times, Father. He's no fine gentleman. He's a classless boor and an all-around nasty human being. I hate him, and I will never change my mind about that."

"What a pity," Granger replied. "I've often wished for him as a son-in-law. Besides, you're exaggerating. He's never been anything but a gentleman."

"To you," Miss Granger shot back. "You're a man. He has nothing to gain by trying to coerce and frighten you. I cannot abide him, and no amount of badgering on your or his part will change that."

Granger gave her a shrewd look under his bushy eyebrows, but let the conversation drop.

Colin eyed the man, wondering what his speaking expression meant. Miss Granger, her shoulders stiff with anger, fixed her eyes on the window and missed it entirely.

Swallowing his last bite of food with regret, Colin rose from the table and carried his dishes to the sink, where others waited, presumably for his host's fascinating daughter. "I hate to run after such a pleasant visit, but my errands won't wait. Thank you both for all you've done for me. I won't soon forget it."

"You may visit me any time you'd like," Granger replied with a grin, his huge hand engulfing Colin's for a manly pump. "I enjoyed my evening off."

"I appreciate that," Colin replied, knowing it would likely never happen. "Mister Granger. Miss Granger." He tipped an imaginary hat, enjoying the role reversal that had him paying obeisance to people who would have done so to him, had they known his title.

Then he made his way out of the kitchen into a sunny yard, where a nearby barn drew his attention as a likely place to find his horse. Sure enough, in the dusty, hay-scented interior, a familiar silver head peeked over a wooden door and whickered in greeting. "Good morning, old fellow," Colin said, stroking the silky nose.

The horse pawed the stall with a noisy clunk.

"I know. It's been a pleasant idyll for me as well, but we must press on. You have a better future ahead of you if only you can make your way to London. My friend has found a place for you to live in comfort on a lush, grassy estate by the sea. Isn't that nice? I wish I could afford to keep you, old man, but caring for an idle animal is beyond me. Once the grass in the pasture dies, you'll need hay, and I need the hay for other animals, but by then, you'll be comfortable in your new home."

He led his companion out into the warm sunshine.

"Wait," a voice ordered, soft and feminine, and filled with sadness. "Wait, Mr. Butler."

He paused. "Miss Granger?"

Like yesterday, she burst out of seemingly nowhere, the light sparkling on her strands of messy, golden hair as they escaped a parody of a tidy chignon. A faint smattering of freckles appeared against the light tan of her face. Her full lips pursed and then turned downward in a showy pout. "Did you really mean to leave without saying goodbye?"

He blinked. "My apologies. I didn't think you meant it."

"Oh, you foolish man." She drew close and swatted his arm in a showy gesture. "Of course I did. In fact, just for that, I'm going to walk you right out of town."

Colin glanced around. "Are you sure that's wise, accompanying a stranger into the woods? What of your reputation, Miss Granger?"

"I'll risk it," she replied grimly and then muttered something under her breath that he couldn't quite make out.

I ought to dissuade her. It would be best for us both not to draw this out. He opened his mouth, intending to urge her back inside her father's inn, but his tongue betrayed him. "Very well. I should be glad of your company as long as I can keep it." *Fool. Why did you say that?*

"If only you could keep it longer." Miss Granger took a hesitant step toward the line of trees that delineated the boundary between town and forest. "So, so much longer."

Colin followed, his attention fixated on his companion. "There are many causes in this life to think 'if only' and be wistful, but what good does it do? 'If only' never fixed a roof, plowed a field, sheared a sheep. Why bother with what cannot be?"

She glanced at him, meeting his eyes, and he blinked to see tears sparkling in the hazel depths. "Why read poetry, or plays? Why look at the stars, or smell the summer roses? We're human, Mr. Butler. We have feelings. No, indulging them doesn't get the work done, but life is more than work."

"Colin," he urged. "I will never pass this way again, Miss Granger, so let this small indiscretion be part of my memory. Let me hear my name on your tongue. If you're right, and I'm to live for more than work, I could think of no sweeter memory to take with me." *Fool, what are you writing your poetry now? Ode to a Daisy, by the worthless Viscount Gelroy.* He rolled his eyes at his own maudlin thoughts.

"Colin," she replied immediately, a sad smile spreading across her lips. "Now you."

"What?" he blinked away self-recrimination.

"Say my name."

Colin froze, one foot on the grassy meadow that edged the town, the other between two gnarled tree trunks, and turned fully to face his companion. A shaft of sunlight fell gently on her hair, creating the illusion of a glow. Again, Colin thought of a fairy. "Daisy," he breathed. A spark of something words could not express flickered to life in the dark core of his being, shedding light through him.

"Come on," she urged, grabbing his hand and dragging him past the tree line. The sudden movement tightened the reins on his hand for a brief, painful moment before the horse consented to move with a grumpy whicker.

The dense spring foliage shielded the town from their view, and they were alone. Yesterday, he'd scarcely registered that they were in isolation. Today, it felt like the most important thing that had ever happened to him. *Infatuation is a strange thing,* he reflected, trying to dismiss, or at least minimize, the irrational feeling. It didn't work. Something about Daisy, something he couldn't name or even fully understand, radiated out from the vicinity of his heart.

"You shouldn't be alone with me," he said gruffly. "It will do your reputation no good."

She shrugged, turning to face him. "I care little about such things."

"You should," he informed her, his solemn concern for her welfare reflected on his face. "You have a long life to live in this village, and if people decide you're…"

"You know nothing about my future," she replied, irritation snapping in her hazel eyes. "I might run away with a traveling theater troupe. I might move to London and seek my fortune in any number of ways. Assuming that I plan to spend my life in this village, running my father's inn with whatever poor idiot he strong-arms me into marrying is… Well, Colin, suffice it to say, I don't think that will happen. I have more in mind than letting myself be steered by those who care little for my thoughts and dreams."

"Dreams are dangerous, my dear," he said grimly. "They will leave you disappointed. It always happens. Pain is our destiny."

She raised her eyebrows. "You're young to have such a gloomy outlook."

"Life has been a hard master," he replied. "I hope you do escape. I hope you do find a future filled with everything you ever dreamed of, and I hope," he added, shyness creeping into his blunt delivery, "that you take a little piece of me with you. There is no other way my soul can fly free."

Daisy bit her lip. "What has happened to you?"

He shook his head. "I dare not say. Why mar the final moment of our idyll with harsh reality?"

She raised one eyebrow. "You started it."

He grinned, a wry twisting of his lips. "So I did. I apologize. My life has been harder than it needed to be for as long as I can remember. I'm out of the habit of happiness."

Daisy stepped close to him and laid a gentle hand on his cheek. "You live in the past… or perhaps a dark future you don't see an escape from, but neither of those things is here with us in this moment. There is only you, me, the sunshine and the trees."

Stormcloud snorted as if to remind them they weren't entirely alone.

"Yes, and you, old boy," Daisy said, laughter trilling in her voice.

Colin's own words stuck in his throat, reined in by the fragrant sweetness of Daisy's hand against his skin.

Without hesitation, she rose on tiptoes, her bare feet allowing the move in the way no shoe ever could and laid a gentle kiss on his cheek.

Colin gulped, heat and tenderness bounding out from his heart and taking up residence in his every extremity. His fingers tingled. His toes curled. The most skillful caress of the most expensive courtesan could scarcely have elicited such a response. He closed his eyes. "Why did you do that?"

"I wanted to," she replied. "No matter that we must now part, never to cross paths again, there is something between us. Something special. I wanted... I wanted to taste it."

Self-control wavered. Shuddered. Snapped. Dropping Stormcloud's reins, Colin dragged Daisy against his chest and lowered his head, claiming her lips.

Daisy froze in surprise, but only for a moment before her warm, supple body melted in his arms. Her hand, still lingering on his face, trailed down to his neck and inched around to embrace him.

Colin's skin tingled, and the tingle had more than a trace of heat. Blood rushed to his groin until he felt dizzy and almost off-balance. *Oh, God. It's better than I imagined. Why, oh, why would I find someone so... perfect, only to rush away and never see her again.*

"Stop that," his heart reminded him. "Savor the moment without weakening it by wishing for more. Just relax and enjoy."

Colin heeded the warning, leaning into Daisy's willing embrace and savoring the eager cling of her lips. The warmth of her supple, young body. The sweet scent of her hair. *If sunshine has a physical form, this is it; she's like a nature spirit.*

Reluctantly, he released her, drawing back a scant inch to look down into her face.

She inhaled deeply through her nose and opened her eyes. "Colin," she breathed.

"I should go," he murmured. "I have another half day's walk to get to where I'm going, and I'd like to arrive before dark."

"One more," she begged. "We may not have a future, but I'm not ready for this moment to end."

"Neither am I, sweet sprite," he replied, his voice going low with longing.

As one, they leaned together in an embrace of the tenderest, most excruciating joy he had ever imagined. *I would love her, given enough time. Dear Lord.*

Long they lingered, as the shadows of overarching tree branches danced upon their faces, until they broke apart, breathing raggedly.

"I must go," he whispered, voice breaking.

"I know." She sniffled.

"Remember me," he urged.

"I swear it. I will never forget you, Colin."

Trailing his fingers down her cheek, Colin turned, scooped up Stormcloud's reins, and walked away.

Chapter 4

DAISY sighed, staring at Colin's departing form through blurry eyes. "What just happened?" she asked the trees. "How did such an event come to me?"

She touched her lips, still wet from his kiss, not quite believing it. "Amazing," she breathed. *I think I just met my soulmate... and lost him, all in less than a day.* The pang she felt hurt tremendously. She wanted nothing more than to run after him... or back to her room to cry. *Instead, I will have to distract myself with work. There are beds to make. Food to cook. Dishes to wash. Papa won't tolerate sloth, and I've already pushed my luck today.* She squinted into the trees to see if she could make out Colin's retreating form, but he had disappeared into the distance. She heaved a sigh, turned and headed back toward the meadow.

She hadn't made it two steps when something heavy crashed into her, knocking her off her feet. She hit the forest floor with a thud, flat on her belly. A branch slashed her cheek. Blood dripped into the withering leaves while she gasped, struggling to draw air into her laboring lungs.

Heavy hands clamped on the back of her dress and in her hair, lifting her and dropping her on her back.

Air rushed into Daisy's lungs. She gasped. The acne-scarred, squint-eyed face of John Orville, her least favorite person, hovered over her.

"What are you doing?" she hissed.

He lowered his face and planted a sloppy kiss on her mouth.

Revolted, Daisy gagged, trying to turn away, but he took a hard hold of her lower jaw, crushing down with a heavy pinch, so she couldn't move.

I have to get away, she thought. Her heart pounded in panic and her belly threatened to invert itself. Especially when his tongue began to probe at the seam of her lips. Unwilling to suffer his touch another moment, she bit down hard on the invader, until blood tinged his saliva.

Enraged, Orville pulled back with a roar and grasped the bodice of her dress with both hands, yanking in opposite directions. The fabric gave way with a revolting rip, but his focus on her clothing allowed her to shift her position enough to insinuate one of her knees between his body and hers.

Daisy screamed.

He grasped her breast, pinching hard at the nipple, and she screamed again. "Stop. Stop touching me."

He laughed. "You're mine, Daisy-girl. Mine for all time."

"Never!" She vowed. Shoving upward with her knee, she created enough space between them to kick at his genitals with the opposite foot. Though she wore no boots, he reacted instinctively, dropping his grip on her breast and drawing back. Daisy shot to her feet in a flash and ran into the woods.

He lumbered after her, his feet crushing sticks and branches with loud snaps that almost sounded like gunfire. "Come baaa-aaaack," he called. "You're mine, Daisy-girl. Come back and I'll go easier on you. If I have to hunt you down, you won't like the results."

Like *the results?* She thought, dodging to the right and bounding down a hill. *As if I could like anything about Orville other than putting as much distance between us as possible.*

A stream loomed up before her. In the second she had to consider, she noticed a thick layer of fallen leaves on the far side. Assuming that would suffice for her landing, she leaped. Landed. Slid on a slick layer of slime and mud underneath, which sent her sprawling.

Immediately, she rolled over, trying to get her feet under her. Orville's boots splashed in the water, and just as she put her foot on the ground again, a meaty hand clamped down on her shoulder.

"Stop!" she shrieked, clawing at his skin. Her nails broke, and he bled, but he did not loosen his grip. "Let me go."

"Oh, no, Daisy girl. I'll never let you go," he replied. "It's all been decided. You're mine."

"No!" she yelled. "No, never." She yanked at her arm.

His fingers dug in deeper, hard enough to bruise her. Hard enough to snap bone. Daisy's arm throbbed with pain.

Then, just as suddenly as he'd grabbed her, Orville's crushing hand let go. He made a croaking sound, doubling over around…

A fist.

Daisy blinked at the image of Colin, teeth set with rage, driving a hard punch into Orville's soft belly.

"The lady said no," he gritted out.

Orville collapsed to the forest floor, and Colin drove a scuffed boot into his belly, reinforcing the message.

"Beast," he snarled. "Cad. There are not strong enough words for the likes of you." He kicked out again, catching Orville under the chin. "Only a coward would force a woman."

The man's eyes rolled back in his head and then fluttered shut.

Colin turned to Daisy. "Are you all right?" he asked, taking in her battered appearance. Then, his gaze fell upon her bared breast.

She made a hasty grab, covering herself.

"Who is that?" he asked, indicating the fallen man.

She shuddered. "A friend of my father's. You might have heard Father mention him earlier?"

Colin nodded.

"I hate him. He's revolting."

"I agree," Colin said, leveling a look of deep disgust on the prone figure. "Come on, love. Let's get you home."

She nodded, hot sobs climbing up into her throat. A whimper escaped.

"Daisy," he said gently, "I know you need a good cry, but can we get away from this first?" he prodded the fallen bully with his toe.

She turned her face to the ground.

He wrapped his arm around her shoulders and led her back, shuffling through the stream and over the uneven ground towards the village.

A cloud passed over the sun, shrouding the pair in darkness. A shiver rolled up Daisy's spine, and her ability to control her emotions took another battering. A tear escaped, and a sob clawed its way into her throat, where she swallowed it back down.

Colin's hand tightened on her shoulder. She huddled against his side.

"We'll go in the back," Colin suggested. "You don't need to march through the public part of the inn, given the state of your clothing… and your hair."

"Am I as big a mess as I think I am?" she asked with a brittle laugh.

"Yes," he replied honestly, smoothing one calloused hand over her head. His fingers snagged in the strands. "Sorry."

She shook her head. "Let's stay in the tree line. I don't want to march through town either."

"Very well," Colin agreed.

She moved to the east, circling the town toward her home/workplace while remaining out of sight. Only when they stood directly behind the inn, facing the rear yard with its newly replenished woodpile, did Daisy dare to duck out of the woods. She darted across the yard, Colin close at her heels, and yanked open the door into the kitchen.

Her father stood inside. He clutched a rifle in both hands. Reverend Williams, the village's vicar, stood beside him, looking formal in his clerical collar and robes. He clutched a leather-bound book by his side.

Daisy pulled up short, staring at first one man and then the other. Her eyes met her father's, locked. A strange, triumphant smile rendered his small, ursine eyes nearly invisible. She flinched. That expression never boded well.

Colin, unprepared for her sudden stop, ran into her back. Granger turned his gaze to Colin, and his eyes reappeared, wide and startled. His neck thrust forward with a grunt.

The vicar made a face. "It seems you were right," he murmured in his quiet voice.

"What's going on?" Daisy asked. "Why are you here? I... I need to go to my room and change clothes. Orville..."

"Where is he?" Her father demanded, rage transforming his low voice into a thundering growl.

"Who?"

"Orville."

"Far away," Colin said gently. "He hurt your daughter, sir. I made sure he won't do that again."

Granger snarled.

"Sir, your protests are far from convincing," Reverend Williams said in his quiet, dignified voice. "Do you mean for us to believe that you came sneaking in the rear door of this fine establishment, with a young lady in a state of... disreputable disarray, and expect us to believe that someone *else* attacked her? I've heard better excuses from naughty children."

Daisy's jaw dropped. "Reverend, Colin isn't lying. That's exactly what happened. Orville attacked me. Colin saved me."

The vicar shook his head. "Nonsense. You're being duped, young lady. You might think this young man is attractive and fine, but if you end up with child from today's... misbehavior, you and your father will both be ruined."

"There was no misb—"

Daisy's mouth snapped shut at the soft click of the rifle.

"Nothing happened, I swear it," Colin said with quiet intensity. "I care for Daisy..."

"Good," the vicar interrupted. "Then you won't object to doing the right thing."

"But I can't..."

"Are you married?"

"No," Colin replied, "but..."

"But nothing. You will not be allowed to despoil this innocent young lady and run away without consequences."

Another threatening growl emerged from Daisy's father. She met his gaze, or at least, she tried to. The dark eyes skated from side to side, confusion obvious in his expression.

"Papa," she said, "Papa, you know me..."

The muzzle of the rifle snared her gaze as it swung in her direction. Daisy froze. *What is going on here?*

Reverend Williams opened his book, which turned out to be not a Bible but a book of liturgy. "Dearly beloved," he began.

* * *

Colin stared out the window of the train, wondering exactly what the hell had just happened.

"Colin?"

He whipped his head around, glaring at Daisy.

She crumpled in the face of his anger, but she bravely pushed forward. "What happened to your horse?"

"I didn't get a chance to look after I saved you and got blamed for it," he snapped. "I hope it doesn't starve alone in the woods."

Daisy bit her lip. "Colin, I... I didn't... I..."

"Don't lie to me," he roared. "That whole scenario was staged. Otherwise, why would the vicar *and* your *father*, with his *rifle* be waiting for us? You planned that, but you won't get what you want out of me. I swear it. I will annul this marriage the first second I can. I don't want you."

Daisy gulped, lip trembling. "I understand what you're saying. It does look suspicious. I'm sure my father was up to something, but I... I don't think he wanted me to marry *you*."

"Good. Then you won't object to me NOT being married to you."

Daisy sniffled.

"Out of curiosity, how did you know?" he asked, trying to pass the time by satisfying his curiosity. *She owes me that much.*

"Know what?"

Colin slammed his fist against the side of the train. "How did you know about my title, damn you? How did you know?"

Daisy's eyes widened. "Title? What on earth?"

He raised his fist again, and Daisy flinched away. "Determined to play stupid, aren't you? My *title*, bitch. I'm Viscount Gelroy, aren't I? That's what you wanted, right? Did that boor even attack you, or was that part of the plot to trap me?"

"No," Daisy snapped. "I don't want that at all. I... title? You never told me that. How could I have known? And look at me. I'm bruised all over. You were there, you *know* it wasn't a ruse."

He shrugged, knowing he wasn't making sense, but his anger, despair, hopelessness and frustration had taken over his mouth, spewing themselves out with more emotion than sense. "But if you didn't know, what's happening?"

"I.... don't.... know," Daisy enunciated slowly, her confusion turning her words sharp. "I no more expected that scene than you did. I had no idea you were a... a viscount? Good heavens. No idea. No. I.... um..." She stammered to a halt, shaking her head.

"Is it your habit to flirt with total strangers?" Colin demanded. "Am I one in a string of conquests for you?"

"You're being rude," Daisy said. "Stop it. There was a time, before all this happened, when I wanted a future in which I could know you, Colin. It's something I've never done before, but... it was a special connection. At least, I thought it was, but now, you're being cruel. I was mistaken about you. I had no idea you had a title, nor what my father was up to, though I suspect it had more to do with Orville than you, but your unwillingness to listen doesn't bode well, to say the least."

"We won't be together long enough for my listening to make a difference to you." Colin turned back toward the window, ostentatiously ignoring his unwanted 'bride.'

Daisy didn't respond.

Her unwillingness to react to his provocation made him even angrier. Fearing his own rage would cause him to strike her, he tucked his fists under his thighs. The countryside blew past, almost too fast for him to take in. *Nice of her to spring for the train,* he thought. *It gets me to my destination faster, so I can unload my unwanted burden. I wonder how much* that *will cost. Damnation, will I never be able to accomplish a simple goal without these accursed complications? Now, I have a damned* wife. *What in God's name did I do to deserve this?*

How on earth am I going to explain this to Christopher? He's got enough to deal with, between his work and his family, and yet he was willing to host me.

"We will be staying with friends of mine in London," he said in a quiet, icy voice, not bothering to turn around. "They are the Bennetts. The master of the house is a busy, hardworking man, and his wife is heavily with child. You are not to bother either of them. Do you understand me?"

"I'm not five, Colin," Daisy replied, her voice dripping with scorn. "I know how to be a polite guest. You may not want me, but that doesn't mean I'll be rude."

"You had better not," he snarled threateningly.

She didn't respond.

The train rumbled along the tracks, eating up the miles between him and his destination.

Alone with his dark, angry thoughts, Colin at last recognized the fear hiding beneath the anger. Fear that he had lost what little control he had over his life. As rage died, bitterness and grim determination took hold.

"I will annul this marriage. A gunpoint wedding isn't legal. No one will force us to stay together."

"Of this, I have no doubt," Daisy agreed dryly. "You go ahead, Colin. I didn't ask for this any more than you did, and with how you've been acting since then, I think it's best we do go our separate ways."

"Where will you go?" he asked, turning to look at her.

She shrugged. "I have no idea. Not home. It's not safe there anymore. Don't worry about me, Colin. I'll figure out how to make my way in the world."

"It's not that easy," he pointed out.

"It's also not your problem. You can't reject me, say such terrible things to me, and still act like you care. I won't allow that."

"I once thought we were friends," he pointed out, a flutter of the old tenderness stirring him and escaping through his mouth before his overwhelmed mind could point out he was being contradictory.

"I once thought you were a reasonable man, one who might listen to me. Apparently, we didn't know each other long enough to have a friendship either."

"I was surprised..."

"As was I," she interrupted, "but no matter how many times I tell you that, you don't believe me, do you? I didn't know Father would be there with the vicar and the gun. I didn't know a trap had been set, and I didn't know you had a title until this moment. But you still don't believe me, do you?"

Colin shrugged. "Whether I do or don't makes little difference. We cannot remain married. It's simply not possible."

"I didn't ask to," she snapped. "So now, since I understand you completely—we cannot remain married—and I agree because I do not like the current shift in your behavior, can you please stop? I've heard all I care to hear on the subject."

Colin, realizing he had nothing new to say, and that she was right, snapped his mouth shut and turned back to the window in time to see the train pulling into the station. The brakes squealed on the tracks. The whistle shrieked and the big beast ground to a halt.

The late afternoon sun hung low above the rooftops, its light diffused by the smog. A heavy, dank and smoky scent hung in the air as Colin escorted his unwanted bride down from the train, a carpetbag clutched in her hand. His own, with whatever rags of clothing he had brought, was lost with the horse and likely never to be seen again.

Though he had no particular affection for those garments, their loss left him even more impoverished.

Daisy eyed the darkening sky, her nose wrinkling at the stink of fog and rubbish. "Where are we going?"

"It's about an hour's walk," he replied blandly.

"Shall we get a cab?" she suggested.

He shook his head. "I'm not paying for that."

"I can," she offered.

He shook his head. "Save your pocket money. You may need it later. It's not that far." He set off at a fast pace that forced her to trot to keep up, but she managed without angst. *She's fit, I'll give her that,* he thought grudgingly, *even though she had to put shoes on.*

Something about the memory of her bare feet struck him, and he pushed it away before he could analyze it.

"Keep your wits about you," he ordered. "This isn't the best part of town."

"Your friends live here?" she asked, eying the grubby tenements with suspicion.

He shook his head. "Not at all. This is only the nearest station. They live in a much friendlier neighborhood. They even have a garden where their child... soon children... can play."

He glanced at Daisy and caught a glimpse of her smile.

They hurried along through the deepening dusk, Colin observing each alley and side street warily, until the tenements changed to homes, the rubbish to tidy cobblestones, and lush trees stood in a few yards, freshening the air.

They finally arrived at a row of comfortable-looking townhouses, where Colin stepped up to the front door of a house and knocked.

A young man in a uniform opened, regarding them with curious eyes.

"Is the master in?" Colin asked. "He's expecting me." He dug into his pocket and drew out a dirty and wrinkled calling card.

"Step inside," the young man urged. "I will get him." He led the couple into a receiving room with a rich, dark-blue settee, on which Daisy perched. Colin also sat, putting as much distance between them as the furniture piece would allow. Whether that was because he remained angry and mistrustful, or because he didn't want to take in her luscious scent and all the sweet memories that went with it—and thus be forced to regret his unavoidable course of action—he didn't know.

A moment later, Christopher stalked into the room. "Colin! I expected you yesterday. What kept you?"

"Strange, strange things, my friend," he replied rising to shake Christopher's hand. "I doubt you'll believe me if I tell you."

"Now I'm even more curious," his friend quipped, running fingers through hair that had only the tiniest sprinkling of gray, much less than Colin's own, despite Christopher being the same age. "After dinner, we should have a brandy and you can tell me your wild tale."

"I shall certainly agree to that," he replied, mouth watering at the thought of the excellent brandy Christopher kept on hand, not to mention tasty dinners the Bennetts' cook-maid always prepared.

"Ahem," a soft voice cut into the reunion.

Conversation fell to an abrupt silence.

"And who is this?" Christopher asked, suddenly noticing the extra person in the room.

"This is Daisy," Colin said, his effusive greeting giving way to clipped, terse utterances. "My wife."

Christopher's warm brown eyes widened until he looked like a frog. A startled croak completed the effect. "Wife?"

"That's right," Colin said coolly. "I did warn you it was a strange story, did I not? In the meanwhile, my... my bride must be tired from traveling. She's had a difficult day. Do you have a guest room available?"

"Of course," Christopher replied. "I was expecting you, was I not? Ma'am? Lady Gelroy?"

Daisy started. "Yuh— yes?"

"Would you like to retire at this time? Shall I have a tray sent up?"

Daisy gave Colin a long, considering look, then nodded grimly. "Thank you, Mr. Bennett. That sounds like a fine plan. It was lovely to meet you."

Christopher rang a bell and a moment later, the cook-maid arrived.

"Burns," Christopher said to the woman.

She looked up at him, ready to receive instructions.

"I think we will all eat separately tonight. Please bring a tray up to Lady Gelroy in the guest chambers, when you bring my wife hers, and then we'll have trays in the study if you please."

"Very good, sir," the woman said mildly. "Please come this way." She indicated the doorway. Daisy, who had been staring at Colin with an unreadable expression on her face, paused long enough for an uncomfortable tension to grow, and then turned and stalked away.

"Good Lord," Christopher exclaimed as he escorted Colin out of the receiving room and down the hall to the study, where he sank into his favorite high-backed armchair. "What have you gotten yourself into this time, man?"

Colin shook his head, collapsing onto a red velvet chaise. "If only I knew."

"Married, though," Christopher said. "I never thought I would live to see the day. And why was I not informed sooner?"

"Well, hell, Chris," Colin exclaimed, dropping formality, "if I'd known for more than a day that this was going to happen, I might have."

Christopher's already stunned expression twisted further.

"But never mind. I'll be investigating tomorrow about procuring an annulment. I can't afford a wife I want, let alone one I can scarcely stand the sight of."

Christopher winced. "Well, that certainly clarifies things," he drawled sarcastically. "How on earth did you acquire a wife you don't want?"

"At gunpoint," Colin replied with a sigh.

Had Christopher not been seated, he would likely have ended up on the floor.

Chapter 5

AISY trailed after a young servant in a white cap and black dress, along a narrow hallway to a staircase and up. The home, though cozy, felt tight and closed-in compared to what she was used to. At the top, a wide landing revealed a long row of closed doors.

"This way, ma'am," the woman said in a low, gentle voice. "I'll show ye to the guestroom."

"Thank you," Daisy replied. She relaxed an iota. *I once had the thought that more time with Colin was a treat to be desired, but no more. Now, every moment I can spend away from him feels like a reward. I understand why he's angry, but… it's a shame he's angry with me.*

A door opened and a tall, dark-haired woman wearing a blue dressing gown stepped into the hallway.

"Oh!" she said shyly. "I didn't know we had a visitor. Sorry, I'm not receiving at the moment." She laid a hand on a belly so swollen, Daisy had never seen anything like it before.

"My apologies," Daisy replied. "I came with my husband, Colin Butler—er, Lord Gelroy. I understood he was invited."

"Husband?" The woman's eyes bugged out. "He married?"

"He did," Daisy concurred. "May I assume you are the lady of the house?"

"I am," the woman replied. "Mrs. Christopher Bennett, but you may call me Katerina." She grinned.

"A pleasure," Daisy said. Then she blurted, "You can't have more than a day or two left." She colored, embarrassed at her rudeness.

"I sincerely hope so," Katerina replied, rubbing the small of her back. "Being in confinement is… well… it's boring. I miss my friends, and I'm ready to meet my babies."

"Babies?"

Katerina nodded. "The midwife is quite certain there are two. Should be… interesting. I'm looking forward to it being over. In the meanwhile, if you can tolerate the sight of me, I'll be thankful you're here. You're the only person I've seen in weeks, apart from my mother-in-law, my daughter and my midwife. She's *your* mother-in-law, incidentally."

"She is?" *Oh, good heavens. What next?*

"She is. Say, would you like to dine with me? I'm dying for some conversation." A pained look crossed Katerina's face.

"I would like that," Daisy agreed, "but, I say, are you all right?"

Katerina relaxed and rubbed her belly. "False labor. I've been having pains for weeks. Sometimes for hours at a time, but labor doesn't begin. I think I might carry these two forever." She laughed without much humor and indicated the open doorway.

Daisy stepped through, wondering how a total stranger whose home she'd just invaded showed every sign of becoming an ally, if not a friend.

* * *

"And so then," Colin said, taking a deep, shuddering sip of brandy, his eyes fixed sightlessly on the massive collection of books with which Christopher lined the walls of the room, "I brought Daisy back to her house, and—no jest—her father was waiting with the vicar and a *rifle*. They forced us to marry on the spot. That was this morning." He drained his cup and grabbed a slice of bread from the basket between them, smearing it liberally with butter and taking a hearty bite.

"Good Lord," Christopher exclaimed. His brandy lay forgotten in its glass on the small table. A chunk of cheese dangled from his fingers.

Colin laughed mirthlessly. "You've said that about twenty times since I began."

"Well, you've had quite the adventure, haven't you?" Christopher said. He claimed his brandy and down the glass in a single gulp.

"I have," Colin agreed, "and the devil can take it. I didn't want an adventure. I just wanted a brief idyll. A moment out of time, where I could feel like a man instead of a machine. Where I could have hope for a normal future." His voice wavered.

"Understandable," Christopher agreed. "At the risk of sounding maudlin, it's not unusual for men of our age to seek the pleasure, not of a willing woman, but of a long-term relationship. Even my brother is happily married. Cary and I have been at it for years. Your turn had to come."

"Wanting my turn to come is surely normal," Colin agreed, splashing more brandy in his glass, "but you must see that it cannot be. I cannot remain married to Daisy."

"Why not? Granted I only met her for a moment, but she looked like a sturdy, humble lass. No high-strung filly there." He spooned up a mouthful of soup.

"Well, apart from the fact that I *can't afford a wife*," Colin snapped, "she and her damned family trapped me. Marriage at gunpoint is not legal. A wedding forced under false pretenses is invalid. The vicar didn't even give me a chance to speak and her father had a gun trained on her."

"On her, not on you?" Christopher pointed out.

"Well, yes, mostly," Colin agreed.

Christopher sat back in his chair, thoughtfully chewing on his slice of bread. Colin could see the cogs turning in his analytical mind.

"Are you certain they were trying to trap you?" Christopher asked at last. He took another bite of soup and leaned forward, dark eyes trained on Colin.

"What do you mean? It was obviously a trap."

"Oh, I agree," Christopher said. "It's plain as day. What I'm less clear on is who was the bait... and who was the prey? I'm not convinced you were the intended target at all."

Colin raised one eyebrow and took another sip of brandy.

"I mean, think about it. Did you introduce yourself as Viscount Gelroy?"

"Of course not." Colin shook his head. "Why would I do that? I hate the thrice-damned title."

"Precisely. You introduced yourself using a humble, everyday name, wearing humble, ragged clothing and scuffed boots and leading a half-dead horse. Where is the horse, by the way?"

"Got lost in the confusion," Colin replied. "I hope he's enjoying the spring growth. He won't survive the winter."

Christopher patted Colin on the shoulder. "He wouldn't have anyway."

Colin pursed his lips but said nothing.

"At any rate," Christopher added as he crumbled a crust of bread into his soup, "I doubt anyone knew of your title. In fact, I'm sure they didn't. For all anyone knew, you were no one in particular. Didn't you mention that your—ahem—bride had a history with the man you rescued her from?"

"She certainly seemed to," Colin realized, thinking back over the brief conversations he'd shared with Daisy.

"Well, then, that seems more likely, doesn't it? Her father selected a suitor for her. She was... less than enthusiastic about the match, and the two of them conspired to trap *her* into marriage. Her, not you. You bumbled into the crossfire."

Colin twisted his lips as he considered a new possibility. "But the vicar..."

"Probably wasn't in on the entire plot and had no idea what man he was looking for. He heard a couple was misbehaving, you two turned up, and he jumped in."

"That makes horrible sense," Colin admitted. He grabbed a chunk of cheese and chewed it while he finally considered the possibility. "But it doesn't matter," he added, swallowing and nearly choking as guilt over how unkind he'd been to Daisy closed down his throat. *If she didn't know... if she was just as shocked as me... that poor girl. Her own father facilitated...* His thoughts veered away as Christopher continued.

"Why not?"

"Because whether Daisy was a co-conspirator or an innocent dupe is irrelevant. I can't afford a wife."

Christopher frowned, acknowledging the dilemma. "You have a point there, sadly. But what will happen to your wife after the annulment?"

Colin shrugged. "I don't care."

"Liar," Christopher accused. "You didn't abandon her in her village with her angry father and his gun. You must care at least a little."

"I can't afford to care," Colin protested. "I can no more fund her relocation to a safer place than I can keep her."

"You'd like to, wouldn't you?" Christopher prodded. "I mean, you mentioned being a bit... infatuated. I remember the first time I saw Katerina. I don't think I truly fell in love with her until we'd been married a while, but that first meeting... it was powerful."

Colin rolled his eyes upward and stared at the ceiling. "Your wife badly needed to marry, and you had the means to follow through. My 'wife' doesn't need a husband, and even if she did, I can't be that man, even if I want to."

"That's hard," Christopher said.

Colin nodded and ended the conversation by shoveling soup into his mouth.

Christopher kept talking. "Very well. If my wife hasn't gone into labor by the morning, I will take you on your investigation. Do you need a loan to cover the cost… or a gift?"

Colin gulped. "I don't want charity."

"I don't want your estate to go bankrupt over this. Please, for once, let me help you."

"Very well," Colin agreed. "This time, I'm in over my head. If you can prevent me from drowning, I'll accept the hand."

Christopher nodded and splashed more brandy into his friend's glass.

* * *

Daisy stretched out on the Bennetts' comfortable guest bed. Tucking her arms behind her head, she regarded the flickering shadows of candlelight on the ceiling. "Mrs. Bennett will be delivering soon, maybe even by morning," she murmured, recalling how many pains her host had suffered. Still, she'd eaten heartily and moved around the room, restless as a mother cat.

"What a lovely lady. I wish I could have met her under better circumstances. I wonder what tomorrow will bring."

The hasty end to your hasty marriage, a sly voice in her mind whispered.

"I know that," she whispered. "Colin has been clear about his intentions. I mean after. I can't go home. I wonder if he will at least escort me to the bank. It's time for me to take control of my future."

Reassured, though still stinging from Colin's harsh rejection, Daisy rolled her side and closed her eyes.

She wasn't sure how much time passed, but the bed sagged, and a warm body slipped in beside her.

Before Daisy could release more than a startled squeak, warm arms enfolded her, and a hot, liquor-scented breath wafted over her cheek. "You smell so good," Colin whispered, "like warm summer peaches and hope." He kissed the side of her neck.

"Did you have a change of heart?" Daisy asked, raising one eyebrow, though he couldn't see it.

"No, never," he murmured. "I knew from the beginning that you were special; that we would be special together. Tell me you didn't know it too."

"Are you foxed?" she asked, rolling in his arms.

Colin laid his lips on hers.

A soft moan escaped Daisy as memories of Colin's bittersweet goodbye washed over her.

"You're more intoxicating than any spirit," he breathed against her mouth.

His tongue slipped into her mouth. The brandy he'd drunk sizzled on Daisy's tongue. Her body relaxed. Overcome by so many unprecedented events, she took comfort in the arms of a man whose connection to her could not be denied. *My husband. A stranger, but my heart knows him.*

It seemed her body did too. John Orville had only to glance in her direction to make her shudder and her blood run cold. Not so, Colin. His hands slid, warm and eager, over her back. She could feel the heat right through the thin fabric of her nightgown.

"Colin," she breathed. "Colin…"

"Daisy," he murmured. "Are you sure you're real?"

"Are you sure you're not angry anymore?" she asked, dragging herself out of the vortex of passion he had unexpectedly created.

"Angry? Oh, yes, darling, I'm angry. Trouble is, I don't know who to be angry at or about what anymore. It's so damned confusing. Only one thing still makes sense in this topsy-turvy mess."

"What's that?" she asked looking into his eyes.

"I want you." His lips claimed hers again.

This time, the touch drove Daisy straight into a maelstrom of confused sensations. Desire. Fear. Uncertainty. Infatuation. She cupped Colin's face in both hands and took charge of the kiss. His hands on her back slipped lower, cupping her bottom.

It seemed the most natural thing in the world for Daisy to let her thigh slip over his hip. He arched his torso, grinding her intimate places against his rigid heat. Liquid warmth pooled at the place their bodies touched.

After the madness of that wedding and everything that surrounded it, I didn't expect a wedding night. And yet, Colin's touch brought her back to those precious hours when he had felt like a dream man. *He's much more complex than that,* she admitted to herself, *and part of the idyll was that I could remember him in his perfection and never need to embrace him as a whole person.* The real man, the man she had yet to learn, had changed again. *Now he wants* us *it seems. A real marriage. Starting now.*

She tangled her tongue with his, enjoying his pleasured growls.

He fisted his hands in the fabric of her nightgown, until it bunched around her waist, leaving her most intimate places bare. Only then did she notice how little he wore. Only a pair of ragged drawers and an undershirt.

Somehow, though she'd always assumed she would marry and share intimacy with a man, she had never quite visualized the moment when her bare, intimate parts touched him. *Or when he touches them*, she realized with a start, as he began to stroke and squeeze her naked bottom. Though the unaccustomed touch felt strange, the tingling and the wetness in the secret opening of her body told her all was well.

Her grip on his cheeks turned to a caress. She traced the lines of his face, feeling the carved grooves, the rough stubble, the fine bone structure. His tongue swirled in her mouth. His erection, still covered by his undergarments, jabbed at the juncture of her thighs.

Without warning, Colin released Daisy's mouth and rose to his knees, dragging his undershirt over his head.

Unable to resist the draw of his heavy, work-strengthened chest, she rose up beside him and ran her hands into the sparse, brown curls there. The contrast of textures left her fingers tingling.

"Let's get you out of this," Colin suggested, reaching for the buttons of her nightgown.

She gulped as he opened her bodice and gripped the fabric again, this time taking it off her.

For a moment, trepidation warred with pleasured desire. Naked with a total stranger took a lot of slow, deep breathing to accept. Her body, on the other hand, seemed to know what it wanted. Her nipples hardened, reaching for contact with his firm, bare chest. Her back arched of its own accord.

"Lovely," he murmured, cupping one breast in each hand.

"Oh!" she exclaimed softly. A slow exhalation accompanied his thumbs coming into direct contact with each nipple. Sweet, sweet tingles chased down her belly. Her knees weakened.

"Oho, easy now," he said, pride in his voice. "Lie back, sweet girl. I have many more touches for you."

"Oh, Colin," she squeaked, positioning herself on the pillows again.

Colin quickly shucked his drawers and stretched out beside her, on his side. One warm hand stroked her entire length, from her shoulder to her belly and below, lightly cupping the place no one had touched before.

He's going to do more than touch it, she reminded herself, not sure if the accompanying movement was a shudder or a shiver. Maybe both.

"Hot and wet. Just as I knew you'd be. Are you so eager for me, Daisy?"

"You know I am," she breathed, "but I'm scared, Colin."

"Don't be afraid," he urged, even as his light stroking turned purposeful and he delved through the golden curls into intimate folds that reacted strongly to his touch. "I'm going to love you so nicely. You'll enjoy every moment." His questing fingers slid along slick, love-dampened folds, finding and testing her opening.

"Oh!" Daisy exclaimed. "Oh, Colin!"

He leaned forward and nipped her throat, distracting her as he pushed ever deeper. When he withdrew and returned with two fingers, opening the portal to unexpected dimensions, the sound she released in no way resembled words.

Hot wetness engulfed one nipple. Colin sucked at the aching tip. More heat and wetness surged. His encroaching fingers curved upward, finding a spot she hadn't known existed.

Colin transferred his attention to her other breast, nipping the tender tip as his thumb sought and found a knot of sensitive tissue that, at his first touch, drew her head up off the bed with a cry.

"That's it, love. Easy, easy. Enjoy it. Enjoy my touch. Let it make you feel good."

At first, she wasn't sure his touch had felt good. Overwhelming, more like. But as she relaxed into his intimate caresses, a pleasure so sharp she could almost have called it pain radiated out from her core. It built. Built until she didn't know how her body could contain it. Her breath shuddered. Her body tensed, tensed... Locked.

A quiet squeak marked the moment as her pleasure peaked for the first time.

Colin shifted, kneeling between her thighs, and lifted her hips. One hand remained on her sex, keeping the folds open. The other, she barely registered through her continuing climax, took hold of his jutting erection, lining it up with her opening and surging home in one smooth stroke.

The pain she'd been told to expect turned out to be little more than a tiny ache and a startling fullness. He leaned down and kissed her as he filled her.

Daisy stilled beneath her husband as he began to drive into her, again and again, taking obvious pleasure in the clinging wetness of her body. A few quick surges had him growling, muscles locking in what she immediately recognized as the match of her own lovely peak.

She stroked his back, exploring the hard, bunched muscles as they relaxed slowly into limpness. He fell off her onto his side and immediately passed out.

Arching one eyebrow, Daisy shook her head in amazement. Grinning wryly, she turned on her side and allowed herself to relax.

Chapter 6

ENTLE comfort lured Colin up from the depths of the most restful slumber he could recall ever having had. He felt warm, warmer than this thin, threadbare blanket could account for, spring notwithstanding. The mattress felt comfortable. *Well, Christopher is able to afford nice things,* he thought. *But wait, I've slept in this bed before. It's a good bed, but...*

The feeling of relaxation was so unexpected, so rare that he struggled to understand it. *I feel like Atlas when he handed the world over to Hercules. Why is that?*

A soft exhalation in the vicinity of his chin dragged his eyes open. Though morning had not come, a big, yellow moon shone in the window. Its light revealed the small, slender figure in his arms. Golden hair strewn across the bed. The scent of peaches. *Daisy. Warm and relaxed in bed with me.* A ghost of a smile crossed his face. *No wonder I feel good. It's been years since I made love to a woman, and it was... magical. Perfect. She's the sweetest, most eager lover. What a blessing.*

Then, Colin's eyes opened wide. "Oh, no!" he breathed.

Daisy stirred, rolling onto her back.

Colin recoiled. "Oh, no! Oh, no!"

Daisy opened her eyes and stretched, apparently at peace with the world. "What's wrong, love?" she asked, turning his direction and propping herself up on one elbow.

"What did we do? Oh, God."

"Um, we consummated our marriage?" she pointed out, phrasing the statement as a question.

Nausea began to churn in Colin's belly.

"What's wrong?" she asked again, more seriously this time. "I know you had some reservations, but last night, I thought you had made peace with this... with us. That's how you were acting."

"That's how the *brandy* was acting," he hissed. "Why didn't you stop me? I thought you were furious and disgusted with me. Why on earth did you let me touch you?"

Daisy lowered her eyebrows. "You did a good bit more than touch," she said.

Colin buried his face in his hands. "Oh, God. Don't remind me."

Her smaller hands grasped his wrists, dragging them away so she could look into his eyes. He caught a quick flash of her naked body. His own responded eagerly, ready for another taste of his wife. It sounded marvelous. So insanely wonderful that he had to fight to stop himself from grabbing her and tumbling her to the bed. "We can't do this, Daisy," he said, his voice rough and painful in his throat.

"Do what?" she demanded, leaning in close.

"Be married," he said. "I can't have a wife. It's not possible."

"I'm sorry, love," she said, biting her lip as her face and chest flushed, "but the fact is, you *do* have a wife. I'm sorry you're upset about it, but as of last night, we cannot change it."

"We must," he insisted. "The marriage was created under false pretenses. We were forced. Surely, an annulment can still be obtained..."

"No," Daisy interrupted his runaway thoughts. "No, Colin. I won't allow that."

"Our marriage was contracted illegally. Your virginity, our intimacy, it won't matter."

Daisy clamped her hand over his mouth. "Stop that. Our marriage is only invalid if one of us protests it. I won't go along with your plan to end it anymore. I'll fight you. I'll tell anyone, everyone, that you married me, took my virginity and now you're trying to abandon me. I'll tell everyone who will listen that you're a despoiler of innocents. I will not allow you to steal my innocence *and* my reputation. You'll pay with your own. I'll make sure of it. Come what may, Colin, you're stuck with me."

Colin opened his mouth and then shut it again. For the first time, he looked at the situation through Daisy's eyes. *She must be so confused.* "You don't understand," he said at last.

"Of course I don't," she snapped. "You've explained nothing. It was all well and good to be a mysterious stranger when our entire relationship was only meant to last a day, but things have changed now, Colin. We're married, consummated, and you won't tell me *why* that's a problem. I might almost have thought we could be happy together."

Colin's teeth ground together, preventing any words from escaping.

"Do you still think I meant to trap you?"

He shook his head. "It was that idiot your father wanted you to marry, wasn't it? Didn't he and your father set out to trap you?"

She nodded. "That seems most likely," she agreed, scowling. "You saved me from worse than ravishment alone."

"And this was my reward." He rolled his eyes to the ceiling.

"I must say, I'm feeling rather insulted," she told him. "This may not be what you planned, but is it really as bad as that? Granted, we're still strangers, but there is some essential draw between us."

Colin shook his head, not denying the obvious, but trying to shake off his inertia and speak. "It's not enough. If I care about you at all, I can't do this to you."

"Well," Daisy said tartly, "if you plan to annul our marriage for *my own good,* even though you took it upon yourself to relieve me of my virginity, you'll have to provide a better reason than these vague comments."

Colin closed his eyes. The words of his predicament clogged his throat. *It's too late,* he reminded himself. *If you wanted to present a case of marriage against your will, you wouldn't have bedded her.* He glanced at the sheets, at the pink-tinged semen stain that had gathered while Daisy slept. *You wanted her for yourself. You have from the first moment. The brandy didn't make you take her. It let you. Now what?* He didn't know. Nothing made sense anymore, but the green eyes shining with righteous indignation in the moonlight pricked at his conscience.

"It may be too much to ask," he said at last, humbly, "but can you trust me a little longer? I will show you everything you need to know… once we go home."

"Home?"

He nodded. "To my estate. I… You would just have to see… everything in order to understand."

Daisy pursed her lips. "Trusting you hasn't done me much good thus far."

"Please, Daisy. I'm sorry. Please."

"Very well," she said at last.

Colin closed his eyes, nauseous again.

* * *

Daisy flopped back on the bed, more confused and upset than ever. *It's one thing after another. As if the hopeless infatuation wasn't bad enough. That, at least, mixed some sweet with the bitter. But adding on Father's betrayal with that pig, John Orville, this forced marriage, Colin's hostile behavior yesterday, the... events of last night.* Her cheeks heated at the memory of wanton pleasure.

Now, he'd turned again. It was beyond frustrating. *Why on earth am I even considering trusting him? What I've seen so far shows me that he's not a good partner, and our bond was imaginary.*

She knew the answer. She was just as stuck as he and just as inclined to be upset about it.

Agitated, she bounced up from the bed, retrieved her nightgown from amongst the sheets and covered it with her dressing gown. Walking across the room, she stepped out onto the balcony that overlooked the street. Even at the late hour, vehicles drove past, sleepy horses spluttering and complaining in a light drizzle.

Here, Daisy could see that the moon was full; bright and yellow, glowing down on her face. She closed her eyes, letting the light filter through her eyelids. *Why is all this happening?* she wondered. A tear escaped from beneath her eyelid and rolled down her cheek. She had never felt so powerfully alone. It felt deeper than words, deeper than tears, as though some essential element of her psyche had been ripped from inside her and thrown over the balcony to wither in the street below.

At last, fatigue overcame distress, and Daisy made her way back to the bedroom. Colin lay perched on the edge of the bed. His rigid posture told her he was not asleep but pretending.

No matter. I have no desire to talk to him either. She assumed a matching pose on the opposite edge and lay in discomfort on the comfortable mattress.

"Colin?" she said at last.

"Hmmm," he replied, not sounding sleepy in the least.

"What will happen tomorrow?"

"I need to see a man about a horse," he replied. "That's why we're here. After that, we'll head home. It's about a three-day walk."

Daisy raised her eyebrows. *Goodness, what strange things he decides to do. A nobleman walk three days in the wilderness? I wonder where he left his carriage.*

Then, she decided she didn't care and closed her eyes, willing sleep to claim her.

It didn't.

* * *

Morning dawned painfully bright on bleary eyes. Yawning and stretching aching muscles, the couple dragged themselves from their bed, turned to look at one another in wary hopelessness, and dragged on clothing.

Unable to form a coherent thought, Daisy trailed after her husband down to the dining room, where a tasty breakfast lay, hot and utterly unappealing, on the sideboard. Daisy claimed some tea and toast, spread marmalade, and sat, staring at the repast without consuming it.

Colin frowned at his food but began to shovel it into his mouth with unmannerly haste.

Good thing our hosts are not around to see this, Daisy thought. "Colin?"

He met her eyes, swallowing but not responding.

"For what it's worth, though I had nothing to do with causing this predicament, I'm sorry it put you in an uncomfortable spot."

He sipped from his cup of coffee. "I'm sorry as well. It was not my intention to harm you. Far from it."

"Do you believe me then?" she asked, pushing her luck. She forced a corner of the toast into her mouth, chewed and swallowed. It stuck, making her cough. She washed it down with a swig of tea.

"I'm trying to," he replied with painful honesty. "I mean, I can see the explanation you've laid out, and it does make sense, but..."

"But you don't trust people in general?" she guessed.

"It's a small number," he agreed. "I'm sorry, Daisy, but I just don't know you well enough yet."

"Fair enough. Will you allow yourself to get to know me since there's no other option?"

"I'll try." He sighed deeply. "I wouldn't think less of you if, after you've seen my estate, you decide that the loss of your maidenhead is a fair price to pay for escaping."

"What odd things you say," she commented. Again, she lifted her toast, but then she set it down again, scowling.

"I know. I swear it will all make sense in time."

"All? Do you mean that in the end, we'll find a way to make peace, and live as a couple, and try to make a family together?"

Colin choked on his coffee. Clearing his throat, he shook his head. "If, after you've seen... everything, you decide to stay—which you won't—and you also decide that you don't hate me—which you will—I don't know. I think... I think I just need some time. Can you give me that?"

"I don't know," she replied honestly. "Do you deserve it?"

"Not in the slightest," he replied. Then he shoved a large bite of food into his mouth, cutting off the conversation.

Daisy studied his face, her teacup sloshing in her hand. He didn't look angry this morning. He looked... defeated. The sunlight filtering through the warm, golden draperies set the silver strands in his dark hair shining and reflected off the lines bracketing his eyes and mouth. *He's not old, but he looks it,* she thought. *What could have etched so much pain on every line of his face?* Another question with no answer made her grumpy, and she frowned at her unwanted food.

"I must say, you two are gloomy this morning," Christopher said, bustling into the room and helping himself to a hearty breakfast of eggs, toast, sausages and coffee. "I see the sun is shining, but it's not too hot yet. What's the trouble?"

Daisy shrugged and hid her face behind her teacup.

Colin shook his head. "It's beyond explanation," he told his friend. "Were you planning to go to the factory today?"

"Not a bit," Christopher replied. "My father forbade it. He said, as close as my wife is to delivering, I must stay with her until the moment comes. I almost wish I could buck convention and assist her in the delivery."

"Why don't you?" Daisy asked. "Surely, in your own home, with your own wife, you can do whatever you want..."

Christopher grinned wryly. "The women in question won't allow it. They tell me birthing is women's business and no place for a gentleman. That I'll be underfoot. My task has been clearly laid out. I'm to summon the midwife and then take my daughter somewhere so she won't be troubled if Kat gets... loud."

Daisy rolled her eyes. *If I had a baby on the way, I wouldn't let my husband out of my sight. He participated in the begetting, he can assist* me *while I deliver.* Then it dawned on her that any child she bore would be Colin's, supposing every 'if' he'd laid out came to pass. *I might decide to hate him,* she thought, *if things don't start making sense soon. This is ridiculous.*

"So, what are you two planning to do today?"

"I'm going to call on Jeremy Ralston," Colin explained. "Remember he was a few years behind us in school?"

"That's right," Christopher agreed. "You tutored him in mathematics. He had no head for numbers, isn't that right?"

"Oh, he did," Colin replied. "He only had to get past *thinking* he had no head for numbers. Once I showed him, he was bright enough to open a stable and breed, train and sell some prime racehorses. Years ago, he promised me a favor—which I forgot until now. He's just retired his stallion Pesadilla and I hope to acquire him for stud."

"Brilliant!" Christopher cheered.

"Will you be going on to see about… what we discussed?" Christopher asked. "Do I need to come with you?"

Colin shook his head. "That will not be possible after all. Stay, tend to your wife. I'll be back by luncheon, I hope, and then my…" he looked at Daisy with an unreadable expression, "my wife and I must depart."

Christopher looked from Colin to Daisy and back, and a knowing expression spread across his face.

He's just as handsome as Colin, Daisy thought, blushing as she watched him make sense out of the vague comment. *In fact, they could be brothers, but it's clear Mr. Bennett has lived a more comfortable life. Wait, does that even make sense? He's a man of business. He works hard every day. Why does he resemble a gentleman of leisure when Colin, who has a noble title, is more haggard than a laborer?*

"Do you mind if my wife remains here?" Colin asked. "Being around a stallion who is uncomfortable in an unfamiliar environment in the noisy city could be dangerous."

"And yet," she interjected, "you want me to walk with him for three days to your estate. Will that not also be dangerous?"

He regarded her without speaking again. "Do you have another option?"

"I do," she replied. "I have no great desire to walk and walk until I wear my boots out. Is there a train that crosses your estate?"

"Near it," he replied, "but I will not be able to buy tickets."

"I will," she volunteered, "for us and your horse."

"You might want to save your money," Colin suggested.

"I'll decide what to do with my money," she snapped.

He shut his mouth, blinking.

Daisy's face heated as she realized that she'd not only been rude, she'd done it in front of their host. *Our squabble is not Mr. Bennett's business.*

"Very well," Colin agreed. "If you give me the money, I'll arrange it, all right? There's still about an hour's walk once we disembark. Will that suit you?"

"Yes," she said firmly, and then let silence fall.

A short time later, Colin departed, the promised banknotes in his pocket. Daisy took a seat in the Bennetts' library, appropriated an interesting-looking book and tried to lose herself in the story. Distraction overtook her every time she began to settle, filling her mind with useless, pointless ruminations.

A moment later, the door opened, and Katerina lumbered in, holding her belly with one hand. She made her way to the bench of an unadorned, black pianoforte set in the center of the room and took a seat. A moment later, glorious music poured from the instrument, raising the hairs on the back of Daisy's neck.

When the impromptu concert ended, Daisy said softly, "That was lovely. What was it?"

"Chopin," Katerina replied. "I didn't realize you were here. I do hope I didn't disturb your reading."

"Not at all," Daisy replied. "I couldn't have concentrated to save my life. Everything has been so topsy-turvy lately."

"I know what that's like," Katerina agreed. "Thankfully, I've come through the fire and now, I only have normal-people problems, like how to get these two babies on the outside before I topple."

Daisy regarded her hostess skeptically. Katerina didn't look like someone who knew intimately about the travails of life. She looked like a dark-haired fairy princess, willowy and serene.

"Oh, don't look at me like that," Katerina said, her voice grumpy. "I'm blessed now, but once upon a time... well, let's just say that not all fathers are created equal."

"Tell me about it," Daisy moaned. "I believe my father conspired to have me *assaulted* so he could force me to marry the man he chose, a man I hate. I might be fortunate that the result is I'm stuck with Colin, who seems quietly to despise me. The alternative is much worse."

Katerina frowned. Then she drew in a slow, deep breath and released it over a long course of moments. "Sorry," she said at last, panting. "That hurt a lot. I'm sorry to hear it. Mine assaulted me directly."

Daisy's jaw dropped. "He… he did what?"

"Beat me," Katerina admitted freely. "With anything he could find, including his fists. I have scars you would not believe. Good thing they're mostly hidden. Let reassure you that marriages can be happy, even when they begin with disaster. Lord Gelroy is a good man. He's been a family friend since before I entered the family, and he's dear to me as a brother. He's just had a very hard life. If you can get into his heart, I think… I think he'll be a good man to love. Oooh." Another pain tightened Katerina's belly, and she closed her eyes. This time, her slow exhalation sounded like a moan.

"I say, Mrs. Bennett, are you all right?" Daisy asked, concern growing.

Katerina held out one hand in a 'stop' motion and continued her low moaning, pausing only to snatch a quick breath before continuing as more than a minute passed.

"Oh, God," she whispered as it passed. "No, Lady Gelroy, I don't think I am."

"Is it time to summon the midwife?" Daisy guessed.

Katerina nodded, her eyes pinching in the corners.

"Shall I help you to the settee first?" Daisy offered.

"I'd rather not," Katerina replied, her voice raspy. "I want to get to my bed."

Daisy found the bell cord and rang for the cook-maid, who appeared in record time.

"Please send for Mrs. Turner," Katerina rasped the moment a young, brown-haired woman poked her head into the room.

"Shall I help you to your bedroom then?" Daisy suggested.

"Please," Katerina agreed, hoisting herself uncomfortably to her feet. Immediately, another pain took her, and she swayed.

Daisy hurried to her side, wrapping an arm around her waist to support her.

Katerina pressed heavily on Daisy, moaning loudly in her ear. This time, the low toning rose in pitch until it was nearly a scream. She sobbed, breath catching as the pain clenched down on her.

Helplessness consumed Daisy. She could do nothing to ease the moment, only prevent her new friend from falling into a pregnant heap on the floor.

The moment the pain passed, Katerina moved. "Come on," she urged. "I only have a short time before the next one begins. Please help me."

Nodding, Daisy supported Katerina out of the music room and carefully up the stairs.

"Hurry," Katerina urged. "I don't want to get stuck here!"

They made it safely to the top, and Daisy stared in dismay at the matching doors all up and down the hallway. She recognized the guest room in which she'd slept, but the others remained a mystery.

A door opened, and Christopher popped his head out. "What's going on?" he asked.

"It's begun," Katerina replied miserably. "Help me. Aaaaaah!" She wailed and lurched toward the wall, leaning against it with both hands while she shifted her weight from one foot to the other.

"Your servant has already gone to call for the midwife," Daisy informed Christopher as he approached his wife but paused beside her, bewildered.

The pain eased and Katerina launched herself into her husband's arms. "It hurts," she whimpered.

"I know, love," he murmured. "I know. I'm so sorry. It will be over soon, and our babies will be here. You'll get to meet them. Only, you have to endure a little longer."

His tender words caused Daisy's heart to ache. *My husband will never flutter around me, desperately trying to be strong while worrying about me.* "We should get her into the room," Daisy suggested. "I think she needs to be in a place where she can sit or lie down."

"Yes, yes," Christopher agreed. With one swift movement, he scooped his wife into his arms, unconcerned with the hefty weight of her belly, and carried her through the door. Daisy lingered in the doorway, uncertain whether she should enter or excuse herself as her host laid his wife on her bed.

Katerina immediately rolled onto her hands and knees, moaning low and deep again. This time, she seemed better able to control herself through the contraction. The moaning sounded purposeful, not hysterical, though her eyes looked wild.

A door slammed downstairs and feet thundered on the treads.

Christopher, hurried out of the bedroom, calling, "Mrs. Turner! Thank God!"

The woman, a pretty, brown-haired lady who looked to be around fifty, hurried into the room, a simple black skirt clutched in one hand. "How long has she been feeling the pains?"

"Hard to say," Christopher replied. "She doesn't know either."

"I talked to her in the evening," Daisy added. "They kept interrupting her, but they didn't seem to bother her then. This morning, she wasn't even able to talk or walk."

"I would guess since early yesterday, probably, but she has so many, has had so many, that led to nothing," Christopher added.

"Not unusual."

"We're not early, are we?" he asked. "I thought it might be another couple of weeks."

"It might, but her body has decided it's had enough, and that's that. A couple of weeks rarely poses a problem." She reached the bedside and laid her hand on Katerina's forehead.

Lurking in the doorway, Daisy could see the worry on the woman's face.

"Is everything all right?" Christopher asked, peering into his guest's face.

"What?" The woman shook her head and dragged off her hat, tucking it under her arm. "No, I'm fine. I'm just... just concerned because my apprentice isn't available today. That's always the way it goes. Twins to deliver and I'm on my own. Would you like to buck convention, Mr. Bennett, and assist me with your wife's delivery?"

"Um..." Christopher trailed off, then visibly steeled himself and squared his shoulders. "What must I do?"

At that moment, a little girl with dark hair and huge brown eyes stuck her nose into the room. "Papa? Is anything happening? I heard strange noises."

"Oh, God," Christopher muttered, adding a couple of muttered curses Daisy could barely make out before he addressed his daughter in a hearty, cheerful voice. "Everything is fine, Sophia."

"So much for that idea," Mrs. Turner quipped. "Go to your daughter, Mr. Bennett. She's no fool, and you should care for her."

"But my wife..."

"I'll manage." Mrs. Turner scanned the room as though looking for help to appear, and her eyes locked with Daisy's. "You there. Who are you?"

Christopher snorted. "You wouldn't believe me if I told you. She's... a guest. We'll explain the rest later."

"Any chance you might like to assist me?" the woman suggested.

It's an absurd suggestion that I assist the midwife. "Would Mrs. Bennett consent to having me in the room? I'm nearly a stranger to her, and I have no training whatsoever. I've never assisted with the delivery of anything bigger than a puppy."

Mrs. Turner's dark eyes lit up. "You've watched animals deliver?"

Daisy nodded. "Barn cats and my father's hounds. The hounds sometimes needed a bit of help."

"You'll do. All I need is someone to soothe the mother, and then to provide another set of hands when the babies need holding."

"I'll help if she allows it," Daisy decided. "I'd like to be of use."

"Excellent," Christopher said. "Come, Sophia. Let's talk a bit." He escorted his daughter away.

"Come along then. Um, what is your name?"

"Daisy... um... Butler," she said, completely muddling her introduction, as she had nearly forgotten her new last name.

The woman looked at her sharply, seeming to react to the name. "Daisy. I'm Elizabeth Turner. You might have guessed, I'm the midwife."

"I did guess," Daisy agreed. "You should know that I only met the Bennetts yesterday. Mrs. Bennett might be uncomfortable with me being there."

"If she's as far into her labor as I think she is, she probably won't worry about it in the slightest. We'll ask."

"All right."

"Mrs. Bennett? Katerina?"

Katerina's unfocused gaze turned toward the midwife. Her low toning stopped, and she drew in a deep breath, her shoulders sagging.

"My apprentice is not able to join us this evening, but your guest, Mrs. Butler..." a strange note sounded in her voice as she spoke the name Daisy scarcely recognized as her own, "is willing to help. Do you mind?"

Katerina turned to Daisy, finally focusing her eyes. "Yes, that will be fine. Please, will you come?" she extended a hand. "I'm... I'm afraid."

"Now, don't be," Mrs. Turner huffed. "I'm here. I'll be sure nothing bad happens to you."

"I know, I know," Katerina replied, "but it hurts."

"Take a seat beside her," the midwife ordered Daisy, digging in her bag and pulling out a folded square of simple cotton fabric. "Hold her hand. Maybe sing to her. She likes music. Um, do you sing?"

"About like average, I suppose," Daisy replied. "Would that help you, Mrs. Bennett?"

Katerina nodded. Another pain clamped down her belly, and she began her soft toning once again.

Daisy took the note as an indication of what key the laboring mother found most soothing, and began a quiet rendition of "Scarborough Fair," which was the only gentle song she could think of that had lyrics she could remember.

Meanwhile, Mrs. Turner had tugged Katerina's undergarments from her body and hiked her skirt up, tucking the pad under her hips. "Has your water broken yet?"

Katerina didn't answer, intent as she was on her coping strategy. She held Daisy's hand loosely, but her focus remained inward.

"Is she all right?" Daisy asked.

"Oh, yes," Mrs. Turner replied. "Given her reactions, I'd say she's near the end. This shouldn't last long at all. Especially not since she's given birth before. Twins are often small, and so the actual delivery shouldn't unduly strain her."

"Ugh," Katerina grunted, falling limp against the pillows and rolling to her side. "I hate lying on my back."

"You don't have to," Mrs. Turner replied. "Choose any position that feels comfortable to you."

"I have better cloths," Katerina added. "In the bureau."

Daisy released her new friend's hand and opened an ornate, darkly-stained bureau to reveal a stack of cotton squares dyed in a myriad of unusual patterns.

"Scraps," Mrs. Turner explained, "from the cotton mill. These will work nicely."

Another moan. This one began to sound hysterical. Daisy hurried back to her side and tucked her hand into Katerina's. The woman's grip turned harsh, crushing Daisy's fingers.

"No, Kat," Mrs. Turner scolded in a sharp, almost angry voice. "That screaming will only make you hurt more. Keep moaning low. It works better."

Katerina obeyed. Her grip on Daisy's fingers loosened.

Daisy considered what to do next. Her songs had fled, and they clashed with Katerina's tone more often than not anyway. Instead, she pitched her voice to the same note and began to rattle off Shakespeare. " 'Shall I compare thee to a summer's day?' " Rather than the usual intense inflections with which she infused her recitations, she kept her murmur like a drone, only providing a counterpoint for Katerina to consider.

The pain eased, and Kat squeezed Daisy's hand gently.

Daisy looked into her eyes. Her friend shook her head slightly.

"What do you mean?" she whispered.

"Probably she'd like you to stop. At the end of labor, a woman goes deep inward. Some want to be distracted, but... It seems Mrs. Bennett doesn't. I'm not surprised. Artists often have a place inside themselves where they can retreat."

"Is that it? Shall I stop talking while you're... busy?"

Katerina dipped her chin.

Daisy considered apologizing. *But for what? We're all fumbling through this, all but Mrs. Turner.* She patted Katerina's hand. Because her gaze was still locked on the other woman's face, she saw the next surge come over her with a worried furrow of her eyebrow. Then her face went slack. Her eyes lost focus. Her hand clamped down hard on Daisy's. She gritted her teeth and snarled. It wasn't a fearful sound but rather a powerful one, filled with strength and intention.

From her position, lying on her side, Katerina drew her knees up and bore down.

An audible splash sounded.

Katerina whimpered.

"Sorry, sorry," Mrs. Turner apologized. "Your first baby is head down and already emerging. Kat, I know you won't like this, but I think it's best for you to deliver more upright. Daisy, can you help me?"

The two women moved side by side to assist Katerina into a kneeling position over the cotton padding. Her skirt fell around her.

Daisy could immediately see that this would not do. She opened the buttons up her friend's back and urged the fabric up. Katerina cooperated with an irritable raising of her arms. Then, clad only in a short shift that had been altered to stop just above the massive swell of her belly, she leaned forward, gripping the bedposts in her hands for support.

Though she tried to respect Katerina's privacy, Daisy couldn't look away from the tableau of feminine strength before her. Though Katerina seemed fragile before, in this moment, a look of determination tightened her jaw and eyes.

Pain gripped her anew, but this time, she didn't sink into it. She used it. Used it to power herself as she bore down, snarling.

They shouldn't call it a pain, Daisy realized. *Maybe the ones that came before, but not this. This is pure strength.* It impressed her. *Do I have that spirit in me? Could I also call on my inner beast, the ancestors of all women, and engage in the drama of birthing new life?*

Though she could scarcely imagine it, she knew what she was seeing was true, and could be true for her as well.

Time lost meaning. It stretched with Katerina's body as she bore down, bringing her child closer to the outside world, and hurried on swift wings between the surges as she rested. One last push, with a screech like a wildcat, and Mrs. Turner reached between Katerina's bare thighs to cradle a small head fuzzed with dark hair.

"Excellent!" she encouraged. "Next one, we'll have this baby out."

Katerina's body tightened again, and a naked, messy infant slid into the midwife's capable hands.

Katerina sagged.

"Daisy, I'd like her to stay upright," Mrs. Turner ordered. "The second twin has a better chance of staying in position if she doesn't lie down."

Nodding, Daisy scrambled onto the bed and laid her hands on Katerina's hips. This time, she could feel the woman bear down, and a mass of slimy redness dropped onto the bed.

"Oh, dear."

"What's wrong?" Daisy asked. "What is that?" her heart pounded as she feared her friend had lost some vital organ. *Don't be stupid,* she reminded herself. *It's only the afterbirth. Dogs and cats have them too.*

"Nothing, nothing," Mrs. Turner said, eyeing the object with concern.

Working quickly, she tied off the baby's umbilical cord and cut it. She quickly wiped the baby's face and scooped out a mess of slime from his mouth. Unhappy with the outside world's coldness and loudness, the little one howled.

Daisy grinned.

"Let me see him!" Katerina exclaimed breathlessly. "Is it a him?"

"See for yourself," Mrs. Turner replied, extending the squalling infant towards his mother.

"Oh, a baby boy! My boy!" Katerina leaned down and kissed the little face. The infant stopped howling and regarded his mother with solemn eyes."

"Doesn't he look just like your husband?" Daisy suggested.

"He does," Katerina agreed. "Oh, argh!" Her body tensed and she dragged herself more upright.

"Here we go," Mrs. Turner said cheerfully. "Good. Daisy, come here please."

Seeing that Katerina was back in control of herself, clutching the bedposts and bearing down, Daisy slithered off the bed and hurried to the midwife's side.

Mrs. Turner wrapped the cotton square around the infant and handed him to her, settling him against her shoulder. "Here. Keep this little one warm and monitor his breathing. It's fine if he cries."

Though Daisy's instincts wanted to protest—surely, she shouldn't hold this near stranger's baby before his mother did—the delivery of the second twin made it necessary. She cradled the tiny boy, listening to his snuffles and whimpers. They sounded moist but not uncomfortable. She patted his back.

Mrs. Turner eased her fingers into Katerina's birth canal. "The second baby is breech—He's coming bottom first. He's small though. I think it will be fine. Kat... Kat?"

Katerina's head turned toward Mrs. Turner, but Daisy could see she wasn't paying attention. "Let's get your second son born."

A massive contraction clamped down Katerina's body before the midwife could finish speaking, and she gritted her teeth and pushed.

"Is a slow pace such a big problem?" Daisy asked in an undertone. "Is it necessary to hurry the delivery of a breech baby?"

"No," Mrs. Turner replied. "It's not that. Ideally, a breech baby is delivered slowly. However, do you see the second cord here? They shared one placenta, and that can be..." she glanced at Katerina. There was no indication the laboring mother was even aware of their presence. "It can be dangerous to the second baby."

"Oh, dear." Daisy snuggled the baby closer to her. *Please, Lord, don't let this little one be harmed.*

Katerina bore down, growling as before, but halfway through, she stopped, panting.

"Don't!" Mrs. Turner urged.

"It hurts," she wailed. "I can't, I can't." She sagged and tried to sit down.

"You will," the midwife snapped, gripping her arm and forcing her back upright. "You must. You knew this would happen, Kat. We talked about it. You must draw on your inner strength for this second baby. If you want him to live, you must push him out, now!"

Anger creased Katerina's pretty features, and that anger lent her strength. She straightened her spine and pushed. A round, plump bottom emerged, then legs and torso, bent into a bundle. Arms crossed over the little chest. Katerina paused, panting.

"Now the head," Mrs. Turner barked. "Push."

Katerina obeyed, and sure enough, the second boy slipped into the midwife's hands. Mrs. Turner exhaled noisily as she laid her hand on the baby's chest. Even from a few steps away, Daisy could see the pulse throbbing in his neck.

He's alive! Thanks be to God!

The midwife worked quickly, almost roughly to rub the baby with a clean cotton square. She wiped his face and patted his thighs and cheeks until the boy howled in protest.

The women in the room all sagged. Katerina collapsed backwards onto the bed with a groan. She threw one arm over her eyes.

Mrs. Turner, her shoulders slumped, wrapped the baby in cotton and made soothing noises.

Daisy lowered the child she was holding away from her shoulder and looked down into his face. He regarded her for a quiet moment before screwing up his face and wailing.

"Mrs. Bennett?" Daisy said, drawing the exhausted mother's attention to her. "I think your son wants you, not me. Are you feeling well enough to hold him?"

Though she looked pale and her hands trembled, she reached out her arms. Daisy laid the child on Katerina's chest. She rolled to her side. "Oh, my darling," she breathed, leaning down to kiss his face.

Exhausted, Daisy sank to the floor, not in a faint, but just to take her weight off her legs.

"How's the other one?" Katerina asked.

"He's just fine," Mrs. Turner replied, cutting the umbilical cord and wrapping the boy in a blanket to bring him to his mother as well. She set the second twin beside Katerina's belly, just below his brother's feet. Katerina reached down and laid a hand on his abdomen. "Oh, my precious sons. My perfect boys." Her voice broke.

From her spot, cross-legged on the floor, Daisy could see Mrs. Turner examining Katerina's genitals. The mother had crooked one leg to allow the examination but was otherwise ignoring the midwife, fixated on her sons.

"You didn't even tear," Mrs. Turner said, "and your bleeding is normal. I imagine you're plenty sore though."

"A bit," Katerina said, though she still looked a bit shaky.

"Let me give you some soothing salve and a sanitary napkin." She turned to rummage in her bag.

Now that the crisis had passed, Daisy found herself studying the room, which had not been able to see well the previous day, as the light had been poor. Now, in the morning, she could see that the room had been draped in luxurious fabrics—rich gold paisley for the draperies and deep blue on the bed and upholstering the armchairs—but the walls were plain and white. *A complementary color and pattern would enhance the room. Perhaps they prefer it this way?*

Mrs. Turner smeared some herbaceous-smelling substance on Katerina and helped her into a huge, padded undergarment.

That's a lot of blood, Daisy thought. *Is that really normal? I guess it must be.* The sight quenched some of the primal hypnosis she'd experienced from participating in the birth.

"And now, love, it's time to put the babies to breast," the midwife explained to her patient. "Are you certain you want to feed them both and not hire a wet nurse for one?"

Katerina shook her head fiercely, one hand on each baby as though to protect them from some undefined threat. "Mine," her expression seemed to say.

"Then let's get you settled upright. Feeding them will help your womb clamp down. It's healthy for you."

She helped Katerina scoot up to the pillows in a seated position.

"Would you like your nightgown on?" Mrs. Turner didn't wait for an answer. Tugging the sweaty shift over her head, she lifted a white garment and settled around the mother's body, opening the bodice. "Remember how this works? How many years has it been?"

"Eight," Katerina said. Her color had improved, but her voice still sounded hesitant. Raspy from so much roaring. "I remember some."

The midwife assessed the two infants and chose the one with the louder bellow. "We'll start with you, noisy boy." She handed the baby to his mother, placing Katerina's hand on the back of the tiny, fuzzy head. Together, they positioned the lad, tickling his cheek with his mother's nipple. A moment later, he was attached.

I wonder what that feels like. For the first time since the ordeal began, Daisy remembered the previous night; Colin's mouth and hands on her intimate parts. Heat rose in her body. *I could get pregnant. I could already be. Good Lord.* She shuddered. *I'm not ready for all this. Mr. and Mrs. Bennett have a wonderful, loving bond. These boys will be a blessing to them, and wasn't Mr. Bennett lovely with his daughter? Colin and I... we're nowhere near ready for this. I hope I didn't conceive.*

A bit of maneuvering had both babies settled, one on each of Katerina's breasts. Soft smacking sounds filled the room. Mrs. Turner began to massage Katerina's belly vigorously, below the pillows on which the twins rested.

Daisy's attention wandered away, suddenly focused on herself, on her ridiculous marriage and the possibility that last night's impromptu deflowering might be even more significant than she'd thought. Her heartbeat increased, not quite pounding, but definitely harder than normal. She drew in a deep breath through her nose and focused on a single curved shape on the curtain.

"Are you all right, Mrs. Butler?" Mrs. Turner asked, extending a messy hand to Daisy. "Did you get lightheaded?"

"I'm fine," Daisy replied hauling herself to her feet without help. "I just needed to sit down for a moment. This was... intense."

"Birth always is," Mrs. Turner informed her. "Now that mother and children are situated, I'd like a cup of tea. How about you?"

Daisy's stomach growled. "Yes, most definitely, as well as something to eat."

Mrs. Turner smiled. "Good. Then, you can tell me just who the devil you are."

Daisy flushed. "What do you mean?"

"I know the name Butler very well, but never mind about that just now. Let's ring for some food and drinks. I'm certain Mrs. Bennett could use something as well. Kat, are you hungry?"

Katerina lifted her head. "Starving," she replied. "I think I could eat everything in the house."

"Shall we start with tea and sandwiches?" Mrs. Turner suggested. "It's time for luncheon."

A quick ring of the bell had them set up with a tasty repast and a pot of steaming tea—and a lap tray for Katerina to use in bed. She tucked her sleeping sons into a cradle stationed at arm's reach beside the bed.

"How are you feeling, Kat?" Mrs. Turner asked.

"Better, now that labor has ended and my boys are here, safe and sound." She reached across to caress one sleeping face and then the other.

"I suspect your struggles have only begun," Mrs. Turner commented dryly. "You are going to have your hands full with these two little men *and* Sophia. Have you decided what to name them yet?"

"I'll wait until Christopher returns," Katerina said. "We need to be sure we still agree." She turned to Daisy. "Thank you for your help."

"Think nothing of it," Daisy replied. "I only hope you didn't feel your privacy too badly invaded. I mean, we only met yesterday."

"It's no bother," Katerina replied. "I appreciate your assistance."

Daisy smiled. *I suspect I've made a friend for life.* "Shall we stay in touch by letter? I have no idea when I'll be back to town." She took a bite of her sandwich.

"Where will you be going?" Mrs. Turner asked, staring at her with a shrewd look on her face.

"My husband's estate, apparently," Daisy replied. "I beg your pardon, Mrs. Turner, but I don't know much myself. I... we... we married yesterday after a *very* brief acquaintance and I'm a bit at a loss what to think of any of it."

"So then, who is your husband?"

"Your son," Katerina said, chuckling. She shoved a sandwich into her mouth at reckless speed, chewed and swallowed, washing it down with a swig of tea.

Daisy's jaw dropped. Realizing her mouth was full, she snapped it shut again. "Oh," she said. "I didn't realize."

"I mentioned it," Katerina pointed out.

"You did, but... but... I didn't put it together. Butler... Turner..."

"Yes, my son and I have different last names," Mrs. Turner said, still scrutinizing Daisy. "I remarried after his father died. Why did you marry him?"

Daisy bit the inside of her cheek, wondering how best to answer. "Neither of us had much say in the matter. My father... he misunderstood something that was... harmless. When there's a weapon involved, conversation and... and sense tend to get lost. Now, here we are, wondering what to do next."

"Have you considered an annulment?" Mrs. Turner asked. "Or are you afraid of returning to your father?"

"I wouldn't return," Daisy replied. "That option is no longer safe for me. I have the means to live independently. However, an annulment... isn't an option I'm willing to entertain." Her face heated.

"I see. Has my son told you why marriage isn't wise for him?"

Daisy shook her head. "He keeps hinting but refuses to explain."

"Means?" Katerina asked from the bed. She sipped her tea and sighed. "If your 'means' are substantial, you might be able to stay together. That is if you still want to."

"Are you certain you just delivered twins?" Mrs. Turner asked. "You're might feisty."

Katerina grinned. "I feel better than I have in months. I know I'll be sore later, but right now, I'm euphoric." Her gaze strayed to her sleeping twins. She yawned.

"You should try to rest," Mrs. Turner urged, "now that you've had a bite to eat. Before you know it, those lads will wake up and keep you running. You must rest, Katerina. You're doing well so far, but you're not out of the woods, yet. Infection and hemorrhage are possible. Rest. Get help with the boys from anyone who offers it. Your only tasks are to feed them and rest. Let your husband and your staff handle everything."

"I understand," Katerina agreed. She scooted down and closed her eyes.

"We should go," Mrs. Turner urged Daisy. "Let her sleep. I'll check on her a bit later."

Setting her napkin on the small table near a bookshelf crammed with volumes, Daisy rose and followed the midwife into the corridor.

At the railing along the edge of the staircase, Mrs. Turner whirled to face Daisy. "You married my son."

"Yes, ma'am," Daisy replied.

"And you refuse to seek an annulment?"

"Yes, ma'am." Daisy gulped. "Can you please explain to me why it's such a problem? I mean, no one wants to be married to someone they've known a day. I don't either. But… since it's too late to change it, I'm making peace with it. No one else is. What's going on?"

Mrs. Turner shook her head. "If Colin has decided not to tell you yet, I won't interfere. I hope you can forgive that one day. I must leave your marriage to the two of you to work out. I'm simply… stunned. Stunned, Daisy. You seem a nice girl, but…"

"But the situation is wildly unexpected and troubling?" Daisy supplied.

The woman nodded.

Downstairs, the door banged open and the young girl Daisy had seen earlier pranced into the foyer. "Mummy! Mummy!" she called.

"Hush now, Sophia," Mrs. Turner hissed, hurrying down the stairs to meet the girl and her father, who had just entered the house. "The twins have arrived, but your mama is resting."

"Is she well?" Christopher asked, eagerly approaching and grasping Mrs. Turner's arm with one hand, holding his daughter's wrist in the other.

"She came through it. She's as well as can be expected. I will remain to monitor her throughout the day and night and will return frequently over the next couple of weeks to ensure nothing happens."

"And the babies?"

"You have two fine, healthy sons, Mr. Bennett."

Christopher beamed. They made their way up the stairs to meet the new arrivals.

Another man appeared in the doorway. Colin. Daisy slowly walked towards him, descending the stairs as if in a dream. The powerful images of the delivery would not soon leave her. "Was your task successful?" she asked him.

"Yes," he replied. "I got the horse and the train tickets. We leave in an hour."

"I watched two babies being born," she blurted.

He tilted his head and regarded her with an unreadable look. "My mother attended the delivery, I presume?"

"Yes," she agreed.

"I'm sorry to have missed her. She will be busy with the new family, exhausted and in no mood to answer a thousand questions. Meanwhile, we need to get underway. I'll send her a letter."

"I believe I shall as well. I quite enjoyed her company, despite the... excitement of the situation. How is the mother of a viscount a midwife?"

"It's a long story," he said.

"You have a lot of stories," she pointed out. "I'd like to start hearing them soon."

Colin didn't answer. "Do you need to pack up?"

"I do," she agreed.

"Go do it then," he suggested, brusquely but not rudely. "The answers to most of your questions await."

"Come with me," Daisy urged. "I feel strange, and you're my man, I suppose. I don't want to be alone."

"Very well." He walked along after her, back up the stairs to the guest bedroom. Daisy tucked the few items she'd removed from her baggage; her nightgown, yesterday's clothes and her hairbrush. Then she sank, overwhelmed, onto the edge of the bed.

"Are you all right?" Colin asked.

She opened eyes she didn't remember closing to see his boots. Scuffed and messy, standing toe to toe with hers. "I'm not," she said softly. "I didn't sign on for any of this. I can't be upset because the alternative, had you not been there, is unthinkable." She did think about what her father had planned for her, and a shudder ran up her spine. "That doesn't mean I'm happy about being married to a man who hates me, stuck in a situation I don't understand with no information, no idea what the future holds. Nothing. Colin," she looked up into his eyes, "I don't think you should drink brandy anymore."

Colin's unreadable expression transformed with a wry twisting of his lips. "I rarely do, except when I visit my London friends. I don't invest in such useless, indulgent distractions. That's why it hit me so hard." He extended a hand and she took it, allowing him to help her to her feet. His support felt necessary, as her legs didn't have their usual strength. "I wish I could say I was sorry. I know that… that last night wasn't wise, but…"

"But something in both of us wants us to be together, even though your conscious mind rejects the idea and I have no clue what is going on?"

"Yes, that's it. I don't hate you, Daisy. Not at all. If I were a superstitious man, I might say something about fate or… or soul mates."

Daisy gulped. "That makes it worse!" she cried. "I *am* a superstitious woman, and it *does* feel like fate. If you feel it too, what on earth could hold you back from at least trying to find out what fate has in store for us as a couple?"

"I'm trying," he said softly. "I…" something seemed to break in Colin, and he tugged Daisy forward, enfolding her. "I wish you could understand."

"I wish you would tell me," she replied. "You don't understand so I'm not allowed to try?" She shook her head, and yet, heart to heart with her husband, something essential felt as though it had to click into place. *We fit together like the cogs of a machine, but the machine is broken, and the technician won't explain what went wrong.*

"I'm sorry," he said simply. "I'm sorry, Daisy. I'm sorry I'm not the man you thought I was. I admit I pretended to be something I'm not. I didn't think there would be any harm in it. I only wanted someone to remember me fondly."

"I do," she replied, her cheek against his shirt as she listened to the slow, steady beat of his heart. "I do remember that man fondly, but I don't think you misrepresented yourself. You wouldn't have been able to do it so convincingly if it isn't at least part of who you are."

"It was who I wanted to be," he said, his voice aching in her ear.

"Then, once all the mysteries are revealed, once the terrible secret is known, *become* that man. He's part of you. Turn him loose."

Colin's arms tightened around Daisy. His cheek rested against her forehead for a moment. She could feel waves of longing and regret buffeting her. *The man I met might be real, but this tortured soul is as well. I must never forget that. Despair is his natural state, and that won't change easily, if ever.*

Then, a curtain fell between their hearts. He stepped back, and his cool, unreadable look had reappeared. "I can't do that, Daisy. I'm sorry. Let's go."

Chapter 7

"ELL, here we are," Colin said as he and his wife stepped out of the forest into cultivated land crisscrossed by ragged fences and filled with animals. The stench of cattle, birds and sheep rose up from to meet them, and flies buzzed irritably in the heavy air. His new horse, Pesadilla, whickered and pawed the ground with one foot.

He's better-natured than I expected, Colin thought, patting the glossy black coat. *I hope it helps enough.*

Daisy paused and scanned the scene. Before her, the fallow fields had been transformed into grazing pens. In the distance, crumbling tenant homes, their walls warped, barely managed to hold up their slate roofs. Children in ragged garments sat in front of their homes, digging in the dirt with sticks, but lacking the energy to run and play after a late-winter infection swept through the estate.

They still look ill, though most are on the mend. Then, his gaze fell upon young Bobby Bullock. The child leaned against the wall of the house, coughing miserably into a handkerchief. The sight of them made Colin's heart clench. *Will we have enough time to save him? We couldn't save Mrs. Billings, nor Mrs. Smythe when the fever set in. How many will die before we can afford a physician?*

"Where is here, precisely, Colin?"

"My estate," he replied. "Welcome to Gelroy land. Isn't it dreadful?"

Daisy turned to the left, toward the noisy, quacking and honking pond. Then, she turned to the right and stilled at the sight of the crumbling manor house. Colin saw the exact moment when she noticed the entire east wing had collapsed, the stones and boards lying in a pile of plaster rubble. The central portion sported gaping holes in the walls through which it was easy to see decaying furniture and rotting fabrics. Only the west wing stood strong and solid, its walls defying the slow march of time.

"What happened here?" Daisy demanded, staring at the wreck.

A bead of sweat sprang onto Colin's brow. *It's muggy for spring, or maybe the animals themselves are lending to the heat and humidity.* Though the sight of so much manure on his fallow land caused a swell of pride, Daisy's presence beside him quickly turned it to shame.

"Nothing outside the ordinary," Colin replied, frowning at the ruins of his life. "Over a century ago, my great, great, many times great grandfather was a minor advisor to the king. He gave the king good advice, so the king created the Gelroy Viscountcy and gave him a small piece of land. He managed it well, as did his son and grandson, but over the years, the idea of leisure took hold of the Gelroys, and they forgot to work hard, forgot to be wise. With an estate this small, it didn't take long for poverty to set in. By the time my father inherited the title, the land was depleted, as were any funds set aside for the maintaining of the manor or the estate. Debts had begun to mount up. This is what I inherited."

"Good God," she breathed.

"At the risk of sounding sacrilegious, God hasn't been particularly good to me thus far." He sighed. "This is the great secret, Daisy, the reason I never planned to marry. The estate is deeply in debt. We live month to month in the worst of conditions. There are five families under my care, and at this time, they are all unable to buy even a scrap of fabric to repair their clothing or a single nail to repair their homes. If all goes well, at midsummer and at the end of summer, we should be able to take animals to market and bring in a bit of income to pay the taxes and make another payment on to the creditors. If the sale fails, we go under."

"That's a wise plan," she said softly.

"It's not enough," he said bleakly. "Debts must be paid on schedule. We've delayed too many already. Even if the creditors don't foreclose, what do we do until then? One of the tenants has a son who has an illness. He needs medical care. Without it, he may not live another year. I cannot supply it. His family cannot supply it." His voice broke.

Daisy's hand sneaked into his, and she squeezed his fingers gently. "I'm so sorry," she told him. "That must weigh on you like... like a slate roof."

"Apt analogy, my dear," he said, feigning lightness. Her hand in his felt like life, like a life he dared not embrace. "This is why I doubt the wisdom of you remaining. To be blunt, Daisy, I cannot afford you. If I had any money, I would pay down the balances on the estate's debt or use it on my tenants. I would repair their homes or hire a physician. Honestly, this may be the thing that finally finishes us off." He bit his lip. "Come on, wife. Let me show you to our manor." The irony dripped in his voice.

Don't be a bastard, he scolded himself. *You know she didn't do this. Even basic logic will tell you that. She doesn't want to be here any more than you do. Be angry, as always, at your own impotence, but leave Daisy out of it. Her sunshine beauty has no business being in this dark place.* Even the passing thought showed how much he'd grown to care for her, and how quickly, and it upset him. *This is the most unfair thing of all. Why do I deserve to meet the woman who could very well be my soulmate, when I have nothing to offer her?* The setting sun illuminated her golden hair and her tanned, freckled face, so she shone like a spring flower in the dirt.

"I would like that," she said at last.

He led her forward, angling toward the ruin in which he lived.

"Are you sure the west wing is solid?" she asked, eyeing the structure doubtfully.

"It seems to be," he replied. "At any rate, the kitchen is in decent shape, and it's warm. I've been sleeping there for a year."

"In the kitchen?"

He nodded, angling a glance at Daisy. Her surprised expression did not surprise him. *Not what she expected, is it.* "At whatever point you decide to leave, I won't hold it against you. I will make no attempt to fight the annulment. I cannot help you, and I do not know what you will do, but I have no malice toward you. Not at all. I only wish I could have been the man you need."

Daisy turned her head and looked at him for a long moment, seeming to be on the verge of saying something, but then she fell silent, eyes fixed ahead, and walked along.

Crossing the fields carefully, as each step contained a different risk, they arrived at the crumbling façade of the manor house. Up close, it looked worse. Bricks lay scattered. Huge holes revealed the overgrown garden at the back. The front door had fallen in. All the windows seemed to be broken.

"Step carefully," Colin urged. He turned his stallion loose in a penned field filled with sheep and led his wife up to the gaping maw that had once been a front door. Inside, the structure had collapsed to the extent that the sky was visible through two floors of construction. "Never go upstairs," Colin urged. "The stairs aren't safe, and the floor above..."

"I see it," Daisy replied grimly. "Colin, are you sure any part of this structure is safe?"

"I don't know," he replied honestly. "The kitchen isn't beneath anything, so I don't think the ceiling will fall in. It isn't drafty. I've set up... a sort of nest there. It isn't much, but it's comfortable if you have low expectations."

He turned her sharply to the left and twisted a doorknob, guiding her over uneven floorboards and into a room that contrasted sharply with the rest of the house. Solid and cozy, the large kitchen had been well maintained. A modern stove gleamed in the light filtering through unbroken windows. A long, wooden counter had a couple of chairs set at one end, to create an eating area. In the corner below the window, a bed had been dragged in and simply dressed in a thin blanket and flat pillow. Beside it, a small shelf that must have once held cookware housed...

"Books!" Daisy exclaimed. "Why, Colin, do you still make time to read?"

"You know I do," he reminded her. "Is it wrong that I take a moment each evening to escape my troubles?"

"Lord, no!" Daisy replied. "I love to read. It was a habit my mother picked up in her youth and passed on to her daughters. We all adore reading, no matter how many people protest. I think it's healthy to cast off your cares and take part in someone else's adventures now and again. Do you have any favorites, other than Shakespeare, that is?"

"Many," he replied. "Did you bring any of your own books? There's room."

She eyed his meager collection, a sad look on her face, and then she brightened, though it looked less than convincing. "I did, and I appreciate a spot on your bookshelf. I'll unpack later if you don't mind. Um, what's through that door?"

"The pantry," Colin replied. "There are a few potatoes and onions in there, and I think an apple or two, but nothing of any great interest."

"All right then," Daisy said, regarding the kitchen. "So, we'll be living small. Good. Less to clean that way. Shall I prepare onion and potatoes for supper?"

"If you'd like," he agreed easily. "There may be something growing out back, but it's early to find much. Make free with any of the cookware. It's a surprisingly extensive collection, all things considered."

Daisy nodded, dropping her bags beside the bed. She meandered around the kitchen, examining the supplies closely. In the end, she claimed a saucepan and set it on the stove.

"You say you've been sleeping in here for a year?" she asked in a soft, neutral voice. "What about before?"

"Oh," Colin replied, unlacing his boots and falling back on the bed. Fatigue, exacerbated by not knowing what Daisy had in mind, left him unable to rise for a time. "I had a bedroom in the east wing. Upstairs. It leaked like a sieve for as long as I can remember, but I didn't realize how bad the structure had gotten. I spent several months in London, trying to get a loan. When that didn't work, I sold the townhouse. I used that money to supplement the taxes and credit payments, and to compensate my tenants for a poor harvest the year before last. When I came home, the roof had fallen in completely and crushed most of my furniture and belongings."

"Oh, dear," Daisy said gently. "That's a terrible shame."

"I agree," Colin said, his voice carefully neutral. It did not convey in any way the despair he'd felt upon arriving and finding half his home and most of what was left in the world that he cared about destroyed. "I salvaged a few books, some of my clothing, and the bureau in the corner there. This bed was in a downstairs bedroom that wasn't ruined, as was this bookshelf, but both came from guest rooms, so I don't have any particular attachment to them. Perhaps it's better that way."

"Perhaps," Daisy agreed cautiously. "I'm going to take a look in the pantry."

"Don't expect much," he warned.

"I don't," she replied, ducking out of sight.

Colin stared at the ceiling, letting his overwrought mind finally go blank. He didn't know what the future held. Not even the next ten minutes, and he didn't care. He only wanted to rest. *Rest, ha. Rest forever. Sometimes I wish I could just die and get it over with. This is a miserable existence.*

"Look what I found!" Daisy called, hurrying back into the room with two fat potatoes, a huge onion, and... "Did you know there was a crock of butter in here?"

"I had no idea," he replied, not sitting up. "Sometimes the tenants bring me things if they have excess. I wish they wouldn't, but… they wait until I'm out and sneak it in, so I don't know who to return it to. Go ahead and use it, I suppose."

"I aim to. Don't return gifts, Colin. Your tenants probably feel badly that they're not living up to their part."

"I would never ask it of them," he explained. *Who's not living up to what, woman? My family has taken advantage of these people for ages. I owe them far more than they owe me.*

"You don't have to ask it. Clearly, everyone feels equally responsible for life on this estate. It's a healthy way to live, you know, caring for one another."

"That's one way to look at it, I suppose," he said, though it didn't much dispel the sense of overwhelming failure with which he'd lived his whole life.

A loud hiss told Colin that Daisy had lit the stove. A few moments later, the wonderful smell of onions hitting hot butter wafted through the room. His mouth watered. Soft snicking sounds told Colin Daisy was peeling and slicing the potatoes. They hit the pan in a series of thuds and then silence fell.

He tried to think of something, anything to say to the wife he wanted but couldn't afford to keep. Thus far, she'd accepted the news kindly, but he knew she wouldn't tolerate their poverty for much longer. *Who would? This is beyond anything anyone would want. No, she'll move on. Go back home with a stern word for her brutish father. Or go back to London and take a position in a shop or perhaps in a restaurant. She's good with food and knows how to cook for a crowd. I hope she can manage it safely.*

"Colin?" Daisy said gently. "The food is ready. Are you hungry?"

He sat up, considering how he felt. His stomach growled painfully after such a busy day. His mind did not connect to it. In fact, the idea of food made him ill. Still, he needed to fuel himself. *There's a lot of work ahead. Fill your belly.*

He joined Daisy in the chair at the large worktable. In front of him, a lovely pile of crispy, brown food sent a luscious aroma that tempted him not in the slightest. Lifting a spoonful on his fork, he put it in his mouth and chewed. It stuck, dry despite the savory butter that bathed each piece. In the end, he succeeded in swallowing it, and when it hit his stomach, something strange happened. A tingling surge of energy radiated out from his belly, traversing up to his head, where lingering dizziness he'd long since stop noticing faded away. Strength flowed into his legs and fingers. It allowed him to raise his fork again. His mouth watered on the second bite, releasing the flavors in his mouth. Between one bite and the next, ravenous hunger awoke and sent him shoveling the tasty dinner into his mouth in monstrous chomps.

"Easy, love," Daisy said, laying a hand on his arm.

He whirled, staring at her with feral eyes, and she recoiled. Moving slowly, she scraped half of her portion onto his plate. He consumed it without reflection.

As the last morsel slid down his throat, his wildness eased. His eyes focused on Daisy. She was staring at him, concern crimping her eyes and gauging lines in the corners of her mouth.

Colin had no idea what to say to her. "That... that was delicious," he finally blurted. "Um, did you get enough?"

"I'm fine," Daisy replied. "I'm glad you enjoyed it. Next time, I'll prepare a larger portion. Men who work hard tending animals and plowing fields need a good supper."

"There isn't enough food for it," he replied.

"Let me be the judge of that," she said stubbornly.

She is stubborn, he thought. *She hasn't conceded defeat. Probably still embarrassed to leave after her deflowering.* He knew he ought to be ashamed of taking her virginity, but he wasn't. Though he'd been tipsy enough to overcome his restraint and take her, he still had the memory of every moment he'd spent touching his wife. *It was delicious. Daisy is an excellent wife. If only I could be a decent husband.*

"Well, Colin, now what?" Daisy asked. "It's too early to go to bed. Will you show me around?"

"Around what?" he asked. "You've seen the manor and the estate. What do you think is left?"

"I stared at your estate," she said, "from the edge of the forest. I doubt I saw all there is to see."

"Perhaps not," Colin agreed, "but I'm tired. I have a lot of work waiting for me tomorrow."

"Starting with gathering your tenants and introducing me," Daisy replied, firm as always.

Looks like she's here to stay, for the time being anyway. "Yes, fine," he agreed, fatigue making him snappish and irritable. "You can meet everyone in the morning. It's five men. Two are widowed, three married. Two of the married ones have children. The third has a child on the way."

"Good," she replied. "I won't forget anyone's name then. Um, where are we sleeping? Are we sharing? The bed is big enough."

"You take the bed," he grumped, angry that she had addressed the question rather than just letting things flow in their own way. "I'll find somewhere else to sleep."

He stomped out of the kitchen into the ruined east wing, looking for a safe corner to curl up in.

* * *

Long after darkness fell, Daisy sat on the edge of the bed, writing a letter by the light of the stove. When she finished, she tucked the missive under the pillow and settled down. *It's not going to be easy getting Colin to listen to me, but I'll do whatever I can.*

Alone in an empty room, thoughts she'd suppressed throughout the last two days finally filtered up to her awareness.

Father betrayed me. He knew I wasn't interested in Orville, and he decided my desires didn't matter when it came to choosing a husband. He thought his choice took precedence over my own. For my marriage. For my body.

"My father arranged to have me raped," she whispered aloud, her voice cracking and her eyes stinging. "He thought an assault on me would be a worthwhile means to an end." A tear spilled over. "I can never go home now. Can never be near him again. My own father committed this crime against me."

Closing her eyes, buried her face in the pillow to muffle her sobs.

Chapter 8

 ORNING dawned cloudy and cheerless in the home of the unhappy Viscount and his equally out-of-sorts wife.

Colin stumbled blearily into the kitchen to find coffee, tea and porridge waiting, hot and ready to serve. Daisy had even ferreted out a pot of honey and a few early berries to flavor the breakfast.

Ravenous again, Colin devoured most of the pot before he stopped to think whether Daisy had eaten. Sadly, she was nowhere to be found, so he couldn't ask.

"Well, she's an excellent cook," he admitted to himself.

Not able to see his wife anywhere in the kitchen or the pantry, Colin shrugged and stalked out to the field, where he found his five men waiting to hear new instructions.

"Hello, all," he said lightly.

They stared at him, eyebrows drawn in five matching lines.

"Are you well, my lord?" Bullock asked.

He shrugged. "Fate has played a nasty trick on me. I'm married. I don't yet know what it means for us all, but for the moment, she's determined to stay. She would like to meet you, your wives and your children later on."

The men stared in silence, mouths agape to show stained teeth.

"Sir, what?" Bullock asked.

Colin shook his head. "It's a strange age in which we live when an innocent kiss on an innkeeper's daughter ends up with a vicar and a shotgun. It remains to be seen what the next course of action for her will be. I make no promises, but it seems, for the moment, she's here. Now then, what's been happening while I was away? Anything of import?"

He looked from man to man, but all were too busy gaping at him to answer the question.

"Men!" Colin barked.

They shook off their astonishment. "Um, my house has a new leak," Bullock said at last.

"Damn." Colin frowned. "I'm sorry, Bullock."

The older man scrunched up his face. "It's still mighty cold at night."

And your boy isn't well. Damn, damn, double damn. They can patch it, of course. They know how, but at some point, they will need to repair the walls, not just patch them.

"The animals are doing well," Jones added. "Most of the chicks and ducklings and all of the lambs have survived. They're growing fast. Another couple of months and the birds will be ready for market. And there are eggs aplenty."

"That will help," Colin agreed. *A couple of months with no income,* he thought, the old sense of helplessness rising. *There's food but no money.*

"The calf is growing and will be born any day," Farrell added.

Nods greeted this. "Milk from her as well as from the goats," Bullock pointed out. "Butter and cheese to sustain the children. Perhaps a bit to sell, not in London, to be sure, but at the market."

Murmurs greeted the information.

Crumbs, Colin thought. *Crumbs of future hope, yet they grasp at it. They should all leave. Move to town and get jobs. Leave this wreck to the ravages of time.* And yet, they stayed. Against all odds. Against sense or wisdom, they remained loyal to a man who had never yet provided them with any relief.

"Well, there are good things on the horizon," he said blandly. "Show me the livestock."

The men hauled themselves to their feet and led the way out of the manor yard and into the pens.

Colin's new horse, black as its namesake nightmare but surprisingly gentle for a stallion, stared at the milling, bleating sheep, but consented to graze on sweet spring shoots. Lambs bounced and played in the sunshine, each one representing another moment of survival.

The pond beyond the meadow rippled in a spring wind, which ruffled the feathers of so many ducks, each leading a string of ducklings. Geese honked and squabbled in the reeds along the bank.

So much life here, he admitted. *Will it be enough? Will the birds stave off disaster until the lambs are grown? Will the calf be born alive? Will the old cow survive the delivery? Will she make enough milk to nourish our children and hers? So many questions and as usual, no answers.*

"You've done well," he said in a raspy, unsteady voice. "Since everything seems to be under control for the moment, would you all gather your families? I'll go find Lady Gelroy and bring her here."

The men nodded and scattered. Colin leaned against the fence for a long moment, looking out at the future of his farm.

Then, with nothing answered, as usual, he returned to the house.

Again, he found no sign of Daisy. *Did she run off already?* But no, the breakfast dishes had been washed and lay on a towel on the counter to dry. The bed had been made. *Where is she?* "Daisy?" he called.

"Just a minute," came her reply from the vicinity of the pantry. She popped out, dressed in a gray skirt and matching blouse. "Here I am. What's going on?"

"Where were you?" he asked. "Is there anything that interesting in an empty pantry?"

"Oh, Colin, wait until you see. Um… how often did you come into this part of the house before… before the main wing collapsed?"

He shook his head. "Rarely. I might have ducked into the kitchen now and again, but… but father's servants didn't like me milling around. They got all sullen and, well, rude, when I did. Not to mention, Father didn't want me mingling with the servants. If he found me where I didn't belong…" Colin broke off, shuddering.

Daisy considered him for a thoughtful moment. "I know why the servants didn't want you around. Come on." She grabbed his hand, dust and grit crunching between them as she dragged him through the door into the pantry.

There, another door stood open, and she hurried toward it.

"Isn't that the root cellar?" he asked, curious why she was racing in that direction. "I never got that far because… why bother? Any produce in there would have long since rotted by the time I got back to London."

"It isn't," she told him as the moved through the dark, cavernous room filled with shelves. "The root cellar is outside. This is… something a lot more interesting."

She pulled him through the door into… a parlor. A small sitting room with a dusty sofa and two armchairs positioned in a U around a stone fireplace. A dirty but attractive rug sat on the floor.

"What is this place?" he asked.

"I would guess it's the servants' quarters," Daisy replied. "It's in excellent repair. Just look at this room. The sofa could benefit from new upholstery, and the whole thing needs a good cleaning, but it's a usable space, and look here!" She tugged on his hand again, toward two doors that stood open off the back of the room. "Bedrooms! The mattresses are not trustworthy. There are mouse droppings everywhere, but the walls are solid and each one has a fireplace. The bedframes, the wardrobes and the chairs are usable. All the walls are solid. All the windows are intact. There's even a water closet. Someone invested a fortune in this room while the rest of the manor crumbled."

Colin stared in shock. A comfortable living space had lain, beyond his awareness, only a few steps from where he'd been squatting like a vagrant in his own home.

"I think I know," he croaked, "how this happened." He continued as though talking to himself. "I never could figure out what happened to all the money my father's land steward embezzled. I fired him, but… he built this place for himself and his wife, the cook/housekeeper. They must have done it while I was away at university."

"It is odd that you didn't notice," Daisy pointed out. "Couldn't you see this room from your bedroom window?"

"My bedroom faces the front, not the rear. The opposite bedrooms were in worse shape, so I just didn't go in them. Besides, the second I inherited, the estate manager informed me of the grim conditions of the estate, the back taxes and generations of debt we owed. We created a repayment plan that required so much effort just to meet each responsibility, I didn't have time to be curious."

Daisy frowned in sympathy. She reached for Colin's hand, but he withdrew, not wanting her pity.

When she spoke, it was to return to the subject at hand. "They built this for themselves, not realizing that it would one day house the lord's son. We should move in here as soon as I finish cleaning it up."

"I agree," Colin said, still dazed. "Thank you for the breakfast," he added. "It was tasty. Where did you find the berries?"

"There's quite a garden in the back," she told him. "It's wildly overgrown, but there's a surprising amount of food there. Berries. Asparagus. Herbs. Who knows what will pop up as summer comes."

Colin nodded absently. "I see you've been busy."

"It's in my nature," she told him. "Colin, why did you never explore this place? Did you even know there was food back there?"

"Honestly," he replied, "I never had the energy. The struggle is too great."

"Melancholia?" she asked kindly.

"I..." His voice cracked. The diagnosis made him sound unbearably pathetic, and yet... "It's true. I have little strength. It's mental exhaustion. Once the day's work is done... I collapse."

This time, she did grasp his hand, and she squeezed gently. He allowed it but quickly changed the subject.

"I told my men about you. I told them to gather their families so they could meet you."

"All right," Daisy agreed.

"Would you like to change clothes?"

"Good idea!" Daisy dropped Colin's hand and darted back through the pantry while Colin sank into one of the armchairs. A cloud of dust wafted up and set him coughing. *Good Lord. This place has been here all along and I never knew. Daisy found it in a second because she still has hope and energy enough to be curious. Well, I don't know what good it will do, but this apartment is nicer than sleeping in the kitchen... and much nicer than trying to find a comfortable spot in one of the ruined guest rooms.*

"Colin!" Daisy called. "I'm ready, love. Let's go." She bounded back into the room, eager as a gazelle, a fresh, light blue dress floating around her curvaceous figure. "Silly man, don't sit there. You'll hurt your lungs with all that dust. Let me clean it first. Come on!"

Covered in grime, his boots caked in mud, Colin hauled himself to his feet and took Daisy's hand. Her fingers felt right in his.

The realization made him grumpy. *There's still no future for her here. No matter how sweet, cheerful or clever she might be, it would be wrong to keep her here.*

Still, he let her lead him back through the kitchen, through the ruined hallway and out into the spring sunshine.

"Where do we start?" she asked.

"Shouldn't we wait for them to come to us?" he suggested.

"And line up like horses in a stall?" Daisy protested. "I don't need any such formality. They're people. We call on people in their homes. Who do we begin with?"

"Bullock," he grunted, pointing to the tenant house furthest to the left from the door of the manor yard. "He's my foreman. He's married to Miranda. They have four children: Kate, who is nearly grown, Alice, William and Bobby. Next, there's Farrell, my second. His wife is named Mary. They have one son, Robin. In the third house is Jones. He has a wife, also called Mary, and they're expecting their first. Billings, who lives in the smallest house, is the oldest. His wife passed away two years ago, and all his children are grown. Last is Smythe. He's also widowed but younger. His late wife was Billings's daughter. I think he has a sweetheart in town, but this is no place to bring a bride, so who knows how long he will stay. Are you ready to meet them all?"

" 'Lay on, Macduff,' " Daisy urged. Her casual allusion to Shakespeare captured some forgotten lightness in Colin's heart.

He responded in kind, " 'And damned be him who first cries, hold, enough.' "

Daisy beamed.

Sighing, he tugged her hand, leading her past the animal pens. Pesadilla trotted over to the fence and whickered at Colin.

"Hello, friend," he said, petting the horse's black nose.

"Here you go, sweeting," Daisy added, holding up a wizened apple.

The horse eyed the wrinkled fare warily but eventually gobbled it up.

"Good boy," she praised him.

"Daisy, this is a stud stallion," Colin pointed out. "Don't turn him into a pet. He needs a bit of aggression or no one will want him to breed their racing mares. He's already too friendly."

Daisy giggled. "No promises, my lord. He's a lovely horse." She patted his nose. The attention-greedy animal accepted her caresses eagerly.

"I thought you wanted to meet Bullock and his family," Colin said sourly.

"Don't be gloomy, love," she urged.

Colin wanted to snarl. Her casual endearment hit him in all his weak places. He clamped his lips together and escorted his wife toward the largest of the tenant houses. Though a small, three-room space, it had once been an attractive home, with decorative strips of wood adorning the dormers and a mossy slate roof.

Colin knocked on the door. His foreman appeared, his silvering blond hair more neatly combed than he'd ever seen it.

"My Lord," he said to Colin, winking at the unaccustomed formality. "My lady."

"Oh, please, don't!" Daisy exclaimed, dropping her hold on Colin to grasp Bullock's hand in both of hers. "I'm no lady, just an innkeeper's daughter from a village outside London."

"Well, you captured Lord Gelroy's eye," the man teased.

Oh, God. Colin thought, rolling his eyes. *I'll be hearing about this for years.*

"It was a stroke of fate," Daisy said, her face deadly serious. "I think we can all be good for each other, and for this poor, abused estate."

"That's what we're all trying to do, ma'am," Bullock said kindly, clearly enamored by Daisy's sweetness. "Achieve some good. Won't you come in?"

Colin led Daisy into the Bullock family home. Inside, a crack in the wall admitted extra sunlight as well as drafts of April chill into the large central room. More cracks had been repaired with mud and straw over the years, many more. Too many more. *We should tear this place down and rebuild*, Colin thought, shaking his head.

Inside, a middle-aged woman with prematurely gray hair rose to meet the visitors. Her dress was ragged, but her manner had an almost-painful dignity. Three attractive, half-grown children stood around her, neatly combed and washed but lacking the energy they should have had, as they were still recovering from a late-winter illness. It grieved Colin in particular to see the youngest, Bobby, with his crooked back, coughing into his hand.

"Hello, all," Daisy trilled. Her cheer had taken on a rather fixed aspect, but she kept it in place, nonetheless. "Please, call me Daisy."

"You look like a daisy," Bobby said. Then, he coughed again.

"Thank you," she said with a warm smile, handing the boy a handkerchief.

Well, Colin thought, *they seem to like her, and I don't blame them.*

* * *

Stepping out of the overstuffed hut into the sunlight, Daisy took several deep breaths and closed her eyes as the late-spring sunshine fell on his face. That is until a loud, quarrelsome chatter interrupted. "I won't have it, I tell you. No one shall invade my privacy!"

"No one is invading, Mary," a high-pitched male voice protested. "You complain we never have callers..."

"No one!"

"What goes on here?" Colin asked.

Daisy opened her eyes to see a woman storming toward them, her wild gray hair bouncing above her head. She bustled straight up to Colin and Daisy and blurted without preamble, "Are ye a Christian woman, lass?"

"Mary," Farrell piped, "that's no way to speak to Lady Gelroy."

"Bah." She waved her hand in front of her face and stomped up into Daisy's face. "God is no respecter of persons, and neither am I. Are ye a Christian woman?"

"I am," Daisy said, raising one eyebrow.

Mrs. Farrell nodded, her loose, graying curls bouncing above her head. "Then ye can stay. I'll not have visitors though. No one told us you was coming, and I ain't prepared."

"Very well," Daisy said amiably. "I'm not here to invade anyone. I only wanted to meet you. Um, I'm pleased to meet you."

Mrs. Farrell ducked into a mocking curtesy and skittered away. Farrell tossed them an apologetic glance and trailed his wife back into their house.

With all the commotion, the door to the third house opened and a much younger couple popped out. The man, young and handsome, though thin, had a mop of curly hair. The woman, blond and fragile, wore a dress that barely fastened around her belly.

She's expecting, Daisy realized. *About halfway. That must be hard with so much stress. This has to change.*

The woman dropped into a curtsey that looked both elegant and awkward. "My lady."

Daisy smiled sadly at the woman. "Pleased to meet you."

She lifted her head and returned a matching expression.

"Daisy, this is Jones and his wife, also called Mary, as I mentioned earlier. Jones's father worked for my father. Now, Jones works for me. This is my... my wife."

The young man bowed.

"I'd invite you in, Lady Gelroy," Mary said, "but I haven't felt up to cleaning, and the place is a mess." She laid a hand on her burgeoning belly.

"I quite understand," Daisy replied. *Maybe lining people up has a purpose. I didn't intend to intrude.* "The manor isn't in excellent condition either. I'd hate to have a guest pop in without warning before I can get it under control."

The woman's wry grin turned genuine.

The path outside the tenant houses transformed into a de-facto lineup as two men, one middle-aged, the other verging on elderly, joined the Jones family.

"Ah, here's everyone else," Colin said mildly. "Daisy, these two rascals are Billings and his son-in-law, Smythe. Both are widowed, so there's no one left for you to meet. Men, this is the new Lady Gelroy."

They bowed.

"Pleased to meet you both," she said, wishing there were something more to say. *Words will not help in this situation. Not at all. Only actions will make a difference. Thank you, Lord, that I have the power to act. I only hope my husband will allow it.*

* * *

Exhausted after forcing cheer while meeting so many desperate families, Daisy collapsed onto the edge of Colin's bed in the kitchen of the manor house.

"Well, wife, have you seen enough?" Colin asked, leaning tiredly against the wall. He left plenty of space between himself and Daisy.

"What do you mean?" she asked. "This is your life. This is their lives. Why would it be too much for me to see? Do you think I'm as fragile as the flower I was named after?"

"Are you?" he asked.

She shook her head. "It's sad, but I've seen poverty before. I... I think I understand your concerns better now."

He nodded. "Well, then, If we can just hold on until we can get the ducks and chickens big enough to take to market, we'll have enough to make our quarterly payment on the estate's debt, but it will be late, and I don't know if the creditors will wait again. Then, the geese and lambs will bring a bit more, perhaps half of what we need for the taxes. Then... I don't know. I don't think that Bullock's son will last long without medicine. He has a lung infection—we all had it, but over a month ago, most of us have recovered. Sadly, with his deformity, it's harder on Bobby. He can't get clear of it. That's the grim reality?"

"That's hard. Very hard. Please, won't you sit by me? I want to talk to you."

He shook his head. "I'll listen, but I'll stand over here. It's better this way, Daisy. Surely, you can see that. What future can I offer you?"

She shrugged. "Maybe you don't need to offer me anything. Maybe I have something to offer you."

"What do you—?"

Daisy cut him off. "I'll explain, of course. Just give me a moment. You've shown me your story. Now, let me tell you a different tale. One that might surprise you. It begins in a whorehouse in France."

Colin lowered his eyebrows, but Daisy rushed on. "The company was quite successful, and the madam had grown quite rich. Her daughter, who worked for her, also managed to put away a tidy sum of money, but in the end, the daughter grew tired of the Venus trade and decided to marry one of her clients—an Englishman—and return home with him. Eventually, they had three daughters together, but the mother always kept what she'd earned as a dowry for her daughters. She even had legal documents drawn up, keeping the money in trust until her girls came of age. She died only a few years after the youngest was born. Then, more recently, the old madam died and also left all her money to the three granddaughters. The older two refused it, saying it was 'dirty' money, but the youngest... well, she decided that money is like manure. Just because it's dirty doesn't mean it's useless."

Colin gave her a rare half-grin. "If there's one thing I understand these days, it's the value of manure."

Daisy smiled. "So, at any rate, that granddaughter... well, I'm not without resources, Colin."

"I'm glad to hear it," he said intensely. "I was worried about what you would do once you'd had enough of this place. Is it enough to keep you comfortable and far away from your father?"

"Plenty," she replied.

"Then why have you stayed with your father so long?" Colin demanded. "He hasn't been particularly kind to you, has he? Even before he cooked up a plan to trap you in marriage with that... that creature... he was always a bit of a brute, am I right?"

"Oh, yes," Daisy agreed. Taking in a deep breath, she released it in a shuddering sigh. *Don't cry, Daisy. Not now. He's proven more than a brute. He's a villain, but I have no time to mourn that realization now.* "I'm used to it, I suppose. Anyway, his brutish ways were only a minor annoyance until recently, and I always did plan to move on, when the time was right. In the meanwhile, I enjoyed the work. Business is in my blood. But, Colin, I don't think you're understanding the point I was trying to make."

"Oh? What was it then?"

"I have money. I want to help you and your poor tenants."

Silence crashed louder than any wave at the seashore over the occupants of the manor kitchen. Colin stared at Daisy, unable to form a coherent thought, let alone a word. His ragged respirations, like the gasping of a fish on the bottom of a boat, added no sound and drew no air into his laboring lungs.

Daisy, a look of concern crumping her pretty face, bounced up off the bed and hurried to Colin, wrapping her arms around him and drawing him into an embrace.

"How... what..." Words still fought him, refusing to form anything like a sensible comment.

"I suppose you've had estimates done long since," Daisy rushed on, covering his awkwardness with pertinent questions. "How much would you need to fully restore the estate, pay off the debt and cover this year's taxes? I mean, I surely don't have enough for that, but..."

"Thir—" he coughed, swallowed and tried again. "Thirty thousand pounds. That's what it would take to fully repay the debts, the taxes, restore the manor and all the tenant houses, purchase new farming equipment, a bull, several cows and compensate the tenants for not planting this year. But there's no way..."

"No," Daisy agreed. "My inheritance is twelve thousand pounds, with another five thousand in my dowry. If you don't mind, I'd like to keep the dowry for myself. As the 'lady' of the manor, I have responsibilities that, in their own way, are just as important as yours, for the estate and its inhabitants. Colin, are you sure you're all right? You look pale."

He shook his head.

"Come on, then." Though not a large woman, she managed to maneuver him to the bed. Then, she plunked to a seat beside him on it. "I think, with careful management, that might be enough to make a difference. There's no need to restore the manor. In fact, if we tear down the ruined east wing, there might be materials enough to repair the tenant houses without needing to purchase much. It needs to come down regardless. It's dangerous in there, and we run the risk that, when the upper floor finally falls altogether, it might damage the rest of the structure."

Still, Colin couldn't speak.

"Love, please, say something."

"Twelve thousand pounds?" Colin managed to croak.

"Yes. There may be a bit of interest on it, after all these years, but I would need to check with my solicitor. I don't think restoring the house is the best use of the money, though."

"No, of course," Colin said quickly, so quickly she was quite sure he wasn't thinking about what he was saying. He paused, he brow furrowing, and he blurted out, "The debts. The taxes."

"Exactly. I'm sure I can cover the taxes. And the debt?"

He nodded. "Not all."

"But would it be enough to restructure the payment plan; reduce the payments to a manageable level?"

He nodded, though his eyes remained wide and startled.

"And then, the money from selling the animals—and breeding Pesadilla—would more easily cover the taxes and leave enough for the tenants to have a more comfortable life?"

Colin blinked but didn't directly answer the question.

"And just maybe, if your tenants have a decent life, you could finally feel worthy of one for yourself?"

"Why are you doing this for me?" he croaked. "Why not take your money and go to London? Rent a flat and live in leisure? Or you could open a shop, since you like business, or write a novel, or take to the stage. Your lack of middle-class sensibility means the world is open to you. Why stay here, in a ruined home, on a ruined estate with a ruined man?"

"I don't see any ruins here," Daisy said, growing serious. "Well, perhaps that *other* part of the house where we don't live. I only see a chance to make a real difference with my money. You're right, I could take to the stage. That might be enjoyable. I could write a novel. I could create a business. I could also do all those things here while helping you and your people. The money is no great matter to me. I'd rather see it go to something useful. Now, then. If apply my inheritance to your taxes and debts, how much of a difference would it make?"

"There are no words for how important that money would be to me, if I accepted it."

"Then you had better accept it, Colin. As my husband, my inheritance already belongs to you. In fact, I'm surprised you didn't marry some wealthy businessman's daughter long ago."

He shook his head. "I may be a fool, but I won't do that. I won't drag some spoiled merchant's girl to this place. She would hate it, and me, and there we would be."

"I don't hate you, Colin," Daisy said gently. "Once upon a time, we found a special connection with each other. Now, I understand why you felt unable to act on it, but I can help. I can make a contribution to your estate. Then, if you're not so desperate, maybe we can go back to where we started. Where our hearts touched, if only for a day."

Colin bit his lip. The picture she was painting looked so appealing, but he feared to take hold of it. The endless litany of lack and despair now played in his mind. *It isn't enough. It won't be enough. You are not enough. Nothing will ever be good enough.*

"Colin. Colin." Daisy patted his hand.

He drew in a shaky breath and met her eyes. The glowing green, like life, like spring tried to take root in his heart. Tried to grow, but too much anguish stifled it.

"I... I don't know if I can manage that," he said, despair ravaging his voice. "I'm more ruined than you know, Daisy. I cannot in good conscience refuse your gift. Not when it might mean the difference between life and death for Bullock's son, but..."

"But accepting charity goes against the grain?" she suggested. "Don't think of it as charity. It's only a hand up, just the same as if you fell into a pit. If I lowered a rope, would you refuse it?"

"It's too much."

"It's barely enough," she insisted. "Look, Colin, you've already done the hard work. You took a failing estate and found a way to save... not the crops, but the people, and we so often forget that every business is for people, not people for business. Your idea to raise animals is pure genius, but it's slow. Let's take the pressure off this year. Pay your taxes. restructure the debts. Then, when the animals go to market, the tenants can keep their share. That's all I'm offering. Just a bit of leeway to stave off the reaper. Before you know it, the estate will become self-sufficient. It's already OUR money. Please, use it."

"I—ugh. Yes, Daisy. I will accept your help. I must. I cannot refuse the funds to compensate my tenants. Write to your solicitor as quickly as you can. Argh." His voice died. "I cannot… I need to…"

"Take your time, Colin," Daisy said gently. "It's a large change in thinking." She laid her hand on his.

He recoiled, right up off the bed and out the door without looking back at his wife.

Colin flew through the field, heedless of the messy piles the animals had left in the uncultivated ground. Unformed thoughts and a vague sense of shame kept him moving aimlessly away from… from everything. From the estate he had given his body and soul to save and failed. From the wife who had offered to rescue him from his failure, which was, in itself, a failure. *A failure I must embrace, lest my people suffer. It's my pride or our future. There is no question which route I must take.* And yet, humiliation burned in his guts. "I gave my life to this place, and I couldn't save it. Daisy waltzes in with her whorehouse money and sets the whole thing to rights. And she's right. Demolish the east wing and hand out the materials. If my father hadn't terrified everyone into submission—myself included—we might have done that long since. Pay the taxes. Reduce the debts. Give the tenants a fighting chance to make a life for themselves… and bring in a physician to care for Bobby. Not a rich life, but a decent one, lies suddenly in our grasp."

Why are you so angry? a voice in his head that sounded remarkably like his mother scolded.

He couldn't answer. He only knew that in his heart, this success was his ultimate failure. *I'm worthless.*

Darkness closed in around him, and he glanced up, surprised to find himself past the tree line into the forest. Out of sight of prying eyes, a scream of pure frustration ripped itself from his raw throat. He collapsed to the mossy, leaf-littered ground and beat his fists against the soil as impotent rage tore into his soul until fatigue claimed him and he lay still.

How long he lay in the cool loam, he could never have said, but at last, he stilled. He rested his cheek on a mossy stone and closed his eyes.

With a loud rustling sound, a shower of leaves and sticks rained down onto his back.

Colin sat up, staring into the tree and expecting to find a sassy red squirrel.

The dense foliage was moving, but he couldn't see any creatures.

Well, I know it's there, anyway. "Say, what do you mean by all that?" he asked the unseen rodent. In response, an acorn clunked down on the top of his head. "If you're trying to knock some sense into me, it won't work. If I had any sense, I would have sent all the tenants away and let this land go to ruin years ago."

More acorns fell. A whole shower of them. They bounced painfully on his skull and shoulders.

"Say, now. That's a bit much. I was only looking for some peace here, not to have an encounter with a territorial squirrel. You mind your business and I'll mind mine."

The next object that dropped onto Colin was a good-sized rock.

He shot to his feet. "What the devil?"

The rustling mass in the treetops bounded away. He could see its movement among the branches, though of the creature itself, he could make out nothing. It seemed strangely large. *That was no squirrel.*

Shaking his head in confusion, he beat a hasty retreat out of the forest and back to the pasture. Pesadilla whickered and trotted over to him, thrusting his black head through the fence in search of treats.

"Sorry, amigo," Colin told the horse. "I haven't got anything for you." He patted the silky neck. "I need to let people know they can bring their mares to you. You'd like that, wouldn't you? To have a lady friend now and again?"

The horse bobbed his head and snorted.

"Just like any red-blooded male. I wouldn't mind a lady of my own. Might be relaxing." Then, he recalled that he did have a lady, and bedding her had indeed proved relaxing. *She still thinks we have a future. I can't think that way. It would be unfair to take her again. Not when I'm still struggling to understand what the future holds.* Confused, conflicted and frustrated, Colin made his way to the pond to check on the ducklings. *At least I can keep on working with our animals. That's something.*

Chapter 9

"'ll be going to London," Colin informed Daisy at the breakfast table one morning two months later. *I can't believe how much lighter I feel with taxes paid and the debt restructured. The payments will be so much easier to make now. I wonder if Daisy regrets giving away her fortune. She's stuck with me now.* He eyed his wife curiously.

"Oh?" Daisy spooned porridge into his bowl, sprinkled berries and honey on top, and joined him, digging a spoon into her dish. She looked completely comfortable at his table, though the way her gaze lingered on him spoke of volumes still waiting to be uttered.

Our table, he reminded himself. *What's mine is hers, such as it is.* "Yes. The ducks, geese and chickens are grown enough to go to market. The men and I need to figure out who will buy them. Make connections. This will be our income for many years to come, so this first sale is particularly important."

"I'd like to come with you," Daisy said. "I'd like to visit with the Bennetts and pay a call on your mother. I also need to arrange the purchase of some more furniture. If you're determined to sleep in a separate bedroom, wouldn't it be nice to have a bed?"

"I have a bed," he grumbled, spooning porridge into his mouth. The sweet, sharp flavor of the berries tasted like sun-soaked heaven.

"You have part of a bed," Daisy replied, "that you salvaged from the rubble of the east wing. Aren't you worried about splinters?"

Colin shrugged. "It's better than the pile of dirty clothes I used to sleep on. I'd hate to use our limited funds on an unnecessary indulgence like that."

"Colin, a bed is not an unnecessary indulgence. You work hard. You deserve to sleep… when you're able."

He raised his eyebrow.

"You think I haven't noticed your sleeplessness? You rustle around the house like a mouse at all hours of the night."

"I'm sorry if I disturbed you," he said, his voice flat and neutral. "A bed won't help. Sleep has always been hard for me."

"I know," she replied. "I was already awake. Do you think you're the only one who ruminates over dark thoughts in the night?"

She has a point, he realized. *She's been through a hell of her own.*

"I'd also like to add some wallpaper to the bedrooms. They're so relentlessly plain."

"Now, come on, Daisy, that is an indulgence," Colin argued. "Wallpaper is expensive. Isn't there a better use for your money than that?"

"It's not expensive at all," she replied. "I don't buy premade wallpaper. I make my own out of fabric scraps. I have a feeling the Bennett mill might have a few they'd part with for little or nothing. A bit of ink and a few inexpensive ingredients and we'll be able to brighten our space quite cheaply."

"You make wallpaper?"

"I do." Daisy smirked. "I'm not much of an artist, but I can handle a simple geometric design, and I have a good eye for color. I made all the wallpaper for Father's inn. Do you remember it?"

Gamely, Colin wracked his memory, and sure enough, an image floated up. "Green, wasn't it? With a pattern of brown leaves. It looked… attractive."

She beamed. "I did the bedrooms too. Stripes. Squares. I tried circles once, but I'm not as good at curvy shapes. Do you have a pattern you'd like in our home?"

Our home? The words touched a deep place in his heart. *I remember home. After Mother married Jack Turner and moved into a cozy London townhouse, and I would go to them and their daughters on holiday from school. Small, humble and filled with tasty smells.* The aroma of the slow-cooked lamb stew Daisy had begun preparing for their supper wafted to him. *She's like Mother. Warm. Homey. Also smart and business-like. I could love her…*

"Don't fool yourself," the smug voice of his interior accuser sneered. "You have less than nothing to offer."

He shook off the intruding voice. Like a magnet, she drew him in her direction. Settled in a chair at his side, her sunny hair and sweet smile looked like…

like home. She looks like home. She's trying to make a home for us. For me. All I have to do is reach for her. She'd love to kiss. I know it. Torturous memories of the handful of kisses they'd share warmed his lips.

All I have to do is accept, just like I accepted her money. It was all good. The men are so much happier now that they have repaired their homes, their paddocks and even their garments, and of course, Daisy has been helping them. She brought them seedlings from the wild plants in the manor garden to supplement their own. She hired the women to help her clean what was left of the manor while the men and I dismantled the damaged portion. In short, she's worked herself to the bone to ensure the women are just as healthy, happy and confident as the men. Now, she wants to work on me—on us.

The thought still surpassed his ability to comprehend, let alone embrace, and he shoved it—and Daisy—out of his heart for the thousandth time.

"You may come," he said shortly. "In fact, why don't you go on ahead. Take the train. I'm sure Mother will let you stay with her, and you might pay a call on the Bennetts, though given that Mrs. Bennett has two-month-old twins, she might not be receiving. If that's the case, wait for me, and we can call on Christopher and the mill together."

Daisy raised both eyebrows toward her golden hairline. "I had hoped we might travel together."

"Daisy, love. I'll be traveling with a flock of juvenile birds. It's going to be a loud, slow, smelly process. You won't enjoy that."

Daisy bit her lip as her expression changed from invitation to irritation. "I'm not such a fancy lady that some chicken droppings will offend me, but I understand. You still need 'time.' Very well."

Leaving her half-eaten breakfast abandoned on the table, she stalked out of the house, slamming the door behind her.

"Good," Colin muttered to himself, wishing he could believe it. "it won't do for her to get too close, no matter how she thinks she wants to."

Knowing he had a busy day ahead, he gobbled his breakfast and scooted out their door.

* * *

"Damn, damn, damn," Daisy cursed as she stormed into the sunshine. "Soon, it will be the summer solstice. Everything is better. Everything except my marriage. It seems as though Colin couldn't refuse my help, and he'll never stop blaming me for offering it."

Suddenly craving greenery, she skirted the fence, admiring the half-grown lambs that would fund the tenants through the winter and provide the funds for next year's taxes. They bleated happily as they nibbled lush summer plants. Daisy ducked into the forest and wrapped her arms around the fat trunk of an oak tree. Laying her face against the rough bark, she took deep breaths of its green, living scent and tried to center herself.

The warm summer sun filtered between the trees, dappling light onto her face. She closed her eyes, letting light and shadow play on her lids. "I will take the train," she breathed. "Much as I might be ready to make our marriage real, I cannot force it on him. I'll take the train to London. I'll ask the Bennetts for fabric scraps for my wallpaper and see how Katerina is doing after that challenging delivery. Then, I'll pay a call on my mother-in-law. Maybe she can give me some guidance about how to deal with her son. I'll move my own life forward while I wait to see what Colin is willing or able to do."

Something thudded against Daisy's shoulder.

She opened her eyes, brow furrowed as she looked at a medium-sized round stone that still rocked in the leaf litter on the forest floor.

"Is anyone there?" she called. "Bobby? William? Robin? If that's you, you shouldn't throw rocks. Do you want me to tell your mothers?"

Silence. A heavy, waiting silence that meant someone was out there, not responding but not retreating. Just waiting. The tense mood seemed to pulse. *This isn't one of the tenant's children making mischief.* She swallowed hard and took a step backward toward the meadow and the safety of the sunlight.

Another object zipped out of the forest.

Daisy dodged another, larger rock and whirled, racing out of the forest. A third rock slammed into her back, almost knocking off her feet as she raced into the meadow.

Colin stood in the pasture, patting a docile, patient ewe.

Daisy leaped over the fence and raced to him, throwing her arms around his middle.

"Daisy, what?" He looked bewildered, his whole face drawing inward, but his arms encircled her anyway.

"Someone's in the woods. Someone who shouldn't be there. They threw rocks at me."

"What?"

"I'm afraid, Colin. Please, don't let him hurt me."

Colin hugged her tighter, and she gasped as his hand compressed the bruise forming on her back.

"What?" he asked again, loosening his hold.

"It hurts," she said. "He hit me twice. Colin, what's happening? Why would someone do that?"

"I don't know," he said. Then, he turned to other parts of the pasture where some of his men were examining the lambs. "Bullock, Ferrell, there's someone in the woods throwing rocks. Go see if you find him. Probably a child being naughty, but we can't allow it. Someone could get badly hurt."

The men nodded and stomped toward the woods.

"It wasn't a child," Daisy said.

"How do you know?"

She shook her head. "I can't explain. I could just feel it. There was no giggling. No slinking away when I called out. Nothing."

Colin paused, his tight expression easing to thoughtfulness.

"You do believe me, don't you?"

"Yes, Daisy. I do believe you. You see, a while back, I went into the woods, and someone threw a rock at me from up in a tree, but the leaves were thick, and I couldn't see. I did notice that the person who retreated from me through the branches was big. Too big to be a child."

"Why would someone do such a thing?" she asked. "Everyone knows it's dangerous to throw rocks at people."

"Who can say?" Colin said. His gripping hands softened to a soothing stroke up and down her back. "Some people get a sick thrill out of making others afraid. They have no other purpose. Others seek to cause harm because they are mad, and in their madness, they justify dangerous behavior."

"Will your men be safe? I worry about them. If this person attacked you, the lord and master, what will he do with two tenant farmers?"

"Probably nothing," Colin assured her, hugging her closer to the muscular wall of his chest. His hand slipped to her face, stroking away a stray tear and a strand of messy hair.

She leaned into his comforting touch. The unspoken something that had connected them from the moment they met flared in his touch and flowed into her, reawakening hope.

"I mean," he continued, not seeming to notice how his demeanor toward her had changed, "most likely it's the first type. True madmen are rare. Someone who just wants to stir up trouble is essentially a coward. He won't stand and face two burly men bearing down on him. He'll run."

Daisy took a deep breath, taking his essence deep into her. "You may be right, but it's still a danger. The children play in the woods. Women and girls gather firewood, mushrooms, and search for wild berries. We're all in the woods every day. What's to stop this troublemaker from harming someone, or from sneaking into the pasture after the sheep and birds or—heaven forbid—the cows. What's to stop them from doing something even worse? Colin, this must stop now!"

"Hush, Daisy. Hush. I know. I won't let it get to that. We'll find this person and make him leave before any worse harm is done. Now, love, are you injured?"

"A couple of bruises," she replied, leaning into the hand that still lingered on her face. "They're not serious, but I'm still so frightened."

She looked up at her husband with wide, helpless eyes.

His hand on her cheek tightened, holding her in place. He lowered his head. She pursed her lips ever so slightly in invitation.

"There was no one there, my lord," Ferrell's voice shrilled out, shattering the moment. "We found ashes from someone smoking and some trampled leaves—not to mention quite a pile of rocks—but no person."

Daisy sagged in disappointment, a litany of swearwords running through her mind as Colin straightened and his arms fell away from her body.

"We'll have to set a watch on the animals," he said gruffly, "and tell your wives and children to keep out of the woods until we find out what's going on."

"Yes, my lord," the men said in unison.

"Ferrell, spread the word, won't you? Bullock, watch the pasture. I need to take my wife to town."

The men nodded.

"How long do you need to pack?" Colin asked. "I mean, we only just had this conversation. You can't possibly be ready."

"I'm not," she said, "but my needs are simple. I should be able to ready myself in a quarter-hour or so."

"Please get started then," he suggested.

You want me when you forget you shouldn't, Daisy thought, her eyes locked on his. *I must work with this. You're my husband and my soul mate. I will not rest until you stop fighting me.*

Colin broke eye contact and turned towards a little lamb that had wandered, bleating, up to his leg.

Scowling, Daisy picked her way across the pasture, climbed over the fence and entered the manor—which now resembled a farmhouse with an oversized kitchen—through the rear door from which she had emerged a short time ago.

* * *

"Ahhh," Daisy sighed as warm tea slid down her throat, relaxing her. It helped dispel the stark white walls of the Turner family's parlor. "Thank you, Ma'am. This is just what I needed."

"Not much tea at the estate?" Mrs. Turner asked kindly.

Before Daisy could answer, three adolescent girls whose brown hair matched their mother's to a shade tumbled into the room, giggling. "We're going to the park for a walk, Mother," the oldest said.

Mrs. Turner raised thin, light-brown eyebrows and rotated on the green brocade upholstery of her sofa to regard her daughters. "Daisy, these are my three younger children, Christine, Samantha and Marjorie." She turned to the oldest. "Will young Henry and his brothers be meeting you there?"

The oldest daughter blushed until her face flamed. "I think so."

"You know so," the youngest tattled, sticking her pert, upturned nose in the air. "You just received the note."

"Stuff it, Marjorie," the middle daughter said, elbowing her sister.

"Girls," Mrs. Turner said sharply, "is this really how you want to behave in front of company?"

"Isn't she Colin's wife?" Marjorie asked, showing her youthful tendency to argue over everything. "If she's family, she'd better get used to it."

"I don't mind you going to the park, and I don't mind you meeting with Henry and his brothers, but you must remain in the public eye, girls. There is to be no nonsense, do you understand? Henry has not talked to your father or me yet, Christine. If he's not ready to make a declaration, it's not a courtship, and friendships can be conducted in public. Is that clear?"

"Yes, Mother," Christine said with painful decorum. Daisy noticed that she too elbowed her sister as they scooted out the door.

Mrs. Turner shook her head. "Getting those girls safely grown may be the death of me," she commented.

Grown, not married. How interesting, Daisy thought. *I think I like this woman already.*

"So, what brings you to see me today, my dear?" the midwife asked.

Not midwife. Not only. She's your husband's mother. Don't let her professionalism distract you from the familial connection you're trying to draw on.

"Well, we were in town…"

"Were you? I didn't expect Colin to return, and certainly not so soon."

"It's the spring fowl," Daisy explained. "The ducks and chickens were ready to come to market, so I begged to come along for a visit. I stopped by to see Mrs. Bennett and her twins, and goodness those boys are handsome already."

"Aren't they just?" Mrs. Turner agreed. "They're going to be heartbreakers when they're grown. Their sister dotes on them."

"I don't blame her. I'm the youngest, and I would have loved a little sister to play with growing up. Mine are older, and while they made a pet of me for a while, the oh-so-serious concerns of adolescence interested them more. They're married now and scattered across the country, but they send a letter now and again."

"Well, that's nice, I suppose."

"Better than nothing," Daisy said, "but we're so different both in age and, well, attitude, that it's hard to communicate with them sometimes. They became rather… I don't know… stuffy after their children came along."

"That can happen," Mrs. Turner replied cautiously. "Why do I feel that this is building up to something? I mean, I could be wrong, but it seems like you're doing more than just getting to know me as your mother-in-law. Is that right?"

"You are remarkably astute, ma'am," Daisy said. "Yes, I'd like your advice about my marriage. I don't have a mother, I live far from my sisters, and I want more information about my husband, so I'm here to beg you for insights."

"I'll do what I can," Mrs. Turner replied mildly, "but I'll not get into the middle, you understand? Your marriage with my son is for the two of you to work out."

"I don't want you in the middle, Mrs. Turner, and I don't want you to take sides. I just want to understand Colin better. Has he always been so gloomy?"

"Oh, yes," Mrs. Turner said. "He was my moody boy, but that should be no impediment. Moodiness is also a sign of intensity, and intensity is wonderful for passion."

Daisy felt her cheeks heating. "He's certainly passionate about his tenants."

"Well, yes, dear," Mrs. Turner said gently. "They're his responsibility. He's worked so hard to save them from poverty. I do hope the sale of the spring fowl will ease his worries."

"He doesn't need that," Daisy mumbled.

"What was that, dear?" the matron asked, sipping her tea from a cup with a gilt and rose pattern Daisy found unnecessarily fussy.

"Nothing." Daisy took a bite of cake and closed her eyes, savoring the sweetness of the sugar on her tongue.

"Come now, Daisy. At least be honest. Oh, and you are welcome to call me Beth, or even Mother if you'd like. I won't mind a bit."

"Beth, then," Daisy said firmly. "I don't know you well enough to call you Mother."

"That's fair," the woman conceded without offense, shoving a long, gray-streaked strand of brown hair back into her simple, functional bun.

Daisy took a deep breath. *Don't be shy. You won't get what you want that way, and this seems like a blunt, honest woman.* "I inherited a tidy sum of money, and I encouraged Colin to use it to pay this season's expenses. He did. He paid the taxes in full and made a large enough dent in the debt that it is no longer threatening to crush them. Yes, he needs this sale to keep things moving forward, but the burden of this year's expenses is already a distant memory."

Beth's eyes went sharp. "How did he take you handing him money?"

"Badly." Daisy sighed. "I thought it would help. I thought it would make him feel less hopeless about our marriage if he had more money for his estate, but it didn't. He accepted it, but he became even less open and caring than before. It's like I offended him somehow, but I don't even know what I did."

"I don't think you did anything wrong, dear," Mrs. Turner said gently, sipping her tea again. Her cake lay ignored on her plate. "A timely infusion of cash was just what the estate needed, but... you'd have to understand Colin. That was a deeply hurtful thing, not for you to do, but for him to need."

"But I don't understand Colin. I don't understand at all," Daisy cried. "Sometimes, he seems so passionate, like he's on the verge of sweeping me off my feet and carrying me… I don't know… somewhere private. Other times, he's furious, but there's never a reason for it."

"The reason has nothing to do with you." Mrs. Turner sighed and crumbled a piece off the corner of her cake. "Daisy, listen. Colin has been struggling to turn the Gelroy estate around since he reached his majority. Even longer, really. It's his mission. His lifeblood. He's so tied to that land and his people, he can do little else. He's been fighting to save them for so long."

"Then why—"

"Think, Daisy. He's been fighting, giving the very food off his table, to keep the estate afloat for years. Then, you swoop in, unasked for and frankly unwanted, and throw the money he needs but was never able to earn into his lap."

Daisy lowered her eyebrows. "I wasn't trying to insult him."

"Of course not. He's angry at fate, not you. I imagine he doesn't know what to do with you. You're everything he's ever needed, but he cannot accept that anything other than tragedy will ever come his way. It's all he's ever known. He's simply out of the habit of hope."

"How can I restore it for him?" Daisy asked.

Mrs. Turner shook her head sadly. "You cannot. He must decide to embrace it for himself. He must decide to retrain his thinking to include happiness. Until he does, there's nothing you can do, and he may not. He expects you to grow tired of rough living and run, doesn't he?"

"He seems to," Daisy admitted. "He says things almost weekly that show he thinks of me as some kind of fragile flower, perhaps a member of the nobility. Ma'am, I'm an innkeeper's daughter. Neither hard work nor mess worries me. He seems to have forgotten that. He's also forgotten that, in the last couple of months, we've really turned the estate around."

"Please tell me you're not living in the old manor house," Mrs. Turner interjected.

Daisy laughed. "Not really. We tore down all the 'manor' parts of the manor house and distributed the materials to the tenants. Not only were they able to repair their homes, but several are planning to expand. We found servants' quarters, and the kitchen was still in decent condition, so now we have a small, safe, comfortable home. It's more than enough for our needs."

"Well, that's good to hear. What have you been up to since your arrival, Daisy? I regret we didn't get a chance to get to know one another the day we met, though I wasn't surprised Colin wanted to hurry back home."

"Me? Oh, I've been tidying up our home and taming the manor garden. It's been plenty to keep me busy, though I'm not quite sure what to do now. That's why I'm hoping to get your help. A good next project would be to address our marriage, but it seems Colin still has reservations. I was hoping you could give me some insights. I'm not going anywhere, but this isn't the way I want to live, with a husband who will make bland conversation at the breakfast and dinner table, but sleeps in another room and..."

"And never stops by yours for the evening?" Mrs. Turner guessed.

Daisy's face heated, but she nodded. "Is that wrong of me? I'm sorry. I know this is a very indiscreet question, but I have no one else to ask. I hope, as a midwife, you know things about the body that the average person doesn't."

"I'd like to think I do," Mrs. Turner said blandly, not seeming upset by the turn in the conversation. She sipped her tea, her face a study in neutrality that set Daisy's mind more at ease.

Though quite certain her cheeks were red enough to warrant a call to the fire brigade, she plunged forward. "I mean, as a midwife, you must deal frequently with the intimate questions of total strangers, given how babies are made and delivered. Mrs. Bennett may be a family friend, but not all your clients are, right?"

"Correct, Daisy," Beth said patiently. She crumbled another chunk off her cake.

"Right, then. Colin and I, we... we consummated our marriage in London before returning to the Gelroy estate, and it was nothing like I expected. My sisters always told me how vile and painful and revolting marital intimacy is, but..."

"But you didn't think so?"

Daisy shook her head. "It was... nice. Barely any discomfort, but... but there was something else. Something powerful. I had hoped to experience it again. The way my sisters talk of their husbands and their demands... Well, I was expecting Colin to approach me often, but he won't go near me. We haven't shared so much as a kiss since that night, and when I touch his hand, he often pulls away. Is there something wrong with me? My sisters would be overjoyed if their husbands left them alone, and all I can do is long for mine." She didn't think it was possible for her face to grow any hotter without bursting into flame.

"Daisy, Daisy, no. There's nothing wrong with you at all, I promise." Mrs. Turner set aside her teacup and joined Daisy on the sofa, patting her hand.

"Human desire is a complex thing. It incorporates the mind as much as the body, but both male and female bodies are designed to enjoy sexual contact. You have parts that exist solely for sexual pleasure, as well as other parts that serve multiple functions, one of which is sexual."

"Are you sure?"

"Yes, dear. I cannot speak to your sisters' experiences, as they're not here. It may be that, if they have small children, they don't want to be touched more, since little ones give their mothers neither space nor peace. It happens to most young mothers at one time or another. Just imagine chasing after multiple small, busy people with no sense of safety all day long and being smeared with... whatever slimy substance they've just touched... or produced."

Daisy shuddered, remembering just how sticky small children could get.

"It may also be that there's some lack of closeness in their marriages that interrupts the flow of affection. Or, they may simply be repeating what they think they're supposed to say in order to keep their baby sister out of 'mischief,' and they don't actually believe it. Last, they may fear they're doing something wrong if they don't say what they're expected to, even if they don't mean any of it. Regardless of the reason, what they're saying is erroneous. There's nothing wrong with sharing pleasurable moments with your husband."

Daisy gulped. *My husband is her son. This isn't the best person to have this conversation with, but what choice do I have?* "It's good to know, but we don't. I... How can I encourage him to... to reclaim that? How do I let him know I'm... available? He seems to think he's protecting me, but..."

"But he's disappointing you instead?"

Daisy nodded.

"It is a thorny dilemma. I think a passionate marriage might be good for Colin. Such a powerful, physical connection is hard to deny. That's probably why he's fighting so hard against it."

"What should I do?" Daisy set aside her empty teacup and half-eaten cake and laced her fingers together, twisting them in discomfort.

"Be direct," Mrs. Turner advised. "Tell him that you'd like to move your marriage back into the bedroom and that when he's ready, you'll be waiting. Sadly, you cannot simply order him to stop being a ninny. He isn't, though it might seem like that. What he's been through... it would put anyone off from enjoying everyday life. But if you are persistent, kind, and keep letting him know that your bed is available to him, his resistance may eventually crack. I think, if it does, a lot more closeness will follow. Only time will tell."

"He won't think badly of me if I boldly invite him to my bed?"

"I'm sure he won't," Mrs. Turner assured her. "I didn't raise my son to have strange and illogical attitudes about female sexuality or what it means about the woman in question. He knows better."

Daisy took a deep breath and released it without speaking. *Can I be that bold? I don't know. Especially not if he's going to reject me. He still seems so angry.*

"In the meanwhile," Mrs. Turner continued, not seeming to notice Daisy wandering off into contemplation, "I can give you a recipe for a tea that helps dampen conception. It's not a failsafe, but it will help. You can increase its effectiveness if you keep track of your menstrual cycle. Do it for at least three months and if it's regular, you can avoid pressing your suit on your more fertile days. After that, the tea should suffice. Colin would stoically accept a pregnancy, I'm sure, but I doubt he's ready to find joy in it. Do you know about plants, or do I need to sketch what they look like?"

Daisy shook off her meandering thoughts. "Um, I'm not bad with plants, but no expert. Sketches would be appreciated. As for, um… As for keeping track of my cycle, I always do that. My mother was… she started life in the Venus trade and taught my sisters how to track their cycles. My sisters taught me. They said it was important for everyone to know the particulars of their bodies. They also told me that being able to delay conception and try to space children a bit more widely is a great blessing."

Mrs. Turner stuck her lips out in pleased surprise and nodded. "I agree with both of those ideas, though they're rare. I imagine both of them are uncomfortable with their sexuality, at least in part, because they're uncomfortable with your mother's occupation, and whether any sign of enjoyment might not mean… more than that they are normal women. It doesn't mean that you know. Women selling their bodies for money and women making love for pleasure are worlds apart."

"That makes sense," Daisy said. "For some reason, it never bothered me, you know, about Mother. She grew up in that environment. It was all she knew. I don't remember her being a shy or timid woman, though she died when I was small, so my memories are few. I remember her being like a ball of light, all intensity. Impossible to ignore. She told me never to let anyone dim my brightness." Realizing she was chattering, Daisy stammered to a halt.

Mrs. Turner smiled. "That's good advice." She took a bite, finally, of her cake.

"Mrs. Turner?" A serving woman knocked and stuck her head in the door.

Mrs. Turner turned her head to regard the new arrival and raised her eyebrows in silent communication as she chewed.

"Your son is here."

She swallowed and sipped her tea. "Won't you show him in?"

Daisy's face flamed to its hottest temperature yet as the man she'd just been so intimately discussing strode into the room. His face glowed with compelling energy she'd never seen in him before.

"Good afternoon, Mother. Daisy."

"Hello, son. How was your day? I must say, you look happy."

"Oh, yes! Miss Smith," he called.

The servant stepped back into the room.

"Can you bring me a cup, please?" As Miss Smith scuttled away, Colin claimed a slice of cake and devoured it in unusually large chomps.

Wiping crumbs from his jacket, he perched in an armchair across from the women.

"Did you get your fabric scraps from the Bennetts?" he asked Daisy after he swallowed his treat.

"Yes, without any trouble," she replied. "Mr. Bennett mentioned that they have so many scraps, and they have to have them carted away and burned. It seems like quite a waste."

"I'm sure," Colin said. "It's unavoidable in their industry."

An embryo of thought flared to life in Daisy's mind, and she set it in a fertile corner to mature. "And you, love? Was your quest successful?"

"It was," he replied, a hint of a grin tugging the corner of his mouth. It took decades off his appearance. "We found markets for all the birds. The sellers were quite pleased and complimentary of their condition. They have asked to see the lambs at the end of summer, and most especially the geese for Christmas. We did better than we expected, Daisy. We now have enough for feed and supplies for the rest of summer, with some left over for next year's taxes. If we have another good turnout next year… and a few people breed their mares with Pesadilla—which they will because he's incredible—we will have plenty to pay the debts as well. In short, we're in good shape."

"That's wonderful!" she breathed. "I'm so happy for you. Look what you did! You're brilliant."

Colin's suntanned face darkened a shade. "I just did what needed to be done," he mumbled.

"No, love. You innovated a solution to what seemed like an unsolvable problem. You implemented it and you succeeded. Don't deny your success."

The corner of Colin's mouth twitched again. "I did, didn't I?"

Daisy nodded, wishing she could embrace him. "You did."

"You should be proud of yourself, son. I imagine you're proud of your tenants for all their hard work, aren't you?" Mrs. Turner pointed out.

"Of course. They've worked harder than anyone should have to. They've endured more than any man should have to."

"So have you," his mother told him bluntly. "You've endured more and worked harder than even they have, so allow a moment of pride and success for yourself."

"I think we should have a party," Daisy blurted.

Colin blinked at her.

"You all *have* worked too hard and endured too much. We should buy some beer and cook some meat and celebrate. It's almost the summer solstice. It's a lovely time of year to have a party."

"I would hate to waste money that way," Colin began.

"It's not ever a waste to celebrate success against great odds," his mother pointed out. "Your men and their families need to know that you, the lord, want them to be happy. Don't they deserve that? Relax together, son. You, your wife, your tenants and their families. It's not wrong to celebrate. It's human, and it's never a waste to live in balance."

"I see your point, both of you," Colin said slowly. "Let me think about this."

Mrs. Turner whispered to Daisy, "He thinks slowly. It's important to remember that."

"I've noticed," Daisy whispered back.

"Say, now. Are the two of you telling secrets about me?"

"Oh, no, never," Daisy protested.

At the same moment, Mrs. Turner, a smirk on her face, said. "We might be, but you'll have to wait to find out."

Colin regarded the two of them with amused suspicion stamped all over his face. "I think I'm alarmed."

"You should be," his mother told him.

Though she hadn't eaten or drunk anything in several minutes, Daisy choked.

* * *

"What's that you're mixing, ma'am?" Katie Bullock asked, creeping into the former manor yard—now a tidy and well-kept garden—behind the Gelroy family home.

Daisy looked up from the mushy mess of fabric scraps and water she was grinding under a heavy stone pestle.

"I'm making wallpaper, Katie," Daisy said. "Want to help?"

"What do you do?" The adolescent crept forward. A waft of warm summer wind puffed past then, dragging a strand of light brown hair out of the girl's untidy bun. She tucked it back.

"I grind these fabric scraps with water to start with to make a mash. I chose red, brown and white fabric because I want a light maroon base color."

"Interesting." Katie crept forward again. "How did you learn to do that?"

"I read it in a magazine," Daisy explained. "I tried it out in my bedroom back at my father's inn, and it was so nice to be able to choose exactly what I wanted. That first one wasn't the best, but it was good enough I kept trying, and now I'm rather good at it, not to be immodest. I'm not an artist, but as long as the design is simple, I can make something pretty."

"It doesn't look pretty now," Katie commented.

Daisy paused in her grinding to gather up more small squares of scraps from the bucket of water in which they were soaking.

Katie reached out to touch the mash. "It feels like potatoes."

"A bit, or maybe like applesauce."

"You've made applesauce?" Katie asked.

"Yes, and potatoes too. Remember, I wasn't born a lady. I became one more or less by accident. Life's a funny thing, Katie. Good and bad are in everyone's future, but we can never predict when or how they will come."

"That's for sure. I never thought I would see a day when Mother and Father weren't frustrated and upset. We had food but never quite enough of anything else. Especially pretty things."

Her comment caught in Daisy's throat. "I... ugh." She coughed. "I'm sorry you had to live that way. Is it better now?"

"Oh, yes. I know Lord Gelroy did his best. My Da says he's so much better than his father was, but he wasn't able to do everything. No one expected it of him. He's only one man. I don't blame him, but I was almighty tired of wearing worn-out clothing and being able to peer through the cracks in our walls. We never could keep up with patching them." She blurted out the whole comment fast, as though it had escaped unbidden and she feared punishment for it.

"I can imagine," Daisy said dryly.

"The bricks from the manor have made such a world of difference," Katie added. "The whole house feels solid now, and so much bigger and more comfortable. I can't wait for it to be done!" Then, she blushed, seeming to realize she was babbling.

Rather than pursue, Daisy changed the subject. "Here. Would you like to try the grinding? It's hard work, but when we're done, it will be worth it."

"Surely!" Katie grabbed the pestle and began vigorously grinding the new batch of fabric to mush. The dye seeped from the bits and stained her fingers reddish-brown. "What do you do once it's all ground up?"

"See that vat over there?" Daisy asked, indicating a wine barrel that had been sawed down into a shallow dish. "There's a large frame in it, with a filter inside. We will drop the mash into the frame, add water and spread it thinly over the filter. Then, it dries in the sun and when it's dry, it's a lovely, thick paper we can paint on. We'll glue it up to the walls, and hey, presto! It's wallpaper."

"I like to paint," Katie volunteered. "Draw too."

"Do you?" Daisy asked, enjoying her conversation with the young lady. "That's a lovely talent to have. I always wished I could draw, but sadly, anything more complicated than a line or a circle—if I have something to trace—comes out looking like a toddler drew it."

Katie giggled. "Is this ground up enough, my lady?"

The title grated on Daisy's senses, but she knew she had to accept it. "I think it is. Let's bring it over to the frame."

They grabbed big, mushy handfuls of fabric and carried it over.

Katie giggled again. "My sister would love this."

"Go get her," Daisy said. "The more the merrier. It's a lot of work, but I enjoy it more with company. Plus, it's not a bad thing to learn a new skill."

"Let me go see who I can find," Katie said. "I'll be right back, my lady. Thank you!"

A new skill. The words bounced around in Daisy's mind. *A new skill. A new... job? A new career? A new business?* A thought dawned, mingled with one she'd thought up in London, and blossomed into a flowering idea. "Oh, Lord. This opportunity can't be ignored. We have all the parts readily at hand. Now, all we need is to bring it to life."

* * *

"How was your day, love?" Daisy asked, approaching Colin where he sat at the table and handing him a plate heaped high with roasted chicken with potatoes and summer peas. A buttery, herbaceous aroma wafted up.

Colin grabbed his fork and took a hearty bite, closing his eyes while he chewed.

Daisy waited, taking a seat with her plate and nibbling at her food. *He's not ignoring me,* she reminded herself. *He just appreciates food intensely and takes his time thinking about everything he says.*

After only knowing each other a couple of months, Daisy was only beginning to understand her husband and his habits. *He's a thoughtful man, and he certainly takes his time.* Sometimes, this annoyed Daisy, who bubbled with energy and wanted to move forward *now,* but she was learning to be patient with him. *Impatience doesn't help anything,* she reminded herself in a voice that sounded like the Vicar's late wife. A general busybody, she'd taken it as a personal mission to settle Daisy into a proper young lady. *She failed so badly,* Daisy recalled with a grin.

"What's funny?" Colin asked. "Won't you let me in on the joke?"

Daisy blinked her way out of her imagination and back into the kitchen with her husband. *He asked me a question? He's making idle conversation?* "Oh, it's nothing," she spluttered, unprepared for conversation while food remained on Colin's plate. "I was just remembering the old lady who used to teach at the school in my hometown. She tried hard to tame me, and I think she went to her grave regretting her failure."

Colin chuckled. It sounded rusty.

She reached out, offering the only touch he seemed able to accept and laid her hand on his. His rough, calloused skin felt thrilling under her fingers.

"Taming you?" His brown eyes sparkled with a hint of mischief. It looked beautiful and alive. "It would make as much sense as taming a wild doe and be as sad. Your wild streak is such a huge part of your charm."

Daisy smiled to hide the sudden pounding of her heart. She bit her lip. *A compliment? He thinks I'm charming? Oh, my goodness.* "It's useless at any rate," she said tartly. "I'm comfortable with my wildness. I think being a proper lady sounds boring."

His grin widened. "You can aspire to more than being an insipid little mouse, and I don't think that particular cloak would fit."

"Certainly, it wouldn't." Daisy took a bite of her dinner to give herself time to reflect.

"I believe you asked about my day," Colin went on, relaxing easily into conversation, an activity that had been painful to the point of impossibility only a few weeks ago. He chewed thoughtfully on a bite of peas, swallowed, and took a sip of water. "It was an ordinary day, I suppose. The lambs are growing nicely. We lost a couple of goslings to a fox. The men suggested we get a sheepdog. It's a good idea. I'm surprised there are no dogs at all on the estate. Father used to have some particularly nasty hounds, but when they died, he was already declining, and no one replaced them. I think it's time to consider something more useful."

"It would be nice to have a dog," Daisy agreed, "not to mention some cats. Why are there no cats on an estate that was once dedicated to growing grain?"

Colin shrugged. "There were none by the time I was born, and I must confess, I never thought about them. It does make sense though. Say, what's that look on your face? Are you planning on spoiling the puppies and kittens with kitchen scraps and head scratches, and turning them into pets? They'd be working animals, Daisy."

Daisy giggled. "As if I haven't seen you patting the lambs. Just because an animal is here to work doesn't mean we can't enjoy them as pets."

Colin acknowledged her words with a sheepish grin.

"I'm so glad everything is better on the estate, Colin. The tenants look so much healthier and happier now. You succeeded. It's lovely."

"I didn't do anything," he muttered, his habitual negativity welling up like a cloud and hiding the sunshine. "You did it, with your money."

"No, I didn't," she argued. She noticed her hand still lay on his and squeezed gently. "You did it, Colin. You and the men. You realized grain was hopeless and decided on animal husbandry instead. It was a success. Your efforts have earned enough to last us through the summer and into the fall, and the second round of sales—the lambs and the geese—will bring in more than enough for winter. I didn't save you, love. You did. I only provided the breathing room you needed for the chickens and ducks to mature. You didn't need much because you had already saved the estate before I got here."

Colin frowned at her, his forehead furrowing as he processed these unexpected thoughts.

"Love, you have to understand this. You saved your estate. You did it. I helped speed up the timing, but this would have been the outcome in a few years anyway. Now, you need to lay the burden down. You'll work yourself into an early grave if you don't stop thinking such harsh thoughts about yourself. You have nothing more to prove. Everything is fine. Only, you have to admit it to yourself. You can live a normal life now. Work hard through the day, as any man should, and then come home and indulge in creature comforts—a hearty meal, a warm bed—and let the day's cares roll away."

He shook his head. "I don't know how to do that."

"I know you don't. Will you let me help you? Let me give you new thoughts and opportunities? You deserve to rest, Colin."

"You've done more than your share already, Daisy," he said. "You're fresh as a summer flower. You have no business living in the dirt."

She raised an eyebrow. "Colin, flowers thrive in dirt. It's their proper environment. What happens if you remove a flower from the dirt?"

He paused.

"Say it," she insisted.

"It dies," he rasped.

"I don't feel out of place here, Colin, and I'm far from exhausted. Remember, I'm not some fancy lady who thinks lifting a fork is hard work. I'm a humble innkeeper's daughter. Labor doesn't frighten or offend me. I rather enjoy it. But when the day is done, when the food is cooked and the house is clean, and the animals are settled in their stables, it's time for us both to set cares aside and explore... explore what it means to be a family. That's what we are now, love. You and me. We can... we can make a life together. I want that. I've wanted it from the beginning. Don't you?"

Her heart, which had not stopped pounding since his compliment earlier, took on a painful rhythm.

Colin gulped. "What are you asking, Daisy? Do you want to discuss literature? That's how we started."

"Yes," she agreed, eager to jump on an easy answer. "Or read together. Discover new works."

"I could agree to that."

Daisy swallowed against a ball of fear that seemed to be forming in her throat. "And other things. Colin, you do realize you don't need to sleep alone, don't you?"

* * *

Just like that, the supportive friendliness with which they had started their conversation died, and a sort of wordless intensity rose. It didn't feel like the usual helpless despair that wrapped around him like a ragged cloak of pain. *Did she just say what I think she said? Did she mean it the way it sounded?* "Daisy?"

She didn't answer, merely regarded him with her heart glowing in her wide green eyes.

Colin couldn't look away. He felt trapped in Daisy's eyes. Captured in warmth and peace that didn't feel it should belong to him. One small hand, rough with hard work, traced the scratchy shadow of a beard on his cheek. She leaned in, waiting.

As though unable to stop himself, Colin moved in her direction.

You wanted this once, her expression seemed to say. *You wanted it as badly as I did. Now, here we are, husband and wife. Come on.*

A pull that seemed to come from the deepest part of Colin's soul drew him forward again. It refused to let him pass up this opportunity.

His lips touched Daisy's in a warm, gentle touch. Her essence radiated into his face, into his head, where obsessive thoughts already circled and chased them back into the shadows. Spread down the back of his neck in a riot of tingles to his heart, where the walls he'd been busily erecting since childhood against future pain took a battering. Down into his limbs, the essence of Daisy, of summer sunshine and pure joy radiated.

At last, it arrived at his manhood, which swelled and ached for ultimate closeness. No rank lust, his desire for Daisy had a feeling of rightness he had never connected with passion before. *We belong to each other,* her kiss seemed to say, and his body, at least, could not deny it.

A wild hunger rose up in Colin, and he hauled Daisy out of her chair into his lap.

She went easily, offering no resistance.

He devoured her, seeking to pull every last ounce of her goodness into himself.

Her fingers curled in his hair, and she tilted her head, seeking and finding a perfect alignment. Their tongues mated and coiled.

Daisy exhaled in an eager, breathless sigh. "Please, Colin," she whispered against his lips.

Oh, yes, his unbridled inner self urged. *Take what she's offering—what we both want. Take her peace and joy and return it full measure.*

Into the powerful moment, a dark and sneaky doubt crept. A sly voice that whispered, "To what end? She's offering passion, but she expects love or at least the possibility of it. Can you offer her the love a woman deserves? Can you take her body and give her back your heart?"

Colin broke away with a snarl and set Daisy on her feet. "I'm sorry," he said, struggling to rein in his unruly desire.

"What happened?" she asked.

He shook his head. "I can't do this."

"Colin?" She reached out with fingers that trembled in their air between them, but she stopped short of touching his face.

He recoiled. "I do need to sleep alone. I must. I know you don't understand, but… it's for the best. Someday, you'll understand. I cannot tie you to me. Not when I have so little to offer."

He rose, a move that put him uncomfortably close to her body, where her heat and scent radiated out to touch him, drawing him with a temptation that almost cracked his willpower.

Nearly knocking his chair over in his haste to escape, he skirted his bewildered wife and ran for the door.

"Coward," his conscience scolded him, looming in his mind like a scowling headmaster. "Daisy didn't deserve that. She wasn't asking you to do anything harmful or frightening. You haven't been afraid of sex since you were a sixteen-year-old schoolboy."

He plunged into the darkness outside the kitchen door, hoping the night would blind his thoughts the way it blinded his eyes. Instead, the pressing night sank deep into his awareness, leaving him in a black chamber where his thoughts echoed louder than the summer crickets.

Just when maybe things were getting better, here is another situation I cannot fix. A situation with no solution I can hold onto. If I take Daisy to wife, if I let myself love her, she'll be trapped in this nightmare with me for the rest of her life. She deserves better. If I let her go, I'll have to force her away, which will feel as good as kicking a puppy.

She's falling for me, for some perverse reason. I can see it in her eyes, and most especially in the bold way in which she just invited me to her bed, but I cannot allow it. She must leave. She must. The cost to her will be high. She gave me her virginity, but a better man will forgive that. She's well worth it.

The idea of Daisy with a new lover, a new husband, made him powerfully angry. A wave of anger he had no right to feel since he couldn't be the husband she needed. Hopelessness thickened until he choked on it.

And how will you feel, knowing you took some of the money she should have kept to support herself?

His thoughts swirled around and around in a vortex of bewilderment.

"What do I do?" he asked out loud. "God, you've never paid the slightest attention to my needs before, but if you care at all about the fate of that kind young woman you tossed into my life, tell me what to do with her."

No answer came. His prayer, as always, seemed to rebound off an iron plate and slam back into him with a force that drove him to his knees in the damp, cool grass. He crouched, fighting the urge to retch, while unformed agony bounced through his entire body again.

Chapter 10

HOUGH she had expected it, Colin's rejection stung badly. Particularly in light of how passionately he'd kissed her.

Daisy sat alone at the table for several long minutes, breathing deeply and trying to still the beating of her heart. Leaning forward, she rested her head on her hands on the table. "This is harder than I thought," she muttered. "In some ways, it's worse than simple neutrality or even hostility. He wants me. I can see he does. Why does he insist on pushing me away?"

Without Colin there to answer her questions, they ricocheted around in her mind, violent as birdshot, shattering joy and leaving seeping wounded in their wake.

"I cannot let this break me," she told herself. "I must remember to care for myself, as he's not able to. Another moment, and I'll get up and find something useful to do."

In the back of her mind, in the silence, another voice whispered, "His need to push me away may eventually become a self-fulfilling prophecy."

She sat a moment and allowed herself to understand that she would not live with his rejection and waffling forever and that one day, if Colin didn't change his behavior, she might leave and be right to do so.

"Someday, but not now."

Rising, she began to gather the plates, to pile them up beside the sink, which those sneaky servants had equipped with the luxury of hot running water by installing a cistern adjacent to the stove. "It was a smart move," she admitted, "though dishonest. They surely made kitchen work easier. Now, I don't have to heat water for dishes or laundry on the stove. It saves hours every week."

She stacked the dishes in the basin, added soap and pulled the lever to activate the hot water when an idea occurred to her. Turning as though in a trance, she made her way to the pantry and opened the door. Inside, a portable tub waited for the owners to decide to bathe.

It isn't bath day, she thought, *but our midsummer celebration is tomorrow.* The thought of luxuriating in warm water nearly made her tremble. *This is exactly what I need.*

She dragged the tub into the open space between the table and the cabinets and claimed out her largest stockpot, which she set aside. Then, she drew out a second, smaller pot, which she filled with cold water and set on the stove, muttering instructions to herself as she went, so she could keep her mind focused on irrelevant things.

"Heat some water on the stove because the running water will grow tepid as I move it from the sink to the tub. While it's heating, I can get myself a towel and my bathing soaps. Today, I want to luxuriate."

Once a pot of water sat simmering on the stovetop, Daisy ducked through the door into the parlor and then crossed to her bedroom. Rummaging in the top drawer of her bureau, she drew out a box made of fancy paper and opened the lid. Inside, a collection of sweet-smelling French-milled soaps, a birthday gift from her oldest sister, released a waft of loveliness into the room. She selected her favorite and also retrieved a towel and her nightgown. She took a moment to clean her teeth before returning to the kitchen. As she had hoped, the water had begun to bubble, though it had a ways to go before it boiled.

She set her supplies beside the tub and got to work extracting the hot water from the cistern and pouring it into the tub. It took several trips, and eventually, the cistern grew empty. She frowned, filling the tub the rest of the way with unheated water.

At last, the tub was full and the water on the stove had begun to boil. She carried it to the tub, poured it in, and stripped off her garments.

"I should have used the room-temperature water first," she told herself. "Stupid. Oh well. I've learned that lesson. It's warm enough."

She settled back against the copper wall of the tub and closed her eyes, inhaling the rose scent of her soap and letting her tension drift away.

"I wonder what would happen if Colin came in and found me naked in the kitchen. I've always warned him when I planned to bathe, and he gave me privacy. Today… today he's made me angry. If he sees more than he intends to, I don't feel sorry for him."

She imagined what his reaction would be, if he burst into the kitchen, only to behold his wife's naked breasts in the dim light of the stove, and know she was bare all over. "Would I be embarrassed? I don't think so. Shy, maybe. Maybe I would flirt with fluttering eyelashes and slowly stand. I wonder how long he would be able to resist?"

Too long, a sour voice in the back of her mind groused, shattering her pleasant fantasy. *Probably forever.*

Annoyed with herself for being so grumpy, Daisy drew her legs up to her chest and sat up. This put her in position to look into the window to the dark, sleeping garden beyond.

Something black blocked the view. Something black with a strip of white. White, with two brown eyes staring in the window at her. A flicker of undefined movement that suggested dark gloves revealed a large, white stone.

Daisy screamed.

* * *

"Get up, you dolt," Colin told himself fiercely. "Your wife invited you to her bed. She didn't tell you she was leaving forever. Deep down, admit that you want her to stay—and you want to take her up on her offer—in spite of everything. At least be honest with yourself."

Digging his hands into the moist soil, he pushed himself upright. The cool earth against his fingers soothed him. It felt like life. Like returning to life after a long, brutal winter.

That's what's happening, he realized. *Life is returning. To the estate, to the tenants and to me. I've been in the dark so long, that life, like light, hurts my eyes. I can't see because it's so bright. I shy away. Flinch away, but, my God, do I want the light to shine on me.*

"You don't deserve it," the sly voice of melancholia—his father's voice—whispered. "You don't deserve light or life. You failed, year after year. A decade of failure has been charged to your account, and a dark debtor's prison is your only just fate."

He shook his heat. *Daisy doesn't think that. She wants to share her light with me.*

"She's a fool," the voice replied, "and when she realizes what a fool she's been, she'll run, and you'll be even worse off than before, for daring to reach out for something that will never be for you."

"Wait," he said aloud. "Daisy is smart, like Mother. One of the smartest women I've known. She's no fool."

Ah, but she fancies herself in love with you.

"Shut up!" he ordered the sly voice, not caring that he sounded like a madman. "Shut up with your lies and your meanness. Is it you, Father, who wants so badly to steal even this one small joy? I was never your image of a proper gentleman, so I don't deserve to be happy? You didn't love your wife, so I don't dare love mine?"

Then, he realized what he had said. "Dear God. Do I love Daisy? No, not yet. I've known her only a few months, but I *could*." The thought stole his breath away from his chest. He laid his hand over his heart and drew in a shattered gasp.

His gasp echoed in a scream.

Colin shot up off the ground and ran in the direction of his door. There, framed in the light from the kitchen window, stood a figure clad all in black with a wide-brimmed black hat and a black handkerchief tied over his face.

"You there!" Colin shouted. "What are you doing? Get away from my home!"

A white object flew in his direction and he dodged. The figure to wheeled around and raced for the woods.

Colin ran after him, but within moments knew it was hopeless. The dark clothing in the dark forest, where even the moonlight had to filter through dense summer foliage, would leave the interloper invisible. He, on the other hand, in a light tan shirt and buff trousers—albeit dirty after a long day of work—would glow like stars in the darkness and likely invoke a shower of rocks.

He turned back toward the house, heart pounding. Without any further thought, he raced to the doorway and threw open the door. Racing in, he locked the door behind him with a deft twist of the key.

He looked around for his wife but for a moment couldn't find her in the dimly lit kitchen. The glow that had seemed to pour into the night from the window inside only turned out to come from a couple of candles on the dining table and an oil lamp on the floor beside the bathtub, which had not been out a half hour ago when he left.

Turning, he saw Daisy's pale form, crouching by the window, peering out into the night. Her whole body visibly trembled.

He hurried to her without a moment's consideration and dragged her into his arms.

She screamed, swatting and scratching at his hands.

"Daisy, Daisy, love, it's me. It's Colin."

She continued fighting. "Let go! Let me go! Don't touch me!"

"Daisy," he breathed again, his lips against her ear.

The fight went out of her and she sagged in his embrace. "Colin?"

"Yes, love. I've got you."

A shudder ran up her spine and culminated in a choking sob. She turned in his arms and grabbed two big fistfuls of his shirt, hiding her face in the stained fabric and inhaling deeply. "There…" her voice broke. "There was a man." Several shattered sobs followed, and then she choked, "At the window." Pant pant. "Looking at me."

"I know, love I saw. I saw him. I chased him into the woods."

"Why…" Sob. "Why would anyone do such a thing? Who looks into other people's windows?"

Colin didn't answer. He knew that the answer—normal, healthy people don't. Only sick, dangerous people did—would do nothing to comfort his wife. "The door is locked now, love, and he's gone. You're safe with me."

For some reason, his words invoked a fresh flood of tears. Daisy sobbed against his shoulder, clutching him as though she'd never let go. "For how long, Colin?" she whimpered at last. "How long until you send me away? Until you finally reject me for good? Who will protect me when I have to try to live alone?" Shattered sobs stole away whatever else she might have tried to say.

"I don't want to," he breathed, admitting the dangerous truth aloud as her wounded vulnerability finally achieved what her tempting cheer had not.

"Then DON'T!" she wailed. "Don't send me away. I can't stand it. I want to be here, with you. This is my home. Please."

"Hush now, Daisy. Hush, love." He rubbed one hand up and down her bare, wet back. *She's naked,* he realized, glancing down at the lush, womanly form pressed up against his front. Without consideration, his stroking hand wandered lower to cup the plump curve of her buttock.

Daisy bit her lip and lifted her head. Her red, tear-stained eyes glowed in the dim room. She blinked, thick, golden lashes flashing over the verdant light.

One hand released its hold on his shirt and crept up his shoulder to grasp the back of his neck. A soft pressure drew him down, down.

He obeyed, helpless to resist the unspoken demand, and his lips met hers with an internal reverberation that resounded through his heart like a gong. *There will be no going back. There will be no further talk of leaving or retreating. No thought of it. If you take what she's offering, you will belong to her forever.*

The eager pleasure that responded told him everything he needed to know.

Unworthy though I may be, the lady has chosen me, and I have no choice but to accept. I honestly don't want anything else.

Daisy's lips parted and thought shattered, leaving Colin one raw nerve, eager to be stimulated. Daisy did not disappoint. Still holding him captive against her lips, while her tongue tangled with his in lush provocation, she used her free hand to tug his shirt free of his waistband and slide her hand underneath. Her fingers trailed over his belly, spurring a riot of ticklish arousal. His eyes slid closed as he surrendered to the inevitable.

Daisy's fingers stroked and gently scratched his chest. He could feel the callouses from her life of hard work against his skin. *The hand of a woman who is not afraid to make things happen, no matter how difficult. The hand of a woman who's ready for any challenge, so long as she doesn't have to face it alone.*

He grasped her questing fingers in a gentle restraint and broke their lusty embrace, drawing her hand upward to his lips, where he kissed the pad of her index finger.

Their eyes met in a moment of unguarded connection that told him, though his reticence had strained the essential bond between them, it was not yet broken.

"Is this what you want, love?" he asked solemnly. "Are you sure?"

In response, she reached for his shirt again, this time loosening its entire circumference from around his waist and tugging it up toward his neck.

"Easy, love. I'll help." He stripped it off, but she had already moved, attacking the buttons on his belly with frustrated haste. Unable to manipulate the closures in her current state, she boldly stroked her hand downward to cup his erection.

"All right, all right. Half a moment." Colin nearly ripped the buttons off his trousers trying to free them, but after a few seconds of fumbling, the garment slid to the floor. Though he'd left off an undershirt when he'd dressed that morning, in deference to the midsummer heat, he still had to contend with high-waisted drawers, which he bunched and tangled, with Daisy's unhelpful assistance, until he could kick it off his ankles.

He didn't even have time to remove his stockings before Daisy grasped his arms and dragged him onto the floor. The cool, varnished wood felt hard under his knees, but he barely noticed as the rest of his body compressed warm, sweet woman.

She claimed his mouth again, desperate, it seemed, to merge their two souls into one.

Bracing his weight on one hand, he wormed the other between them so he could stroke her breasts and belly. She felt like heaven under his work-rough fingers, and she squirmed at the touch, shifting her mound against his sex.

The stimulation proved almost more than Colin could bear. He hovered already on the brink of release, but he knew climaxing against Daisy's belly would satisfy neither of them. *She wants the reassurance of intercourse, and at this point, so do I.*

He slipped lower, between her parted thighs, and cupped her sex. Two fingers slipped between the outer lips, and he sighed with relief at the wet heat between. He dipped briefly into her well and found her ready. *Good. I have no time to sweeten this further.*

Daisy, it seemed, also had no patience. She boldly grasped his erection, trying to line it up.

"Now, love?" he asked.

She responded with a sour look that forced a rusty chuckle from his chest.

He left off caressing her sex and grasped her hand, showing her how to guide him. Together, undone by mutual need, they positioned him, feeding the tip of his penis into her. Her hand fell away, reaching up to rest on the center of his back as he arched his hips, easing further and further into her. Her passage fluttered and she let out a low moan, clutching him tight.

Colin's slow advance into Daisy's fullest depth almost set off his orgasm. *I have no time to bring her to climax,* he realized. *Not unless I do something to help her.* His hand still rested near her, and he sat back a bit, not breaking their intimate connection, but giving himself some space.

Holding his hips as still as he could, unable to bear the stimulation of thrusting, he delved again into her intimate folds in search of her swollen pearl. It pulsed under his finger, and he gave her what she needed, spurred on by the pleasured squeaks he drew from her.

Her hips shifted restlessly as he aroused her. He growled and bit down hard on his lip to prevent himself from spilling. *You first, Lady Gelroy,* he thought, as he rubbed her.

"Oh, Colin. Oh, Lord. Aaaaaah!" A flutter accompanied Daisy's wail of pleasure, letting Colin know that he could, at last, move.

Bracing both hands on the floor, covering her body fully again, he drew back and surged deep into her, claiming every inch of her convulsing sex for his own. "Mine," he snarled, still fighting the rising orgasm so he could enjoy the only moment that remained.

Colin looked down into Daisy's face, saw her lost in passion, eyes closed, mouth open, emitting helpless gasps of pleasure. He drew back and thrust home once more, and his own lids slid closed against a shower of sparks. *Home,* he thought. Pausing at the moment of deepest penetration, he shuddered in sweet release.

* * *

Back at the window outside the small remnant of what had once been a grand home, the watcher shuddered in revulsion. *Filthy pigs. Look how they rut… on the floor.*

Lord Gelroy shifted, and the watcher ducked out of sight… for a moment, before cautiously peeking over the sill again in time to see the couple's mouths meet in a fiery kiss.

Disgusting. This will not go unpunished.

Drawing reluctantly away, he again retreated into the darkness.

* * *

The fluttering in Daisy's core finally died away, bringing her back into the reality of the hard floor beneath her back. Her husband lay on her, his body heavy with muscles. His sex still lingered inside her, though its tempting rigidity was rapidly waning.

He leaned in, his brown eyes soft, and laid a tender kiss on Daisy's lips before levering himself upright. Shaking his head, he retrieved his drawers and looked at them without putting them on.

"What?" Daisy asked, rolling onto one hip to face him and lifting herself onto her elbow.

"Was this really necessary?" he asked.

Oh, Lord. Not this again. Not now. Angry that he was again questioning the beauty of their undeniable connection, Daisy snapped. "Yes, it was. Why can't you just admit, Colin, that we're meant for each other? We're *married*, in case you've forgotten, and it's about time we acted like it."

"Wait. Daisy, hold on." He held up his hand, underpants dangling. "I didn't mean that. I… when I saw you so upset, I knew. I knew I couldn't… hold back anymore. I agree. It was past time we began to live as a married couple. For some reason, you want to stay in this pit of hell? Fine, stay. I won't fight you anymore. I can't. What I meant is, we have *two* beds. Why on earth did we need to make love on the kitchen floor?" He snorted. "It's absurd."

"I thought of retiring," Daisy admitted, "but I was afraid that if you lost momentum, you'd change your mind again. I didn't want that."

"Oh, I see. Well, in that case." He extended a hand and she let him draw her upright. He tucked her into a warm embrace, where she could feel his chest shaking.

"Colin?"

Another snort escaped. Then a low chuckle.

"Colin, are you *laughing*?"

"So it would seem." His eyes twinkled with mirth, even as he shook again, muttering, "Kitchen floor," under his breath.

"Well, I'm glad you're amused," she said, a bit of sarcasm creeping into her voice.

"I am, Daisy. Ah, love. You're so good for me. I don't know why you're so determined to waste your time, energy and money on an old relic like me, but… I can't resist you."

"Oh, Colin." Even now, his haunted vulnerability shone through his humor and touched something deep in Daisy's heart. "You're a good man in a rough spot. Nothing more. And you're mine. My husband. My man. What more reason do I need than that? Do you think I'm some venal, brainless twit?"

"No, clearly not." He cleared his throat, though a hint of a grin lingered around the corners of his lips. "Um, I see you were taking a bath, but your hair is dry. Did you not get a chance to finish?"

"No, I didn't. I had no sooner gotten in than… are you sure he's gone? That was terrifying."

"He's gone. Peepers generally don't continue once they've been caught. I doubt he'll be back."

"I hope not. He's got some kind of fixation with rocks that makes me uncomfortable."

"I noticed," Colin said. "Listen, once it's light, I'll round up the men and scour the woods. If he's loitering on *my* estate, we'll send him packing."

"Good idea," Daisy replied. "Our Midsummer festival is tomorrow night. I would hate to have some… some creeping bastard tossing rocks at the children. They've suffered enough."

"I agree with that," Colin said, not reacting to her harsh word choice. "So, now that we have a plan settled, you should get into your bath. You need it now more than you did before." He smirked at her.

Daisy's cheeks and neck suddenly felt warm, but she nodded. "What about you, love?"

"Oh, I'll use the water when you're done."

Daisy frowned. "It'll be stone cold by then. Come on, Colin. Let's not withdraw from this moment. We're newlyweds. Come with me."

"Sure we'll both fit?" he asked, eyeing the copper structure doubtfully.

"We'll have to get close," she replied, shifting her hips.

Colin regarded her for a long, quiet moment. "Very well," he agreed.

She took his hand and led him to the tub. "You're bigger. Get situated and I'll find my spot."

Colin climbed into the tub and sighed. His body went limp. "Aaaaaah."

"Good?" she asked.

"Hmmmm," he replied.

"I hope you don't mind the girly-smelling soap my sister gifted me. I have no interest in tiptoeing into the dark house alone to retrieve a more neutral one. I'm still a bit shaken."

"If *you* don't mind the men knowing our business come morning. They'll assume any womanly smells rubbed off in bed."

Daisy shrugged. "They're no different. They all have or have had wives."

Another grin tugged at the corners of Colin's lips as he helped Daisy into the compact space of the bathtub. It was a tight fit, and she had to adjust her position several times before she could get comfortable, but she managed in the end. Colin reached beside the tub to the pile of supplies she'd accumulated and retrieved a small cup, which he dipped into the water and began wetting the long, golden strands of Daisy's hair.

"I'm still confused," he admitted as he prepared her hair for washing, "why you would call this place 'home.' It's a nightmare living here."

"I understand you feel that way," Daisy admitted, "and I completely understand why. That's been your reality for decades. However, I don't have that feeling. Yes, the estate was rough when I got here, but Colin, take a step back from your memories and look objectively at what you have here. I see a humble but sufficient farm, filled with healthy, happy animals and people, where everyone has enough. It's filled with opportunity. We'll never be rich, but who ever said I wanted that? It's not a pit of hell. It's a perfectly adequate home. The ruins are gone. Only useful spaces remain."

He lowered his eyebrows, not in anger, but in contemplation. Daisy retrieved her soap and began working up a lather between her hands while she let him think in silence.

"I can see how you would feel that way," he said at last. "Without a long history in this place, someone with humble expectations might find our little farm… good enough."

Daisy grinned and began rubbing her soapy hands on Colin's chest.

He claimed the soap and lathered up as well, rubbing the sweet-smelling bubbles into her hair. She closed her eyes at the pleasurable sensation. Connected by touch, but without the intensity of sight, Daisy posed another question. "Will you be joining me in bed then?"

Colin didn't answer quickly. He grabbed the cup and began rinsing Daisy's hair.

Let him think, she reminded herself. *He thinks slowly. It's his way. It doesn't mean anything against you.*

"It's a flattering offer," he said at last. "Are you sure that's what you want to do? It's not typical among the nobility, which you are, now."

The swish of water around Daisy's head stopped, and she opened her eyes, seeing Colin's unguarded expression. *He's asking a genuine question. He's not trying to put you off.* "I may have accidentally joined the exalted ranks, but when have I ever acted like this mattered to me?"

He raised one eyebrow. "Um, all the time, Daisy. You strode right onto the estate and took charge like you were born to be a lady."

"The lady of the house only, Colin. I still cook dinner myself, dust the furnishings with my own two hands, wash dishes—I have the callouses to prove it—and I still swear a bit and fully intend to celebrate the Pagan rituals whether anyone likes it or not."

"You're more a noblewoman than you realize," he said, curling his lip into that appealing half-grin she'd just discovered. He lathered his hands again and began to wash his hair. "Those are *exactly* the kinds of things any 'I don't give a damn' upper-class woman would insist on... well, maybe not the chores, though I know a couple who bake as a hobby and force their guests to eat it, whether it turns out or not. But your unapologetic eccentricity is right in line. It's middle-class women who worry about the propriety of everyday things."

"I wasn't that either," she reminded him. "Yes, my father owns an inn, but as you've pointed out, he's a brute. My mother was a whore. Middle class? Not in attitude, to be sure."

He nodded. "So, in your estimation, one bed is better for us than two? What if I snore?"

Daisy narrowed her eyes at him, even though she could see from the naughty twinkle in his eyes that he was teasing. "Are you not interested? I must say, for a man, you have the strongest resistance to sexual temptation."

"Not as strong as you think," he replied. Sluicing water over his head to rinse away the bubbles, he swished his hands through his hair a couple of times. "Well, are we clean enough now, love?"

"I suppose so," she said. "Why do you ask?"

"Because if you invite me to sleep beside you, we'll be dirty again in no time."

A tingle of excitement ran up Daisy's spine. "I think that would be just fine."

Chapter 11

 "I MUST say, my lord, you smell *lovely*," Farrell teased, wrinkling his nose in Colin's direction as they stomped through the messy fields among a herd of gamboling lambs. "I had no idea you'd taken to using such marvelous, ladylike scents."

"Oh, it's his missus," Bullock added. "She's tamed him and made him all pretty and nice."

Colin snickered. After the most comfortable night he could remember in months, soothed into a relaxing sleep by listening to the hypnotic rhythm of his wife's breathing, he pasted a fake scowl onto his face. "I warned her about this," he said, joining in the joke.

"Too bad no one warned you," Farrell said.

"Oh, I knew you snoopy old women would notice and tease." He shrugged. "It was worth it." He quirked one eyebrow and poked out his cheek with his tongue.

The men guffawed loudly.

Bullock sobered and added, "She's a good woman. My wife and children adore her. They're so excited about the industry she's inventing."

Industry? Colin thought. *I wonder what kind of mad plan my wife has dreamed up now. Somehow, I suspect she'll find a way to make it successful.* "I adore her too," Colin admitted. "I hadn't planned to take a wife, but... I'm not upset with the results. This festival tonight was her idea."

"Three cheers for Lady Gelroy," Farrell proposed. "Hip hip hooray!"

The other men took up the shout.

Hmmm. I had no idea how much a party would mean to them. I suppose I will need to think about how to incorporate more celebrations into our lives. Daisy was right that they deserve that.

"She would add that you deserve it too," a voice that sounded like his mother whispered into his mind. "After all, what are you working for? What are you living for?"

The warm summer sunshine and the friendly breeze chased away deep thoughts, urging Colin to get out of his head and *be*. Though it felt unnatural after so many years of ruminating, he tried. Not for long. "That reminds me," he added, humor dying, "we have a task to do. I caught someone peeping in the window last night. He threatened my wife with a rock and scared her half to death. I can hardly believe the rock hurler is still creeping around the estate, but we must find and evict this person. We cannot risk him harming one of the women or children—or the animals for that matter. Once the creatures are settled for the day, we must scour the woods and send this interloper on his way."

The teasing glances turned grim as each man imagined his own family on the receiving end of such a terrifying experience.

"We'll send him packing," Bullock vowed, and the other men bobbed their heads.

* * *

"That is amazing, Katie," Daisy breathed, unable to believe her eyes. "You have an incredible gift."

The young woman blushed with pleasure.

Spread out across multiple fabric paper pages laid on the large kitchen table in the farmhouse, the young woman had painted a continuous pattern of realistic birds. It almost looked like a schoolbook or a field guide. Every blackbird's feathers gleamed in the light that poured through the kitchen window. The doves looked ready to coo from their perches on matching leafy twigs. On the center of each sheet, a brightly colored goldfinch took center stage, beak open as though ready to release an endless stream of chattering chirps. Swans lurked in the corners, ready to chase the unwary away from their ponds. Owls peeked out from the background, which had been painted a soft sage color.

"I'm glad you like it, ma'am," Katie said quietly, uncomfortable with so much praise.

Daisy dragged her eyes away from the gorgeous renderings and took the young woman's paint-stained hands. "I don't want you to feel uncomfortable, but I must tell you. You have a gift. An incredible gift. If you were a man, I would say you should go to art school. Even apply to the Royal Academy."

"Oh, I could never!" Katie protested. "Go off to London alone? Leave my ma and da and siblings? My brother needs me."

"I understand your concerns. I'm not planning to ship you off tomorrow, certainly, but you have been given a tremendous talent. We must find ways for you not only to share it but to cultivate it."

Katie looked bewildered.

Don't push. This is a radical thought, especially for a young woman not yet grown, who has lived a certain way her whole life. As the lady of the estate, it will be my duty to ensure the children do not miss out on opportunities. "Anyway, this pattern of birds is glorious. I adore it."

Katie's blank stare turned into a shy smile.

"Do you like to paint other things?"

"Deer," Katie replied immediately. "Rabbits. Foxes. Badgers. Even bees and flowers."

"Nature then? Do you ever paint people?"

Katie shrugged. "I've tried, but that's harder. Does anyone want people on their wallpaper?"

"Oh, I wouldn't think so," Daisy agreed. "That would be strange, wouldn't it? All those eyes staring from the wall, not even a frame to set them off?" She laughed, breaking the tension.

"My lady? Is this good too?" One of Katie's younger brothers tugged at her skirt.

Daisy turned to look at the childish scribble of bright colors on a plain white background.

"Now, Bobby, don't bother Lady Gelroy," Mrs. Bullock scolded. "It was nice enough she gave each of you a sheet of her special paper to play with."

"Oh, isn't that nice," Daisy said. She met Mrs. Bullock's eyes and winked, smiling. "I'm ever to thankful your mummy let you all come and play with me today when she might have had you doing lessons. I will have to find a special place to hang this in the manor."

"Oh, no!" Bobby protested, hobbling away, his twisted back and misshapen chest hampering his movement. "I want Mummy to hang it in the kitchen."

"An excellent choice," Daisy affirmed. "I'm so glad I got to see it first."

The boy beamed.

"Is mine good too, my lady?" another child asked, this one not from the Bullock family, but the Farrells' son, who Mrs. Bullock was educating, along with her own brood. Daisy had learned that while Mrs. Farrell wanted her son to read, for some reason she'd struggled to learn herself and relied on her neighbor to help her.

Robin had painted a heavy, dark cross with bloodstains and a rigid and stiff-looking purple fabric hanging on it.

Daisy pondered how best to respond.

"Goodness, Robin. Your mother will adore that," Mrs. Bullock said, patting the boy on the head.

"Such bright colors," Daisy added. "So, are you all looking forward to the Midsummer festival tonight?"

"Yes!" the Bullock children chorused.

"My ma says I can't go," Robin complained. "Says it's the feast of St. John the Baptist and no time for Pagan nonsense."

Daisy raised her eyebrows at Mrs. Bullock.

"Mrs. Farrell is very religious," she said by way of explanation, "as are we all, but she doesn't like anything she thinks is Pagan. I'm afraid neither she nor her family will be present tonight." Drawing close to Daisy, she whispered, "If Farrell shows up, he may end up sleeping beside the bonfire. She's barred him from the house before when she thinks he's being sacrilegious." Mrs. Bullock wrinkled her nose in an expression that mingled sympathy for the man with enjoyment of the juiciest gossip the estate could offer.

"Oh," Daisy replied. "I knew someone like that. The late wife of the village priest in the town where I grew up. She was a lot older than her husband and very bossy. Kept him under her paw. She tried to lecture everyone on the 'right' way to live, in her rigid estimation. Even her husband wasn't holy enough to suit her. She used to nag him like a disappointed mother." *And when she didn't, he said and did the oddest things. I imagine, if she'd lived a bit longer, she would have prevented Colin's and my marriage from taking place.*

Then, she realized she was drawing a harsh comparison in front of Robin about his mother and glanced at the child. He seemed deep in conversation with William Bullock, his eyes fixed on adding rays of light to the painting.

Daisy pressed her lips together.

"Anyway," Mrs. Bullock said brightly, "I'm looking forward to tonight. We haven't had a proper Midsummer bonfire in all the years I've lived here. It's about time we all had some fun."

"I agree," Daisy added.

* * *

"So, um, Lady Gelroy?" Colin tossed a chunk of wood onto the huge pyre they were constructing in the meadow.

Daisy moved behind him, tucking small sticks among the larger logs and adding scraps of the fabric paper she had trimmed away to make the size fit the bedroom where she planned to install it later. "Oh, dear. So formal," she replied teasingly, even though his manner sparked sharp anxiety in her guts. "How can I help you, Lord Gelroy?"

"Bullock told me something today that I didn't understand."

"Bullock has a rather heavy accent," she replied, pursing her lips and trying to look prim. "I don't always understand him either."

Colin stopped, turned and stared at her. Then, a snort she was beginning to recognize escaped his nose.

"Handkerchief?" she asked, pretending to dig in an imaginary pocket while fighting not to drop her armful of twigs.

Another snort escaped. Colin shook his head and turned back to constructing their bonfire. "Bullock said that you had some kind of… industry? Business? Brewing with the women. Is that true?"

Daisy found an empty spot and tucked a leafy branch into it. "I was considering the possibility," she admitted. "Mrs. Bullock, her daughter Katie and I are discussing such things."

"What such things?" Colin pressed.

Damn. How do I phrase this? I hadn't planned to discuss it with him until we had something more solid. "Um, remember how I can make wallpaper?"

"Yes. I like what I'm seeing so far. The maroon one in the kitchen is quite attractive. Did you make the bird pattern that's currently tying up the entire dining table?"

"Katie did that," Daisy replied. "She has incredible talent."

"Katie Bullock? I had no idea," he breathed, and a hint of his old despair crossed his features.

"She is." The side of the pyre had begun to look a bit too stuffed, so Daisy rearranged the wood to ensure airflow. "She didn't know it herself. I mean, she knew she could paint, but she didn't realize... I think she's a true artist, Colin. She deserves to hone it."

"I agree," Colin replied. "Thank you for finding that out. We'll have to find a way to hire her a tutor. I would hate to see such a gift wasted. Now, about that business. What does Katie Bullock's artistic gift have to do with a business, and how do you plan to fund it? I mean, you still have plenty of your inheritance left, but... but a business requires a capital outlay I don't think you're ready to provide. Besides, if there were an emergency on the farm... a flood or a disease among the animals... Let's just say that while I have every intention of leaving your dowry for you, as you requested, emergencies can happen."

Daisy tossed the rest of her sticks onto the top of the pile and approached her husband, taking hold of his arm. "Colin, I would never dream of spending my dowry for something like this. I believe we can create a small industry at minimal cost."

Colin dropped his last log at their feet. "How?"

"Well, as I said, I'm barely thinking this out, but I believe we can get a lot of scraps from the Bennetts. They're happy to part with them. Has Mr. Bennett mentioned how much they spend on hauling away fabric scraps?"

"He's complained a fair amount," Colin admitted. "And?"

"And, if he and we split the cost to haul it here instead, it would save him money and provide us a huge supply of little bits of fabric."

"Which you will turn into paper?" he guessed.

"And decorate and sell. I may not be the artist Katie is, but I have a good eye for color and can make simple patterns, especially if I have a stencil."

"What makes you think people would want to buy that?"

"Oh, I know they would!" Daisy exclaimed. "It's easy to get mass-produced, factory-made goods. That makes hand-painted items desirable for anyone who can afford them, and they pay. You would have choked to see what the vicar paid for custom-painted dishes for the vicarage. His wife was so angry at the expense, I thought she was going to burst into flames right there in the street. Listening to her shouting, I heard that he had spent more than double what Father did on his mass-produced dishes. It's madness, but it's undeniable."

"And if it doesn't?" Colin asked, gloomy as always at the thought of potential failure.

"Well, think of this. The Bennetts already have the cart for hauling, so there's no investment there, just some feed for the draft horse. Perhaps a few pounds. A few pennies' worth of paint and a few hours' time in the upcoming winter and then we see."

"What do we see, Daisy?"

"Whether anyone wants it. If they do, we re-invest and make more. If not, we stop, and we're out very little. Please, say you don't object, Colin."

Colin grasped Daisy by her elbows and drew her toward him. She went easily into his embrace. "Why do you want this?"

"I'm bored," she admitted. "Our home is small, as is our family. There's not enough to keep me busy, and… and housework is boring in itself. I like business. I like earning and managing money, goods, products, customers. I like selling things. Won't you let me try, love?"

Colin looked into her eyes for a long, unguarded moment, seeming to search deep into her. "All right," he agreed. "It's your money, Daisy. If you think this small investment is worth the risk, do what you need to do."

She smiled. Taking hold of the loose, white shirt he wore, she tugged him closer and laid a lush kiss on his lips.

Colin didn't fight. It seemed his will to resist had collapsed. Instead, he layered a dozen—a hundred—a thousand different kisses on her eager mouth.

Daisy smiled in his embrace. *It's much nicer to receive his passion rather than watching him fight it. And wasn't last night delicious?* The pleasurable ache between her thighs reminded her of their startling reunion.

"What's that smile, my lady?" he asked her, one medium-brown eyebrow winging toward his hairline.

Daisy ran her fingers into his hair, pleased that his austere lifestyle provided no budget for pomade. The soft strands slipped through her fingers. "It's just that you're so… different now."

He dragged his lips along her cheek and murmured into her ear, "You're irresistible. Call me weak if you will, but I cannot fight any longer."

"You're not weak," she breathed. "You're the strongest man I've met. The strongest I've ever imagined."

Colin drew back, staring into Daisy's eyes with a look she couldn't begin to read. She didn't want to try. She just wanted his mouth on hers again.

He complied with her unspoken request. His lips crashed into hers. His arms compressed her waist.

"Ahem!" A voice broke into their embrace.

Daisy jumped back with a squeak.

Bullock had appeared behind them, his arm around his wife, their four children milling around in excitement, even Katie. The young lady bounced on the balls of her feet despite the barely maintained serious expression she had plastered onto her face.

Daisy grinned, willing herself to stop blushing, or at least for the sun to come out from behind the cloud that had just covered it, so she could have an excuse for her red face.

"Glad we didn't wait any longer, eh?" Bullock nudged his wife.

She turned a sour look on him. "I'm glad the animals haven't been in the meadow in a while. There are worse pitfalls than newlyweds kissing on this farm."

Daisy giggled.

The smaller Bullock children, unable to contain themselves another moment, dashed away, running to the far ends of the meadow as though pursued by some unspeaking monster—or perhaps pursuing it. Their shrieks of happy excitement echoed off the trees. It amazed Daisy how well Bobby could run, given his deformities.

"What did you bring?" Daisy asked the newly arrived adults, regarding the baskets in their arms.

"Berry cakes," Mrs. Bullock replied. "My mother's recipe, and some herb and flower cordial. I've no taste for ale."

"Are the herbs magical?" Daisy joked.

The Bullocks gave her a sharp look.

"What?" she glanced from one to the other. "I would have thought, Col—uh, that is, Lord Gelroy's mother, being a midwife and general wise woman with such a great knowledge of herbs, would have encouraged the revival of traditional wisdom."

"She did," Mrs. Bullock agreed hesitantly.

"Is that a problem?"

Colin cleared his throat. "Um, it's a long-standing argument, love. Mrs. Farrell... she..."

"I mentioned she was very religious, did I not," Mrs. Bullock jumped in, noticing Colin had stuttered to a halt.

At Daisy's nod, she explained, "Well, she's a bit... a bit obsessed... with witches. She thought the former Lady Gelroy was one and went out of her way to bait her. I wouldn't go so far as to say she made her life miserable..." This time Mrs. Bullock spluttered and shut down.

"She's harmless," Colin added, "but a bit cracked. Mother had enough misery when she lived here, without that batty girl pestering her, but I don't think it was more than a passing nuisance for Mother. Not with leaky roofs, crumbling walls and a husband three times her age, who loved to drink, gamble and chase skirts with the money they didn't have, but it may have been one thing too many. When Father... when he had a sudden heart seizure and died, she was happy to wash her hands of the estate and leave. She never looked back. Mrs. Farrell likely had something to do with that."

Daisy remained silent, taking in the conversation and processing it slowly. At last, she said, "That's interesting. What does it have to do with me?"

Colin cleared his throat again. "Well, love, it has occurred to me that you might have... a Pagan streak?"

"Yes," Daisy agreed. "I honor the old ways and respect ancient wisdom, though I wouldn't really call myself a Pagan. I was baptized in the Church of England like everyone else, and I'm still a Christian. I don't think those things contradict."

"I would tend to agree with you," Mrs. Bullock said, laying a hand on Daisy's arm in solidarity. "I don't see the contradiction in making an herbal cordial that has legendary powers to imbue the land and its people with life and fertility. It won't stop me from going to church in the village. Most people don't fear to mix religion and tradition."

"Except for Mrs. Farrell?" Daisy guessed.

Everyone nodded.

"Oh, dear."

"Without the forced formality of a large manor house and the buffer of servants between you and her, she may criticize you more directly than she was able to do with Mother," Colin added.

"And her prejudice has only strengthened over the years," Mrs. Bullock added. "She sent us these." Reaching into her basket, she pulled out garlands woven out of wispy green stalks with small yellow flowers.

"Devil's chase?" Daisy guessed. "But if she thinks traditional wisdom is witchcraft, why..."

"It's St. John's plant," Mrs. Bullock explained. "For John the Baptist Day. She thinks if we light a fire and indulge in 'Pagan revelry' instead of honoring our Lord, we'll invite evil spirits, but this plant will keep us safe."

"Well, she does sound a bit… off, and I won't lie. Those garlands stink." Daisy rubbed her nose to dispel the acrid odor of the flowers. "I'm not worried about evil spirits, though if we hang these up near the forest, maybe the reek will keep that stone-throwing beast away. Did you men find him?"

Bullock visibly relaxed, now that talk of his neighbor had ended.

Daisy made a mental note of his reaction. *Everyone tolerates Mrs. Farrell, but no one likes her. In a place like this, that must be quite a lonely existence. No wonder her eccentricities have become more concentrated. I'll have to watch myself around her.*

"We found signs of someone loitering in the woods," Colin explained, "but no camp, and certainly no person. I do hope he moved on after I chased him away from the house last night."

"So, we'll have to be on guard throughout the party?" Daisy guessed.

"I'm afraid so," Colin replied.

At that moment, the rest of the tenants—all but the Farrells, of course—wandered into the clearing clutching baskets and bowls from which enticing scents wafted to tempt the hunger of the revelers.

"Come on!" Daisy urged. "We're behind schedule. The lamb and the duck will be done roasting any minute, and we don't have the table set up." She waved at the kitchen table they'd wrestled out the kitchen door of the manor-turned-farmhouse. It had been covered with a crisp white cloth, held down in the corners by river rocks. Daisy had laid out a few items—vegetables from the kitchen garden, herbed sauce for the meat, a couple of bottles of table wine and cakes stuffed with fruit and iced in sugar glaze, but the platters for the meat stood empty and the guests' contributions had not yet been placed. The barrel of ale stood at the corner, where several tin cups had been laid.

The new arrivals clustered around the table, setting out bread, butter, cheese, fruit, sliced mutton and pastries. A lovely fragrance wafted through the meadow, dispelling the lingering aroma of manure and complementing the rich temptation of meat roasted on a spit. Daisy hurried over to turn the crank, making sure their supper cooked evenly.

"Here, let me take a turn," Mrs. Bullock offered.

"No need," Daisy replied. "They're done. They've been cooking most of the day, and the coals are almost spent, though I wouldn't object if you helped me by bringing the platter for this duck. If we get him out of the way, we'll be better able to deal with the lamb."

Mrs. Bullock smiled and retrieved the plate.

* * *

A short time later, the entire Gelroy estate—less the Farrells—savored food, drink, conversation and cheer.

Colin watched his tenants enjoy a good meal. A sense of lightness grew even as darkness closed in on them.

Daisy bounced past, clearly in her element. She beamed from ear to ear. "Looks like rain," she murmured, waving at the darkening sky. "This is the longest day of the year but look at that sky. All those heavy clouds make it seem almost like autumn."

"I hope the storm holds off until we're done," Colin replied. He took a bit of ham rolled around a wedge of cheese, a simple snack he'd always appreciated.

"Me too," Daisy agreed. "Can't have a bonfire in the rain, but if it rains afterward, that would be beneficial."

Colin nodded.

Daisy flitted away.

She's like her namesake, he thought, not for the first time. *All summer sunshine. I don't understand how she thrives in such a dark place.*

"She doesn't see the darkness," his reason reminded him. "She sees a place where she's respected and appreciated, where her ideas can be heard. She sees hope and a future, and although she knows of the suffering that we endured, she didn't share it. So let her not bury herself in it. Let her bring light to the darkness. Let her bring sunshine and flowers and… and wallpaper. Why not?"

"Why not indeed," he muttered aloud.

At that moment, one of those odd silences that sometimes occur fell over the chatter, and his comment rang aloud in the clearing.

The guests turned to gawk.

"Why not what, my lord?" Bullock asked. "Why not have more ale? If you're talking to yourself, you may have had enough."

Colin thought of the half cup he'd sipped, and knew he was sober. *Sober and daft. Shut your mouth, man.* His face felt suspiciously hot, despite the coolness brought by the clouds.

"I'm sure he was debating an idea I proposed earlier," Daisy jumped in, saving him. "He wasn't sure, but it seems our beloved Lord Gelroy has agreed to join me in providing a bit of entertainment."

Colin raised one eyebrow but approached his wife, nonetheless. *What are you up to now, you imp?* he asked her with his eyes.

Her broad grin didn't inspire any confidence. She took his hand and drew him to a place of prominence in front of the table. Then, she stepped back, affected an offended air, and spat, " 'What! Jealous Oberon? Fairies skip hence. I have forsworn his bed and company.' "

Colin gulped. *Do I remember enough to do this with her? She jumped in to save me from looking a fool, talking to myself in public, and now she wants me to perform Shakespeare in front of my tenants?* Though he wanted to run, his lips formed the words, which rasped from him in imitation of anger. " 'Tarry, rash wanton. Am I not thy lord?' "

" 'Then I must be thy lady,' " Daisy snapped back, perfectly presenting a furious demeanor as though she were in truth a wronged fairy queen. As the lyrical verse tripped lightly on her tongue, her eyes flashed in a way that aroused him beyond belief.

He grasped one wrist in the opposite hand and let them rest lightly before him. *Ah, she is my lady, is she not? And not nearly as standoffish or quarrelsome as Titania. She's a wonder and a jewel, my fairy queen. God, but I love her.*

The realization staggered him. *Love Daisy? But how?*

"Because she's your match," the sly voice whispered in his head. "You were meant for each other."

" '. . . to give their bed joy and prosperity,' " she finished.

Colin fumbled, still half-lost in astonishment, but eventually choked out his line. " 'How canst thou thus for shame, Titania.' " His gaze turned harsh, but it was an act. A ploy. A mere evening's diversion to keep himself from dragging his wife away from all these watching eyes and ravishing her in private.

A hint of a shy grin creased Daisy's features, but she quickly suppressed it, returning to her role of a flashing-eyed hoyden.

Colin loved it. Loved the way they had memorized the same text, so that they could play it here together without needing preparation.

" 'Give me that boy, and I will go with thee,' " Colin proposed in Oberon's stead.

The rage that rose in Daisy, though false, almost frightened him. " 'Not for thy fairy kingdom,' " she shrieked. " 'Fairies away. We shall chide downright if I longer stay.' " Line delivered, she raised her chin, turned to the audience, and curtseyed.

Colin stood strong, not willing to bow for such an impromptu presentation, but the tenants applauded anyway. Daisy blew them a kiss, laughing. She reached out to grasp Colin's hand again. Her fingers felt warm in his hand. Pleasant tingles shot up his arm and settled in the vicinity of his heart. So that he could put off thinking so much about his feelings until an appropriate time, he said, "The sun is set. Let's light the bonfire."

Thunder rumbled in the distance, but Colin retrieved the box of matches from the table anyway. Striking one, he tossed it into the pile of wood and kindling he and his wife had assembled. Circling partway around, he lit another, and then a third. The twigs and paper crackled in the center of the cone-shaped configuration. Flames licked upward, tickling the larger logs.

The small group gathered around the growing fire.

Daisy approached again and slipped her hand into Colin's again. He stroked his thumb over her skin. She squeezed.

"Shall we dance?" Daisy asked.

No one answered.

"What? Dancing around the Midsummer bonfire is traditional."

"Love," Colin whispered, "Mrs. Farrell may be eccentric, but she's part of this community, and the other tenants have to live with her. No one will wander that far into the Pagan. This is a celebration of John the Baptist, and anyone who breathes a word to the contrary will create a controversy no one wants to face."

Nodding, Daisy subsided, though her expression suggested she would be bringing up this issue again soon.

The flames caught and held in some of the thicker kindling, holding it against the large logs, giving them the chance to ignite. *It's like us,* he thought. *The flame sparked immediately. It burned hot and bright like an infatuation, but it didn't burn out. Despite the madness of our connection, we could not release each other. She waited so long and patiently while I sorted myself out. Now, I can't imagine not having her with me. She's right. We're a family.*

The big logs caught, and flames shot upward toward the sky.

The Bullocks caught hold of their milling children and kept them back from the hypnotic sight. Warm, smoky smells wafted through the meadow and up into the sky. The sun crept even lower on the horizon, half gone from view.

Colin dropped Daisy's hand and wrapped his arm around her waist, drawing her against his side. She rested her head on his shoulder. The sweet scent of her perfume mingled with the smoke.

Time seemed to bend and jump, years passing in a second, decades in a breath. The sun died in the distance and darkness closed in, darker than dark because thick clouds covered the moon. Only the fire provided light, a shifting, dancing orange light that drew the eye and stung it at the same time.

The restless children settled and stared, sinking into a quiet, trancelike state. Daisy's breathing deepened and Colin's slowed to match. The fire crackled.

After a time, Mary Jones yawned and rubbed her eyes, turning to lead her husband out of the meadow back toward the irregular row of tenant houses on the edge of the woods, their basket now stuffed with leftovers.

Time seemed to jump again. Hours or seconds later, Colin couldn't guess, the Bullocks drifted away, herding yawning, well-fed children home to bed. They too had a significant package of food for their next days' meals. The two widowed men remained the longest, staring at the fire, a peaceful expression on their weathered faces.

"Thank you for this evening, my lord. My lady." Billings heaved a huge sigh. "I didn't know if a night like this would ever come. You're given…" He paused, clearing his throat. "You've both done the impossible, and you've given us all hope again. Thank you."

"I only did what I could, Billings. I wish I could have done more," Colin said, while Daisy lowered her eyelids, hiding coyly under her eyelashes.

Billings shook his head. "It was enough. You did enough." Without another word, he turned, retrieved a plate that had been prepared for him, and followed the other families back to their homes, his son-in-law trailing after him.

"He's right, you know," Daisy said softly, voice wavering with emotion. "You've done enough. You're good enough. Colin, can't you let it be enough?"

"I don't know how," he rasped. "It's been so long since I could please my mother with a handful of summer weeds or a messy drawing of her cat. Since then, good enough has never been good enough. If I didn't get top marks at school, Father would beat me. But he was a coward. A coward and a fool. A damned wasteful beast. Some peer of the realm."

He cleared his throat. "In his eyes, I could never shake the shame of my mother's working-class background or her otherworldly Paganness, and I was allowed to show neither. I was taught to spend without working, work without profiting, indulging in every carnal pleasure but never thinking of anything beyond this world, and any sign of anything other than his shallow pursuit of power and pleasure led to…" He shuddered as the memory of pain bloomed across his back.

"Why would someone so snobby marry a commoner?" Daisy demanded. "It's not like us, that's for sure. Was he struck by some mad passion?"

Colin shook his head. "He wanted an heir, and he was old. Over fifty. He wanted someone young and malleable he could control. Mother's parents forced her into it. She was miserable. I'm glad she connected with her old sweetheart, Colonel Turner, after Father passed. She finally got a chance to be happy."

"What a beast," Daisy said, stepping against his body and wrapping her arms around his back. "You and your mother are well rid of him."

"But I'm not rid of him," he said, despair rising thicker and blacker than ever. The pain clamped down hard on him, excruciating because he'd dared for a moment to take hold of the light. "I'll never be rid of him. He's here." He tapped his temple.

"Then banish him," Daisy insisted. "Send his memory to hell. I'm sure it will join his soul there."

"How do I banish my entire childhood?" Colin demanded. "What can replace such a fundamental evil?"

"You're already doing it," she told him. "Speak it aloud. Say it to the fire and let it be burned away. Midsummer is a time of renewal. The year is turning. You've worked and succeeded. You've built and planned. Now, we look toward the hard work of the end of summer and the harvest. The selling and the buying, and then the long cold winter. Let the end of this year bring about the end of your father's tyranny over your heart. Let this fire burn away his lies so you can finally see yourself as you truly are. I'll do the same. My father needs banishing as well."

Colin stared into the flickering flames. Their height had reduced as the logs burned away, but a strong, red glow remained. Hot coals. " 'Woe is me! For I am a man of unclean lips.' Daisy, I just named my father a fool and a coward. I've thought it so many times. How can there be any mercy for one such as me?"

143

" 'Then flew one of the seraphims unto me, having a live coal in his hand, which he had taken with the tongs from off the altar.' " She laid her fingertips on his lips. " 'And he laid it upon my mouth, and said, Lo, this hath touched thy lips; and thine iniquity is taken away, and thy sin purged. Also, I heard the voice of the Lord, saying, Whom shall I send, and who will go for us? Then said I, Here am I; send me.' " Daisy quoted back, finishing the verse. "Let the fire burn away your words, love, but also let them burn away his legacy. God sent you. He chose you. You didn't fail. Your father's sins are not yours to mitigate. You were only called to strive and to love. You've done both."

"Love, Daisy?"

She smiled, moving her hand so she could stroke his lower lip with her thumb. "No heart as passionate as yours could do anything other than love. Admit it. You love this land. Love it as much as you hate it. You love your tenants. I can see that every time you speak to or about them. And I dare say, if you let yourself admit it, you love your wife too."

Her words hit so close to home, they almost choked him. He gasped, drawing air past her fingers and drawing the essence of Daisy into him again.

The fire burned beside him, and for a moment, he could have sworn he felt the pain of his childhood burning. Burning. All the while, Daisy's light shone into his eyes. Into his heart, where it found... the light he'd buried so long ago. It flared white, brighter and cleaner than any thought he could remember. Her love, pure like his mother's love, like his siblings'. Like how his friends loved their wives, and how their wives loved them. Like how his mother had learned to love her husband and he her. *It is for me too. Somehow, this pure love belongs as much to me as any other man.*

Awed, he tilted Daisy's chin up and lowered his face, touching his lips to hers in a kiss of such pure, beautiful passion, it stole the air from his lungs and illuminated every dark corner of his heart.

Colin's arms tightened around Daisy. Releasing her lips, he looked down into her eyes, his soul unguarded.

Her thick golden lashes covered her wide gray-green eyes and then pulled back to reveal the internal luminescence that had obsessed and tortured him from the moment they met. *This is your moment, man. A turning point. She's a gift from God. An answer to prayer. She's here. She cares for you. You care for her. Make the choice to turn from where you were to a new future. You've lain together twice. You cannot resist her. You have no reason to do so. Stop trying.* "I..." He cleared his throat. "I love you, Daisy."

Her lips curved upward, even as her eyes crimped in the corners and became shiny. She squeezed them shut.

"What is it?" he asked her softly, unnerved by her reaction.

"I never thought I'd hear you say it." She sniffled.

"Well, you did," he replied.

She opened her eyes and snared him again in her glistening gaze. Then she shook her head. "Here we are then. Married beyond all redemption."

"So it would seem," Colin agreed. "Isn't it marvelous?"

She nodded. "I've always thought so." She swallowed hard, throat contracting.

"Not to put a damper on the evening," he made a gesture with his hips, letting her know what he had on his mind, "but we need to consider the possible consequences. I... I'm working hard to be a better husband and understand how everything will be fine, but... I'm not ready to be a father yet. Perhaps Mother could offer some suggestions of how we could delay that for a while. I could get a French letter..."

"I talked to your mother the last time we were in London. She gave me the recipe for a tea that suppresses conception."

"You did? She did?"

"Yes, Colin. I may be eager for us to draw together, but a baby would complicate our already tense meeting and transition more than we need at this time. I've been drinking the tea daily since then. Your mother warned me it was not a failsafe, and I would need to be aware of my body and my cycle to avoid the most fertile days."

"Have you been doing that?"

She nodded. "I was fertile last week, but this week, it has passed. I'll menstruate next week. This is a fairly safe time. Colin, there are never guarantees. The Lord has overruled us once. He may again, but on my end, things are as safe as they're likely to get."

He nodded.

"Will that suffice for you?"

"I suppose it will have to," he replied with a sigh. "I'm glad you took the initiative, and I certainly have no intention of stopping. You're too delicious. Too tempting."

She grinned, though it still had a watery look about it. "Luckily, as we are, the way you said, married beyond redemption, there's no need to resist temptation."

One corner of his mouth quirked. "Good thing. I don't think I could have held out much longer anyway."

"Well then," she suggested, "shall we succumb again?"

"Right here and now?" he asked, stunned. "Will we *never* make love in our marriage bed?"

She shrugged. "Look around. Here is this magical fire. It's a lovely summer's night. We could be so well-behaved and creep into our bedroom as though our lovemaking is some kind of dirty secret. We could do that if it would make you more comfortable. On the other hand, it would be a shame to waste the beauty of the night, the breeze, the dying fire. I mean, isn't this what being newlyweds is all about? We have the rest of our lives to be stuffy, married folks." She stroked one hand down his cheek and ran her thumb over his lips.

He touched her with the tip of his tongue.

"For this short time, we get to be wild, free and natural, let our passion take us over. What do you want to do, Colin?"

Colin considered her words. Though he'd passed thirty, and life had long since killed his sense of being playful, young or free, he felt the draw of her words. *The night is magical,* he reminded himself, *and the tenants have all taken their children home to bed. No one will know. It can be our delicious secret.*

In lieu of words, not wanting to commit aloud to such rash action, Colin nonetheless made his choice. He claimed Daisy's mouth in a kiss that abandoned gentleness and encouraged passion to rise.

Eager as always, Daisy tugged at Colin's shirttails, dragging them out of his trousers, and slid her hands underneath to caress his skin, or try to. His undershirt foiled her efforts.

"There's still so much coming between us," she said sadly.

"You were the one who suggested we not go back to our bed, where we can undress in private and truly enjoy one another. Do you want to be naked in the open?"

She shrugged.

"Wild vixen. Come on."

Colin led Daisy away from the fire into darker night. Clouds floated past the moon, moving fast and revealing shifting patches of denser and thinner darkness. Away from the heat, the breeze grew chilly, teasing skin and disarranging Daisy's hair so it escaped its pins and danced.

Colin tugged off his jacket and laid it on the soft grass of the meadow. Daisy tugged off her dress and added it to the pile. She challenged Colin with an inviting glance, daring him, it seemed, to take the next step.

Gulping, he tugged his shirt over his head and tossed it down. "You're going to have a wonderful time cleaning the grass stains out of our clothing," he said.

"Oh well. I have plenty of paint stains already." She turned, presenting her back to him, so he could loosen her stays.

The boned undergarment dropped, and Daisy stepped away, nudging it aside with her toes. Free of its constriction, she crouched, unlaced her boots, and set them aside as well.

Colin took advantage of the moment to remove his own shoes. Their stockings quickly followed.

Daisy wriggled her toes in the grass. He could barely make out the movement in the sparse, silver light that filtered down on them between the hurrying clouds.

"Your turn, Lord Gelroy," she teased.

Colin's powers of speech deserted him. He opened the buttons and let his trousers fall before tossing his undershirt to the nest they were steadily creating, where their love could take hold.

Bold as always, Daisy reached forward with one hand so she could stroke his firm erection through the fabric of his underpants.

He could see her nipples, equally hard, pressing out the fabric of her chemise. He slipped it from her body, shaking his head. "Naked outside for all to see. What a wild, wicked girl."

"You like me that way," she sassed. His drawers succumbed to her questing fingers, and he stood, nude and shivering, as the night wind caressed him in places he'd never expected. *It is magical,* he thought. *Wild and free, like Daisy. The things this woman does to me.*

He regarded his wife as she fumbled nervously with the fastenings of her bloomers.

"Shy, love?" he asked.

She bit her lip and nodded.

"Don't be. I've claimed this portal before." He cupped her, bold as she had been a moment ago, and slid his hand through the open seam to touch her intimate places. Her private folds parted, and he felt warm, wet flesh that pulsed wantonly under his fingers, "and I will again. And you'll like it again, and make all those sweet, sweet cries that turn me wild. Here, in the out-of-doors. That's what you want, isn't it?"

She nodded.

Colin tugged the drawstring and let the garment fall from his wife's hips. Tugging her around, he reclined onto the nest of clothing and sank onto his back, guiding her down on top of him. Awkwardly, still unsure how all the mechanics of lovemaking worked, she straddled his belly.

Colin slid his hands up her ribs and cupped her breasts, one in each hand, delivering a firm pinch to her nipples.

Daisy squeaked and moisture surged against his skin.

"This is what you asked for," he growled. "Have you changed your mind? We can still make a run for our bedroom."

She shook her head. Straightening her hips, she rose and shifted back.

"Oho, my bold lady. Here, help me." He grasped her hand and guided it to his erection. The touch of her fingers on his bare skin made him groan. Together, they levered the heavy shaft upright, tracing it along Daisy's saturated folds until they found the opening. He laid his free hand on her hip to guide her downward, working his penis deeper into her than he'd ever been before.

"Oh!" she gasped.

"A lot, isn't it?" he managed to growl, though words were failing. Colin grasped both her hips and guided her upward so she could sink down again, tutoring her in the fine art of riding her man.

Daisy's head tipped back, and she released a soft cry of wanton pleasure. Her sex clenched on his.

This position left her pearl exposed. Now that she'd grasped the rhythm, he slid his hands between their straining bodies to caress it.

Another sound, this one choked and rasping, escaped her. Her thrusts faltered, but she quickly resumed the movements, reaching for the peak of pleasure.

"That's it, love," Colin murmured. "That's it."

Daisy gasped, moaned. A flurry of wild bounces drove him deep into her core. He kept his gentle, firm pressure on her most sensitive spot, knowing she wouldn't be able to hold out long, and he would be following shortly thereafter.

Daisy rocked her hips, adding a sideways shimmy to their eager thrusting, and climaxed unexpectedly. She wailed, a sharp, thin sound in the darkness, and her hands came to rest on Colin's chest. Her womanhood compressed in tight squeezes and flutters that had him on the brink in moments. He made no attempt to hold back but shouted his ecstasy to the night sky.

* * *

Filthy pigs, the watcher thought sourly, frowning at the naked spectacle perfectly outlined in the firelight. *Pagan beasts. They deserve what's coming to them.*

* * *

Awareness dawned slowly for Daisy. She found herself lying on her husband's body, his sex softening slowly inside her. She grinned. It had been wild. An untamed mating fit for nature deities. *I hope it's not the last time we make love in the outdoors. How enticing.*

The breeze teased her skin again, and she shivered.

Thunder rumbled again, but an irresistible urge drew her up off of Colin's body and towards an enticing scent. On the fence that contained the estate's largest pasture, wild roses bloomed in heady profusion, their flowers pale pink like flesh. Cautious of the thorns she could not see in the darkness, she gathered a handful of petals and returned to her husband. He lifted himself on one elbow to watch.

"What are you up to now, love?"

"A bit of magic," she replied. She sprinkled the petals over his prone form. " 'Rose leaves, rose leaves, rose leaves I strew. He that will love me come to me now.' "

"I already have, Daisy."

"I know." She bit her lip. "I forgot to mention earlier, though I'm sure you know. I do love you, Colin. I'm ever so glad you're my husband."

He grinned, teeth flashing in the pale light.

Thunder cracked again, and this time, the clouds opened, and a deluge of icy droplets fell on their naked skin.

"Oh no!" Daisy made a wild grab for her clothing as Colin leaped to his feet. Gathering everything they could find in the dark, they ran, laughing like children, to the door of their home.

Chapter 12

"Argh!" Colin groaned. The pink light of sunrise filtered past the curtains that covered the bedroom window, illuminating the couple who lay in a small bed in a small farmhouse on a small estate. Resting his weight on his forearms, he lowered his head to his wife's chest.

Daisy stroked Colin's hair, soothing him down from orgasm to relaxation. She kissed the top of his head and he settled onto her body. "You finally got your wish," she teased.

"Oh?" Colin more gasped than asked.

"You've been asking for days to make love in our bed. Was it all you dreamed of?"

"Oh, yes," he breathed. She could feel his muscles flex as he moved to cover her. He lowered his mouth to hers for a kiss of tender affection. "I love you, Daisy."

Her heart welled with joy at how easily he admitted it. She drew him down again, fully onto her so she could hold him close. "Oh, my darling."

He sighed, and his shoulders and back relaxed in a way she'd never seen in him before. She trailed her fingers up and down his spine.

"I have to go," he murmured, regret heavy in his voice.

"No," she whined. "Don't go. Stay with me. Those smelly geese can live on without your intervention for one day... let the tenants handle them... not working is it?"

"No," Colin told her. "You'd no more take advantage of them than I would."

She grinned. "You're right. I just wish... I wish we could spend a few days together."

"I'm a farmer, love. Winter will come before you know it. Then, you'll have so much time with me, you'll regret wishing for it."

"Not a chance," Daisy replied. "I enjoy your company whenever I can get it, Colin."

He sat back, grinning a gentle, genuine smile. "I may never understand why, but I'm grateful."

"You don't give yourself enough credit," Daisy informed her husband. "There is so much to appreciate about you. I wish you could see it."

"It's enough that you can," he said.

Daisy grabbed him tight with both arms around his neck and dragged him down to kiss his lips. "If you must go, go with my love and come back to my arms at sunset."

"How poetic, but you know I'll be back in a couple of hours for breakfast. Um, love?"

She met his eyes.

"Could you please prepare something hearty? I'm... starving."

She smiled. "Of course."

"Thank you."

He wriggled out of her arms and crossed to an ewer of tepid water set on the washstand, so he could clean their mingled love from his sex. "It was a lovely encounter. I could do that again every night."

"I might take you up on that," she replied. "At least until my next menstruation starts."

"I might let you," he replied with a grin, tugging on a clean pair of drawers and searching for new trousers and a clean shirt.

"Did your clothes get stains on them?" she asked.

"I think so," he replied, tugging an undershirt over his head. "You might have noticed I was a bit busy. I didn't stop to examine them."

She giggled. This new, more relaxed side of her husband had a charm that even surpassed his compelling sorrow she'd seen the day they met. "I imagine not. Busy is right." She sat up, letting the covers fall away from her body, and Colin froze.

"You're a danger to my sanity, Daisy," he said, eyeing her plump breasts. "I could take you again, right now, with no problem. Good God, I feel seventeen."

She grinned. "It's the novelty of it, I suppose. Once we're used to the idea that we can make love any time we want, we won't feel such an overwhelming need to prove it."

"Perhaps." He tugged on a pair of trousers, winked at her, and meandered out of the room.

Stretching luxuriously, Daisy rose from the bed, retrieved a nightgown from her bureau and dropped it over her head, not in the mood to bind herself up in stays and shoes and garters. "Modern clothing, even simple clothing, does nothing for comfort. I was up late, and I have a lot to do around the house this morning. The ladies aren't supposed to come and learn to hang wallpaper until the day after tomorrow, so no one would know if I didn't get dressed at all."

The floor felt cold under her feet as she made her way into the kitchen to brew coffee and consider her options for the hearty breakfast Colin had requested. She couldn't recall a time when he'd made any request of her, and she intended to feed him in every way she could. "Sausage, coddled eggs, toast and fresh jam. That should satisfy his body. I can only hope what we shared last night—and this morning—will satisfy his heart. I know it did mine."

"Oh, Good Lord!" Colin's voice filtered into the kitchen just as Daisy set the kettle on the stove. He sounded... horrified.

"What is it?" she called. "What's happening, love?"

Colin stood in the open door that led from the sitting area into what had once been the ornamental front lawn of the manor. Several summer flies zoomed past his frozen frame and hurried into the kitchen, intent on making a nuisance of themselves.

"Colin, what's happening?" Daisy squeezed past him, peering into the yard and the trees beyond, expecting to see someone lurking. Colin grabbed her around the waist and arrested her movement.

"Who would do such a thing?" he asked, not her in particular, but the universe.

Daisy noticed his gaze fixed on the ground. She nearly gagged at the sight of two gray legs, severed and laid out in an X shape. A pile of innards lay at in the bottom opening of the grisly shape. At the top, a long, gray face stared at them with blank, clouded eyes. Red-brown drops drew her attention to sprinkles of blood thrown over the ground and, as she followed its path, the door and its frame.

"Good Lord," she breathed, horrified. "What on earth? What *is* that?"

"It's Stormcloud," Colin snarled. "The horse I had with me when we met. Remember, I lost him in the woods?" He exhaled in a noisy whoosh.

"In my village? Oh, no!"

"And look at that." Colin indicated the ground near the revolting pile of offal and blood. With a stick, someone had dug deep into the soil in strange lines that swam with blood.

"Is that… words?" Daisy asked.

She felt rather than saw his nod. "I think it says 'sinner'."

Daisy squinted and the macabre display. "I think you're right, but… what sin? And who are they accusing? And why?"

"I can't imagine." He shook himself. "Come away, love. Don't stare at it. We'll clean it all up. I know the men will help me."

She let him lead her inside, back into the kitchen, where the kettle had begun to boil. Daisy sank into a chair while Colin spooned tea leaves into the teapot and then added the water.

"Do you think someone saw us last night?" Daisy asked, her belly clenching and cramping in protest.

He shook his head. "I cannot say for sure, but though we were a bit… scandalous, it wasn't a sin." He rattled around the kitchen, gathering cups and distracting himself as he talked in a thoughtful, detached way. "Besides, whoever did this had to find Stormcloud, butcher him, wash away and preserve the blood, and throw it. This was not an impulse based on our liaison last night. It required weeks of planning."

"That's even more confusing," Daisy protested. "What sin have we ever committed to warrant such a…a…"

"I know," Colin agreed. "Words fail. I've been too damned busy to get into any trouble in years, and this seems harsh for the few curse words I might have said."

"Maybe it was meant for me?" Daisy suggested. "I've brought some Pagan ideas. I know not everyone approved." She thought for a minute, chasing a forgotten crumb over the wood of the table with her fingertip. "No, that doesn't make sense. No one from here would have had the time or opportunity to go back to my village and find your horse and…" She trailed off.

Colin poured the tea into cups and carried them, altogether forgetting saucers, to the table, handing one to Daisy.

She drew a deep, tea-scented lungful of air. "It might have been my father, or John Orville, or both of them. They'd think me a sinner for thwarting their plans."

Colin sank to a seat beside Daisy and let the warmth from his teacup wash up over his face. "That's possible. It makes more sense than anything else, I suppose. They were there. Your father saw the horse. Housed him. They must have discovered where my estate was—who I am—and made their way here. That might explain why they didn't attack immediately."

"And Orville enjoys throwing things. He always has loved sport." She shuddered.

"Do you mean to say," Colin demanded, thunderstruck, "that you think he's the rock-throwing bastard we've been hunting all summer?"

"It fits," Daisy admitted. "It also makes sense why so much time goes by between incidents. He can't just loiter in the woods for weeks on end, can he? He has to go home so people don't notice. But, Colin, isn't that obvious? How could two lunatics be hovering around us?"

"It's the shock, Daisy. We're neither of us thinking straight." Colin sipped his tea and winced. "Ugh, that's strong." Colin's hand began shaking so hard the poorly brewed tea sloshed onto the table. Daisy tugged the cup away and set it down before any damage could be done. Then she hauled her husband into her arms. "Poor old boy. That's not what I wanted for him." His voice shook as hard as his hand.

"I know, love," Daisy whispered. "It's vile. Poor old Stormcloud."

"He didn't deserve it. He worked hard for us for so long."

"I know, love. I know." She ran her hand up and down his back. "I'm so sorry. Sometimes, I wonder if you don't regret ever meeting me. Look at the mess, and it's most likely someone from my past."

"No!" Colin lifted his head from her chest and met her eyes squarely. "Nothing could make me regret you, Daisy. I had forgotten how to live. How to want things for myself. I had forgotten love. I was only existing, had been for years. Now, with you here, I feel alive again. Whoever did this to my poor horse will pay, but I'm not a fool. I know it wasn't you. I love you." He kissed her hard. His lips compressed hers again and again.

Daisy clung to him, revulsion and fear making her feel vulnerable.

Colin, it seemed, felt the same. He trembled in Daisy's arms.

And why not? He's already in the habit of holding himself accountable for everyone's wellbeing. This poor creature was in his care, and now it's... Her mind veered away, just as a loud pounding sounded at the opposite door.

Daisy screeched in surprise, a startled yip, and covered her mouth with one hand.

Colin tugged her to her feet. "Stay behind me."

The knock sounded again, louder than before. Daisy's heart began slamming against her chest with equal force. "Who could it be?"

"I don't know," Colin replied, his voice grim. He hesitated before opening the door a crack and peeked out... and then threw the door wide. "Good morning, Bullock."

"Good morning, my lord. Sorry to intrude, but... something has happened."

"Something more?" Daisy squeaked. Though she hated sounding so foolish, she couldn't control her voice.

"More than what, my lady?" Bullock demanded. "We came to see if Lord Gelroy was going to be joining us in the field, and there's..." He shuddered and broke off.

"An unholy mess on the step?" Colin suggested. "Yes, we saw." He swallowed so hard, Daisy could feel it.

"Was that Stormcloud, my lord?"

Colin nodded. "I think so. Are the other animals well? Is Pesadilla safe?"

"I haven't noticed anything wrong with any of the herd, and the geese are honking away. Pesadilla is kicking up a terrible fuss in the pasture, but I didn't see any sign of injuries on him."

"He must sense something is wrong," Colin said.

"My lord, I really think we ought to invest in a guard dog. Whoever did this has been creeping around the estate for months, and we can't find him. It's not safe for us or the children or the animals."

"I agree," Colin replied. "We'll do it as soon as possible. Today, if we can. Meanwhile, we need to tend to the animals and then search the woods again. Dog or no dog, I want to find this beast and eject him from the estate."

"Wait!" Daisy protested from behind Colin. "What am I going to do? This person has approached the house twice. I won't feel safe in here alone."

"Good point. Um, love, you're in your nightdress. Could you..."

"No," Daisy said firmly. "I apologize for my appearance, Mr. Bullock, but I will not go back into the house alone. Not today."

"Understood, my lady." Bullock turned his gaze to the shrubbery outside the door and studied it with more interest than it warranted.

"We do need to think of a way to keep the women and children safe," Colin agreed.

"My lady, if you wanted to come to my home, you'd be welcome. Yours is still a bit bigger, but I can understand why you'd feel unsafe."

"But that's no better," Daisy protested. "If I go to your home, whoever is after me will be drawn to your wife and children."

"Jones can stay with you all. He was in the army before he came home to the farm, and he's a crack shot. Give the lad a rifle and you'll be safe enough."

Daisy nodded. "I hope you gentlemen can spare my husband another few minutes so I can dress and gather my wallpaper materials."

"Good idea," Colin agreed. "It will give the lot of you something more pleasant to think about. Taking precautions is all well and good, but there's no need to ruminate."

Daisy shuddered. "I hope I'll be able."

Colin squeezed her hand. "Bullock, please send Jones to your house and inform him of what's happening. I'll be along shortly."

"Very good, my lord," Bullock replied.

"Come along, love," Colin said, turning to Daisy. "Let's get you into a presentable condition and gather up your supplies."

"I'm afraid," she admitted. "This person terrifies me. What if it really is Orville? He must think himself a jilted suitor, even though I never accepted his suit. And he's always been violent and unstable."

"I agree he's the most likely suspect, and he's trying to make you afraid. Make both of us afraid, actually. Try not to fret, darling. If I catch him on my property, he'll learn a lesson he won't soon forget about who belongs to whom. His rocks won't help him then."

They entered the bedroom, and the sight of the unmade bed, rumpled after a long night of passion, clashed terribly with the morning's troubles. Daisy shook her head. "How can we ever relax enough to enjoy ourselves again?"

"We will," Colin vowed. "I promise we'll find a way. Besides, I don't plan to let Orville—or whoever it is—lurk on the estate forever. Just as Bullock suggested, we'll be getting a guard dog, and with its help, we'll be sure to find his hiding place in no time. Be strong, Daisy. A few days at most, and we'll send this miscreant running. He won't return."

"No offense, darling, but… you said that before, and instead of running, he escalated."

"I cannot deny it," Colin replied honestly. "I have never seen someone so determined to cause mischief."

She paused, turning away from the wardrobe to level a sour look at her husband.

"Cause terror and pain," he corrected himself.

She nodded, tugging a fresh pair of bloomers over her hips.

Colin had become distracted, staring at her bare breasts.

"Is this really the moment?" she asked, dragging out a chemise and covering herself.

He groaned. "Can I help it if I desire you? You've worked hard enough at ensuring it. I'm not going to tumble you to the bed, love, but I won't apologize for looking."

"You should be looking at the window," Daisy pointed out. She tugged on a simple black dress and ran her fingers through her tousled golden hair. "I had hoped to bathe. Now, I will smell like a campfire—and you—for who knows how long. I hope the Bullocks don't get upset."

"Upset? Unlikely. Bullock and his wife are no fools. They'll understand. They'll tease, but they'll understand."

Daisy felt her face growing hot, first with embarrassment, and then with anger. "This beast. After all you've struggled through. All we've overcome… as a community, to insert himself and cause trouble, just when we were all starting to feel happy and hopeful… it makes me so angry!" Daisy's voice cracked.

Colin crossed the room in three long-legged strides and dragged her into his arms. His embrace shattered her, and a ragged sob broke from her throat. He didn't speak, merely ran his hand up and down her back. A subtle movement revealed him buttoning up the back of her dress.

"We'll find that happiness again, love. Somehow, we will banish this interloper and continue making a normal life for ourselves. I promise."

Daisy nodded against Colin's shoulder.

"Wash your face, love. We have a busy day ahead."

* * *

"What's that you're painting, my lady?" Jones asked, peering over Daisy's shoulder at the table-sized sheet of wallpaper she was stenciling.

"It's a flower," she replied, leaning aside so the young man could see the stylized arrangement of petals she was dabbing over and over with blue paint. The pale blue background complimented the shade, creating a subtle pattern that would look lovely in a nursery. "It's wallpaper," she added, noticing he still looked puzzled.

"How do you hang that?"

"With glue," she replied.

"In small sheets? Isn't that a lot of seams?"

Daisy set her brush in a cup and turned to look at Jones, noticing that while his hair had grown into a wild, overlong mess of curls, it looked healthier, shinier, and he'd put on weight since their first meeting. "It is," she agreed. "How do you know so much about wallpaper and seams?"

"I helped hang some. Back before I came home to work on the estate in my father's stead, I tried my hand as a footman in London. They needed someone strong with good balance to help with the task, so I did. I didn't care for the smell of the glue, though. Made me dizzy."

"Some of them are very harsh," Daisy agreed, glad for the idle conversation that distracted her from cloaked figures who threw rocks at people for sport and butchered helpless old horses. *It must be Orville. Who else would care? Who else would have the vindictiveness and lack of moral fiber to do such things? The horse part does seem beyond his creative abilities, though.*

"Wouldn't a bigger sheet need fewer seams?" Jones suggested. "Maybe so you only need two to reach from floor to ceiling in a regular-sized room?"

"That would be better in many ways," Daisy agreed, shaking herself back to reality, "but I cannot handle a frame that large. I would also need a huge table to lay the paper out on."

"Both a frame and paper could be handled by someone else," he pointed out.

"Are you offering?"

"If there's any profit in it," he replied. "I don't mind plowing and planting, but all these geese are... well... they're geese, if you know what I mean, ma'am."

"I do indeed." Daisy turned back to her work, dabbing more blue paint through the stencil onto the homemade paper. "In the town where I grew up, one family trained a goose to be extra aggressive. She was better than a dog for protecting the family property. Not an amusing animal to live near."

"Most assuredly not," Jones replied. "You know, these flowers would look nicer with yellow centers. Do you mind?"

"No, that's fine," Daisy replied, stepping away from where the young man had claimed a small brush, absconded with the yellow paint from Katie's spot on the floor of her family's home and begun to dab a tiny, brilliant dot in the center of each forget-me-not.

Moving toward Katie, Daisy saw that she had created a pattern of foxes running and playing among thick rows of green shrubbery.

"Beautiful," she said. "I love that."

Katie looked up and grinned.

"If these sell as well as I think they will, we'll be able to hire you a tutor before you know it. Do you fancy being a famous artist now that you've had time to think about it?"

Katie blushed. "I would like that," she whispered.

Daisy grinned. *There's so much opportunity to do good here. As if I'd ever want to leave. These are my people now too.*

"Lunch!" Mrs. Bullock announced, entering the space with a hot pot gripped with two towels. "Can we set that wallpaper aside so we can eat?"

"Let's!" Bobby shouted, struggling to his feet and carrying his sheet of paper to the window. He looked out. "My lady, your husband is coming this way!"

Daisy rose slowly. Her body felt a bit weak and sore, whether from the strain or from the intemperate way she and Colin had been exploring their sexuality, she didn't know. Perhaps all of it. *Or perhaps the confused mixture of the two. What a painful contrast—to fall in love with my perfect match while in fear of an ill-intentioned intruder.*

A moment later, Bullock strode through the door into his home, Colin on his heels. Daisy ran to him but then, she paused, feeling shy. Colin took hold of her arm in a proper, public manner and looped it around his, gently squeezing to add affection to the touch.

"What did you find?" she asked.

Bullock shook his head. "Nothing, my lady. I don't know where this fool is holing up, but there's nothing more useful in the woods than footprints and a few displaced leaves. No camp. No trails. It's like... like he's a ghost."

"Ghosts might pop up and look scary," Daisy said darkly, "but they haven't the wherewithal to throw rocks, let alone..." She shot her husband a glance. "Let alone butcher a whole horse."

Colin closed his eyes briefly before continuing with the practical. "Somehow, this fellow has found a hiding place, near enough to creep in and harass us, but not actually on the estate."

"The village?" Daisy suggested, referring to the small settlement a couple of miles down the road.

"Seems as good a guess as any," Colin replied. "We'll be heading that way after lunch to see if anyone has a dog to help us guard the animals."

"May I go with you?" Daisy asked. "I need ink to outline my design, and we need some sewing fabric. Your trousers are too ragged to patch."

"We need ammunition for our rifles as well," Colin added grimly. "I never thought we'd be fighting in our own home."

Shame pricked at Daisy's conscience again. *They were well on their way to recovery without me, but if I hadn't come, would all this be happening?* She swallowed hard against a lump in her throat.

Ignoring custom, Colin dragged Daisy into his arms, hugging her. "It's not your fault. Anyone who would take the loss of someone who didn't like them and had repeatedly refused their suit with such violent rancor has clearly gone mad. If you had stayed, been assaulted and forced into an unwanted marriage, do you really think that would be better?"

"For you," she mumbled.

Colin tucked a knuckle under her chin and lifted her head. Their eyes met. "Not a chance, love. Not a single chance. I regret poor old Stormcloud's end. He didn't deserve that, but you didn't do it. You didn't ask for it. You didn't promise that man anything. If he made himself insane with disappointment because he couldn't control you, that's his fault, as are the consequences for the mad actions he's taken since then."

"Don't forget," Bullock cut in, "that we don't know for certain if it even is your former suiter, my lady. There is evidence to point in that direction, yes, but no proof. We won't know for sure until we find this man. And as Lord Gelroy said, even if it is he, you didn't cause it. We like having you here, Lady Gelroy."

Daisy smiled a watery smile.

"Stay for lunch, my lord," Mrs. Bullock suggested. "Afterwards, you and your wife can head to town."

"That's a very kind offer, Mrs. Bullock," Colin replied. "Are you sure there's enough, though? I would hate for anyone to go hungry on my account."

"We will be fine," Mrs. Bullock insisted. "It's mostly beans, and I needed to use them up in preparation for this year's crop. The vegetable gardens are doing so nicely, there will be plenty for winter." She beamed. "Children, clear away the painting supplies and let's eat."

The Bullock children jumped to obey, laying out their wallpaper squares around the floor to dry and capping the paint and ink bottles. Viscountess or no, Daisy helped set the table. Mrs. Bullock looked at her long and hard, and then shrugged and dipped a ladle into the soup. When the men stepped out of earshot to wash their hands, she whispered to Daisy, "Don't ever blame yourself, my lady. Some men are just stupid when it comes to women they think they own. What you've brought to us all is worth so much more. You're one of us now, and we love you."

Tears stung Daisy's eyes. "That's so kind, Mrs. Bullock. I... I don't know what to say. I just hate that you and your children are facing this danger because of me."

"Honestly, ma'am, the only ones who have seen anything are you and Lord Gelroy. At this point, I don't think any of the rest of us are at risk."

She's right, Daisy realized, *which makes it even more likely to be my fault.* But all she said was, "I'm glad. Do be careful anyway, won't you?"

"Of course," Mrs. Bullock agreed, just as the men burst back into the room. Even from where she stood, Daisy could hear their bellies rumbling, and she recalled that the hearty breakfast Colin had requested had never been made.

Shake off your guilt, woman, and get yourself together. You have duties as well as the men do, and you cannot abandon them because of a scare, even a really big scare.

The smell of the soup—of beans, bacon and summer herbs—teased Daisy's appetite and she took a seat at the table, surrounded by the Bullock children, and tucked into a tasty lunch.

* * *

"Did you find what you needed, love?" Colin asked, approaching Daisy in the stationer's shop. She stood near the front, examining a display of different colored inks and papers.

"I did," she replied. "I think I have enough to finish the project I'm working on with some left over for Katie. What did you find?"

"Two mastiffs," Colin replied. "A mother who has long since been trained to guard flocks and her son, who is half-grown and almost trained. They should serve us well. Gentle giants, but not easily fooled. Oh, and I picked up some mail. You had three letters waiting for delivery, and I have an interesting note from one of my old school friends."

Colin handed Daisy a bundle of letters. A quick glance revealed two from her sisters and one from Katerina Bennett. Smiling, she tucked them into her reticule to examine later. "Well, don't leave me in suspense. What does yours say? You're practically bouncing on your toes in excitement."

"Do you have your ink already?"

She nodded.

"Then let us walk to the inn for a cup of tea." Taking Daisy's arm, he led her into the summer-warm street.

Here, away from the estate, the constant feeling of someone looming over her faded and the hubbub of people about their everyday business took precedence. *So refreshing.*

"I received a letter, as I said, from an old friend," Colin murmured, his voice barely audible over the clatter of horses and carts and the chatter of random conversations. "He heard I had acquired Pesadilla, and since he has decided to try his hand at breeding racehorses, would like to negotiate a meeting between the stallion and his mare. He mentions a couple of friends who might like to do the same. This is prime horse breeding season, and my friend would like to stop by sometime this month to see if the beasts are interested."

Daisy grinned. "That's wonderful, love. Um... is it safe?"

"We'll have to try all the harder to catch our harasser. I'm sure Beauty and Henry will help."

Daisy raised an eyebrow.

"The dogs, love."

"Someone named a mastiff 'Beauty?'" She giggled.

"I'll call her anything she likes if she helps us get rid of... our problem," Colin quipped.

Daisy laughed again, but it sounded more hysterical than humorous, so she swallowed it down.

Colin squeezed her arm. "Ready to head home, love?" He paused, turning to look at her. "It feels wrong to bring you back home under these circumstances.

I would rather send you back to visit my mother or perhaps the Bennetts until we clear up this mess. I need to know you're safe, Daisy."

Daisy opened her mouth to protest and then closed it again, considering. "It would seem that guarding me is keeping at least one man at a time from either tending the animals or hunting the perpetrator. If I was just... gone... and no one knew where, it might confuse him long enough for you to catch him. I hate to go. Things were getting so lovely between us, but..."

"But it's worth considering?" Colin suggested.

She nodded, even as her throat burned and her eyes stung.

"I'm not rejecting you," Colin reminded her. "I'm not casting you out, and I'm not asking for an annulment. I only want my wife to be safe. Is that wrong for a husband to request?"

"Of course not." She swallowed again, her voice harsh and raspy. "I would need to stop by the house, if only briefly, to pack a bag. It's one thing to pop in on your mother uninvited. It's another to do so with not even a spare pair of bloomers to my name."

Someone near them tutted.

"Oops. I forgot we were in public." Another hysterical giggle tried to break free.

"It's the shock," Colin replied under his breath. "Everything happened... just this morning. It's been a long day with no end in sight and no time to process."

She nodded, drawing in as deep a breath as her stays would allow and then releasing it.

"Here we are," he said, pointing to a café with rentable rooms on the second story, not unlike the one she grew up in.

He ushered her into a dining room with small round tables and simple white cloths.

"Terrible wallpaper," Colin mentioned as he ushered her to a table and into a seat. "I've honestly never noticed it before."

Daisy glanced while her husband procured tea and a biscuit for each of them, though she struggled to focus her eyes. At last, she managed to understand the messy pattern of uneven lines. *I must be more in shock than I realized. It's getting worse, too. What on earth?* "I wonder if it's messy like that on purpose," she guessed, sipping a cup of tea and grimacing because she'd forgotten to add any sugar. "Colin?"

"Yes, love?" He bit into his biscuit, choked a bit on the dry crumbs, and sipped his tea.

"I want to go home, but I'm afraid to go home."

His gentle expression turned grim. "I understand. I feel the same way." He sighed. "We'll leave shortly. Jones has promised to meet us at the edge of the woodland path to the estate, with the dogs in tow. I'm sure no one will try anything funny with two gigantic mastiffs nearby. You can pack, and I'll send you on to Mother with no one the wiser. Once you're safe, we'll put the dogs to work. I just know we're on the brink of a breakthrough."

Daisy tried to smile, but her mouth felt stuck upside-down. She bit her lip instead.

Colin reached across the table and grasped her hand.

Daisy gulped down her tea, ignoring the biscuit, and the couple made their way out into the sun, which now hung lower in the sky. "Will there be time for me to get anywhere today?" she asked. "If we go back to the estate and return, I might be able to catch the last mail coach, but popping up on your mother's doorstep in the middle of the night doesn't seem too mannerly. Not to mention, I'll be all alone in London well after dark."

Colin crunched on his biscuit as he slowly pondered her words. "I see your point. Do you have enough pocket money with you to send a telegram? We could have you go tomorrow and send word that they should expect you. I'm sure Mother won't mind, but you're right. Welcoming a visitor in the middle of the day is better. If we keep the dogs inside the house with us, we'll be safe enough. It's strange, though."

"What is, love?"

"That this… person has never gone after the animals, nor the garden. Nothing. He threatens us directly but does no other mischief."

"He's never shown himself to any of the tenants either. They've only seen the aftermath of his threats. It's so subtle… and so strange. Clearly, he wants us injured and afraid, but… I had no idea John Orville was so clever. He's more the sort to stomp up to someone and punch them in the face. Someone must have given him this idea."

"Do you think your father could have done it?"

"I don't know," Daisy replied. "He might be angry enough at having his plans thwarted, but what would it profit him to wage a scare campaign against us?

Besides, with me gone, he has double the work to do. He wouldn't have time to make trouble, would he?"

"If I were dead," Colin pointed out grimly, "he could try to enact his plan again. That might be worth the sacrifices it required."

Daisy raised an eyebrow. "True, he could try, but he would not succeed. I'm old enough to make my own decisions, and if I were a widow, the law would be on my side. It already was, which was why he staged an assault in the first place, I'm sure. He tried to pressure me. He tried to bully me into marrying Orville. He tried everything except force because legally he couldn't force me."

"That's why he tried the trap?"

"I suspect so. I just never understood why. Orville is an idiot. What would Father get out of forcing us together? Is his lust for control so strong?"

"Control and money," Colin pointed out. "Your mother managed to keep your dowry from him, and your grandmother passed your inheritance directly to you, bypassing him altogether. If you married an idiot, the control of all that lovely money would go to, well, him."

Understanding dawned. "That makes too much sense," Daisy said, feeling the blood drain from her face until she wanted to stagger. "Orville goes along whatever Father tells him because he's not a thinker. I wouldn't put it past them to come up with the original plan, but murder? Father's a brute and Orville's a dolt, but killers? That doesn't sound like either of them."

"Maybe it isn't?"

"Maybe not," Daisy agreed, "but who else would bother? A couple minding their own business on a small, almost unknown estate in the countryside rarely generates such random vitriol."

"The whole situation is mad," Colin said, finishing his biscuit, gulping the last of his tea and sitting back in his chair. "It strains the imagination. Why on earth would *anyone* want to do such things, particularly as there's nothing to gain from it?"

Daisy shook her head. "I honestly cannot imagine. Shall we go, love?"

"I suppose."

Pushing in their chairs, they made their way out of the café and began the long walk home.

But will it ever feel safe like home again?

Chapter 13

ENRY was whining, so I let the dogs outside," Colin announced. "They seem a little... sad."

"They're mastiffs, love. With those wrinkly foreheads and dangling jowls, they always look on the verge of tears." Daisy rolled up a pair of bloomers and tucked them into her carpetbag. "Though I must say, they are surprisingly attractive for their breed. I like the sharp line between their black faces and their tan coats."

"Beauty is still a stretch for a big, drooly dog, though," Colin pointed out. "She's quite lovely for a mastiff, but she's still a mastiff. I do think they're a bit homesick."

"Any idea why they had to leave the farm they grew up on?" Daisy tucked a few dresses into her bag and turned to open the top drawer of her bureau, considering which of her treasures she might want to bring with her for comfort. *One perfume bottle will have to suffice. A scarf. A couple of handkerchiefs and of course, my letterbox... I should add my sisters' new letters. Something to read on the train.*

"The woman selling them said her father passed away. Her brother had gone to America long since, and she didn't want the responsibility of the farm or the dogs, so she was sending them to a new home."

"No wonder they're sad." Daisy lifted the lid of her letterbox, the new documents in one hand, and froze. "Colin," she breathed, unable to force a full sound past her pounding heart.

"What?" He crossed the room in a few long-legged strides. "What happened, love?"

Daisy pointed into her letterbox. On top, instead of one of her many letters from her sisters—the way she had left it—a sheet of thick, gray paper lay in the box, scrawled with a messy message in handwriting she didn't recognize.

Sinners meet a rocky end. Deuteronomy 21:18. Leviticus 20:10. Exodus 22:18.

A fine trembling began in Daisy's hands. Her knees buckled. Colin's arms wrapped tight around her, preventing her from falling. The silence roared in her ears. Spots danced in the sunlight before her eyes. She leaned her head on his shoulder, forcing air into her laboring lungs so she didn't faint.

"What did you see, love?"

"He's been in the house. He left... left a note... in my letterbox."

Colin edged toward the bureau and stared. "Scripture verses? What are they?"

Daisy shook her head. "I can't think." She swallowed against a wave of nausea. "He's been inside the house. Inside our bedroom. Oh, God." Her breathing shattered into sobbing sounds and again, blackness threatened.

"Rocky. Clever." Colin's voice sounded grim. "We thought this person was trying to scare us, but it would seem he had a more.... Biblical end in mind. Not to mention a deep knowledge of sacred text."

Forcing her words past her terror, she pointed out, "It can't be Orville then. Nor Father. Neither one knows or cares about scripture enough to produce something like that."

"I see that. Well, then, the verses are a clue, not only to what this person wants but to who they are."

Daisy nodded.

"You need to sit down, love." He escorted her toward the bed.

Daisy's feet stumbled on the smooth floorboards, and she sank gratefully on the soft surface. The scripture references ricocheted around in her head, slamming into each other as they tried to communicate to her chattering mind.

"I think I recognize one of the verses," Colin said, returning to the box to stare at the missive.

Daisy lay back on the bed. "I'm trying to remember," she whispered.

"The second one is that passage about adulterers, isn't it?"

"I think so," Daisy said.

"But that makes no sense. Are they accusing me of something? I haven't, of course. Even I were so inclined—which I'm not—I've had neither the time nor the opportunity. Even when I was a wild youth, I kept my exploration to professionals, not married women."

"We've both been threatened with stones," Daisy pointed out. "I've scarcely been married long enough to stray. It would seem that someone thinks our marriage is invalid... and that one of us is married to someone else." The rolling dice clicked into place. "It's me. They're accusing me of adultery."

"What? How?"

She shook her head, the pillow displacing her hairpins to dig into her scalp. "The first one. I remember it now. The vicar's wife used to force me to read it over and over when I was young. It's the passage about what to do with recalcitrant children. If a child engages in ongoing and unrepentant rebellion against their parents, they were entitled to have the child executed." She gulped. "I didn't rebel against my father back then, but against her sensibilities. As vicar's wife, she felt strongly that the behavior of everyone in town reflected on her."

"This still points to someone from your village."

She nodded again.

"Is the old woman still alive?"

"She died shortly before our wedding. Only a couple of days before. I was quite surprised to see the vicar out and about so soon."

Colin sighed. "This doesn't make any sense. Someone who is offended that you thwarted your father's plan to force you into marriage has come all this way to accuse us of adultery—as though the marriage between you and Orville had ever actually existed—and stone us. It's madness."

"It is." Daisy's eyes burned, and one tear spilled down her cheek. "Madness. Utter madness."

"But it wouldn't be Orville or your father because neither one knows the Bible enough to produce these obscure verses?"

"Father's a happy sinner, and Orville is stupid. It wouldn't be in character for either of them."

"What is this last reference?"

Daisy studied the bird pattern wallpaper she'd affixed to the bedroom wall, focused entirely on the red-breasted robin that lay at eye level. *Katie is such a talented artist. She deserves to have her work hung in the Royal Academy.* The idle thought failed to comfort her.

Colin's trousers swished as he crossed the room. Another soft sound suggested he was pulling a book off the bookshelf beside the bed.

"Exodus 22:18. 'Thou shalt not suffer a witch to live.'" There was a loud thump as the Bible fell to the floor. Colin's boots stomped on the floorboards as he ran out of the room. A moment later, the outer door of the house creaked open and fell shut again.

* * *

"It makes no sense," Colin argued with himself as he ran, full speed, across the meadow toward the row of tenant houses that fronted the woods.

Each one has a back door that opens out of sight, he recalled.

"But how could she? She doesn't even know where Daisy came from. She rarely leaves her home."

Except to go to church on Sundays... all day long. It wouldn't be impossible for her to take the train. It's not that far.

"But why would she? How would she have even known about Daisy's father and the marriage trap?"

She already thinks Daisy's a witch. She started throwing stones long ago. She must have wanted more ammunition and went to nose around. Anyway, it doesn't matter. It's madness. Don't look for sense in it.

"She's big for a woman. Tall and bulky. Figure like a man. Rough features. Add a hat and muffler, and it would be hard to tell the difference. Especially from far away."

Heart pounding, Colin approached the Farrell family home and pounded on the door. Without waiting for an answer, he wrenched it open to hear Mrs. Farrell's voice whisper, "Hurry. Hide. Get in there."

"Mrs. Farrell," Colin shouted. "You come here right now." Though he was breaking every societal norm and several laws, Colin did not care. *Threaten my wife and no law on Earth or in Heaven will protect you.*

"What do you want, my lord?" Mrs. Farrell, her grizzled hair standing on end, her clothing rumpled and misaligned, stepped out of the bedroom and glowered. "This is most irregular. My husband will not stand for it."

"Where is your husband?" Colin asked. "Not here, I'll wager. Wasn't he tending the lambs today? So who are you hiding in your bedroom?"

"What are you talking about?" Mrs. Farrell shrieked. "You have no right. How dare you accuse me, adulterer?"

Got you. "I'm a faithful, married man, my dear. Who are *you* committing adultery with, and how dare you accuse me?"

"Your marriage is in vain. It's false."

Colin shook his head. "The laws of England disagree."

In his peripheral vision, Colin could see the bedroom door ease open a crack. *There is someone else in here. It's not merely her madness. What can this mean?*

"There are higher laws."

"Which are not binding in this land," he pointed out. "Nor do they apply to my marriage. I have committed no crime, my wife has committed no crime, yet you accuse and threaten. You are the guilty one. You have assaulted us both."

"If the Lord chooses to punish you, that's your problem."

"I don't think the Lord has much to do with it," Colin said, letting the arrogance of his station creep into his tone. "Overall, our marriage is blessed. It's done nothing but good for us and the other tenants. You are the only one who seems to have a problem. I suggest you take it up with God and leave us in peace."

The bedroom door flew open, smashing against the opposite wall, and in one movement, a large white rock flew at Colin's head. He tried to dodge, but he couldn't move fast enough. It clipped his temple. For a moment, he swayed on his feet, and then he crumpled to the floor. Another rock flew at him, and in his prone, stunned state, he couldn't avoid it. It hit him hard on the hip, leaving an aching injury that would become a colorful bruise later. He covered his head and neck with both hands.

"Stop that," he barked. "What are you doing?"

A maniacal laugh responded to his demand, and a chill ran through Colin's body.

Mad is right, but who? He dared to peek at the doorway of the Farrells' bedroom and his jaw dropped in shock. "You?"

* * *

For another long moment, Daisy lay on the bed, staring sightlessly at the ceiling. *Where did Colin go? Did he really leave me alone, knowing someone had been in the house? What if they're still here?*

"I'll get the dogs," she told herself. "They don't exactly know me yet, though. How do I make friends quickly with a set of mastiffs?"

The answer presented itself quickly in a memory of some sausages she had hanging in the pantry. Getting to her feet proved problematic. She still felt shaken and didn't quite know how to overcome it.

An unfamiliar sound rocketed her to her feet a moment later. Her heart thumped and commenced to pounding painfully.

"What is that?" she hissed aloud, taking a couple of steps across the room and leaning in beside the bureau. The sound, a kind of heavy scratching, reached her ears again, this time accompanied by a pleading whine. "The dogs. Oh, Lord. It's just Beauty and Henry wanting to come in."

She moved to leave the bedroom when her eyes fell on the note again. She squinted. The first two scripture references had been writing in a bold, back-slanting hand. *Left-handed,* she thought to herself. The third, the one that accused witchcraft... "It's different," she breathed. It looked as though someone with smaller, more controlled handwriting had tried to imitate the first, using their right hand.

Daisy bit her lip. "There are two of them," she breathed. "One is completely mad, with out-of-control handwriting. He's worried about adultery and obedience. The second... the second is obsessed with witches."

Realization dawned. "No wonder Colin bolted. He saw that last and knew that only one person hates and fears witches enough to do such damage. But did he notice that there are two? I need to warn him. I need help."

The dogs scratched again and Daisy, a plan half-forming in her mind, collected them by simply grabbing the sausages on her way through the kitchen and meeting them at the back door.

The two large, frowning dogs accepted the treats with painful dignity, butting her hands with their heads. "You're a friendly pair," she complimented them. "Come along, good dogs. Let us go and find some help."

Not wanting to take the time to find and affix their leashes, she simply walked toward the field, hoping they would follow.

They did.

Daisy could see several men standing among the flock of summer lambs, inspecting them, and sneaking in the occasional pat.

"Mr. Bullock," she called loudly, pitching her voice high to carry though a light summer wind. "Mr. Farrell. I need you both!"

The men hustled over to Daisy.

"What do you need, my lady?"

She took a deep breath, resting her hand on Henry's head. "The rock hurler, the horse butcherer has been inside our home. Colin chased after him, and I'm afraid, because I think there are two of them, and I don't think he realizes it."

"Do you know where he went?" Bullock demanded, scrutinizing Daisy with a worried expression on his face.

She nodded. "I'm afraid they went to Mr. Farrell's house."

Farrell's head shot in her direction. "My house? Why is he at my house?"

Daisy bit her lip, the panicked need for urgency warring with trying to choose the right words. "We have reason to think this individual went there," she said. "Gentlemen, please. Come. I'm sure Lord Gelroy needs help."

Not waiting to see if they followed, she set her sights on the second tenant house and hurried that way, whistling for the dogs in a less-than-ladylike command.

They galumphed after her. Swishing in the grass of the meadow, the two men hurried her direction, quickly catching up.

* * *

More rocks pelted Colin, never giving him the chance to get up. "Why?" he demanded, sheltering his head with his arms as best he could.

"It is the penalty for adultery. Even King David is not above the law."

"David?"

Mrs. Farrell cackled. "The Lord has chosen us to replay his drama, here in England. Our country is weak and in need of revival. That is why he has brought his messenger to us."

Another large rock slammed down onto Colin's shoulder.

"He's not a heavenly messenger. He's just a small-town vicar who has lost his mind. Mrs. Farrell, he's tricking you."

"Liar!" the man screamed, pelting Colin with a shower of pebbles. "Lair! Cheat! Adulterer."

"Old man," Colin barked in his most authoritative voice, "you know I'm no adulterer. You married Daisy and me yourself."

The bombardment paused, and Colin used the opportunity to haul himself to his feet and duck behind the Farrells' dining table. It offered scant protection from the blows, but scant protection was better than none. He crouched down, wildly scanning the room for something better.

"It was a sin!" Vicar Williams shouted. "She belonged to another. Her father chose her a husband, and she wedded and bedded you instead. You had no right to interfere!"

"I didn't," Colin said dryly. "That idiot was not married to her, and she despises him. She's also legally of age to refuse a marriage that doesn't suit her. Instead of accepting her choice, they plotted to trap her using assault. You played right into their hands. I believe the Lord intervened by having me close enough to save her. No adultery took place because she was not married to him and she never would have been."

The vicar paused, his puffy, white hair seeming to vibrate with a combination of righteous indignation and confusion. "The father has the right to select a husband for his daughter. They were betrothed by the will of the groom and the bride's father. Betrothals are binding, and your interference constitutes adultery."

Colin shook his head. *This man has lost his mind.* "That may have been true in ancient Israel, but here in England, the bride has a say, and she said no to the marriage her father arranged and yes to me. There was no betrothal, so there was no adultery."

"But she's a witch!" Mrs. Farrell screamed. She picked up a rock and hurled it at Colin, but in her rage, she missed, and the melon-sized white stone flew through the window, shattering the glass.

"She's a good, Christian woman," Colin insisted. "She's a faithful wife, and she's generously donated her inheritance to help us. You have no right to accuse her. Stand down, Mrs. Farrell."

In response, she threw another rock, and from her angle, she was able to toss it around the table and hit Colin in the knee. He sidled away, still scanning for a route to either an exit or a useful weapon.

Silver flashed, and Colin could see a hefty kitchen knife in her hand.

Vicar Williams stood between him and the door, and Mrs. Farrell, to his right, had him pinned. If he ran for the rear exit, she would be on him, too close to miss.

Making a wild dodge, Colin ducked into the kitchen and grabbed a heavy, iron pan from the stove. *Not much of a shield, but better than nothing.*

In the second his attention shifted, one rock and then another flew in his direction. One missed, clattering against the metal of the stove. The other, he deflected with the pan. Sensing movement in his peripheral vision, he whirled to face Mrs. Farrell, who had rushed him with her knife.

He swatted at it with the frying pan, keeping the sharp end away from his flesh. That is until something heavy struck his shoulder.

His arm tingled and his hand threatened to release the pan.

"We have the sinner now!" Vicar Williams screamed. "May God have mercy on your soul!"

* * *

As Daisy and the two tenants approached the Farrells' house, indistinct shouting reached them. Two male voices contended vigorously while a woman screamed in anger. Glass shattered, and a white rock flew through the window, bouncing on the ground and rolling away.

"Oh, good lord," Daisy breathed. Without thinking of her own safety, she darted for the door, wrenching it open.

The scene inside stole her breath. Colin stood, clutching a saucepan, which he jabbed at Mrs. Farrell. The woman stabbed at him with a kitchen knife.

More rocks flew through the air, and one hit Colin, nearly disarming him.

Thinking of nothing but helping her husband, Daisy grabbed wildly at a stone that lay near the door. She hurled it with all her strength.

The rock flew straight and true, hitting… *Is that the vicar? What on earth?* Blinking, Daisy watched the projectile connect solidly with the side of the man's head. He dropped something from his hand and clutched his temple.

"Don't like it, do you," she screamed, hunting for another and throwing it again. This time, the rock slammed into the vicar's nose and blood sprayed, just as Bullock and Farrell strode into the room, Beauty and Henry panting at their heels.

Bullock paused to stare at the scene for a single heartbeat, before ordering the dogs with a pointed finger and a whistle.

Unprepared, confused, Mrs. Farrell paused in her attack to blink at the galloping, pony-sized beasts barreling at her.

Colin took the opportunity to swing the frying pan, connecting solidly with her wrist. The knife clattered to the floor, and a moment later, she joined it, with a monstrous dog crouching on her chest.

Drool dribbled onto her neck and chin. She shrieked in wordless rage, trying to dislodge the animal. He growled in warning, and she subsided.

Beauty, meanwhile, approached the vicar, eyeing him in canine curiosity.

"What is going on here?" Farrell demanded. "Mary, what are you doing? Who is this?"

Colin set his weapon back on the stove and embraced his wife. Daisy could feel him trembling. "He's the vicar who married us," she said. "He must have lost his senses."

"So it would seem." Bullock grabbed the man, wrenching his arms up behind his back. Blood dripped onto the floor.

Meanwhile, Farrell approached his wife, shooed the dog away from her and lifted her to her feet, pinning her to his chest with both arms.

She wriggled. "Let me go."

"Not a chance. Have you gone mad? Why would you attack Lord Gelroy? He's our... our friend."

Daisy saw Colin's throat work in a rough, dry-looking swallow.

Tears stung her own eyes. *It might be considered unseemly by some, but after they suffered so much together, what else could anyone say?*

"He's a sinner. He married a witch."

Farrell shook his head. "Lady Gelroy is no witch, and your obsession, Mary, has gotten out of hand. This stops now."

"You cannot stop me!" she screamed. "I am a vessel of the Lord and his messenger."

Farrell's nostrils flared.

Daisy could feel Colin tense in her arms.

And no wonder. What is she admitting?

"He's no messenger of the Lord," Colin said darkly. "He's a madman. He doesn't even know where he is." He shook his head.

"What do we do now, my lord?" Bullock asked.

Colin sighed. For a moment, his arms tightened around Daisy. Then he straightened to his full height, looking for once every inch the nobleman. "I would say we turn them over to the authorities. They can spend some time in gaol for their assaults on innocent citizens. They might even be transported. However, it would seem that both have lost their wits. It would be best to summon a doctor and have them both committed to an asylum, where they can do no further harm."

Farrell made an inarticulate sound.

"Sorry, man," Colin said, taking several unsteady steps across the room. "At this point, she's a danger to everyone. She needs treatment."

"What's happening?" Jones burst into the room, panting, hand on his chest.

"Ah, excellent timing," Colin said. He remained in his power position, though he looked stiff and sounded strained. "Please hurry to town and bring back the sheriff. We're going to need some assistance."

"Right away, sir!" The youth bounded out the door again.

Colin wavered, and Daisy tightened her grip on his waist.

"You should sit down, my lord," Bullock suggested.

"He should burn in hell," Vicar Williams shrieked. With blood pouring from his nose, he looked deranged.

"That's quite enough out of you." Releasing Colin to sink into a chair, Daisy scooped up a rock from the floor and showed it to the man. "Shall I try again to convince you to mind your own business?"

"God will judge you," he muttered darkly.

"I agree," she said, "as it's his job. He may judge me as he will. You, however, have no such right. Now pipe down."

He snapped his mouth shut and scowled ferociously at the floor.

Bullock stepped toward the man with a pinched frown on his face. His expression, normally mild, turned ferocious. It seemed to speak of all they had worked so hard to build being threatened with this act against their leader.

Colin pulled Daisy into his lap, ignoring discretion, and rested his forehead on her upper chest.

She stroked his hair. "It's all right, love," she breathed. "It's all right. We got them. We're safe. It's all right."

Colin took a deep breath, drawing Daisy's essence into his lungs, into his soul. He exhaled pain, shame, and fear, and the stress he'd been carrying so long. As it fell away, he felt almost giddy, despite his bruises. For the first time in as long as he could remember, a sensation awakened in his heart. Nurtured by Daisy's love, the spark grew in strength and brightness until he finally recognized it.

Hope.

Chapter 14

CHEERY fire crackled on the hearth, warming a room she had never entered before in a home she had never seen.

She shivered against the bite of autumn that slipped under the door into the garden. *Summer has ended. The lambs and geese have gone to market. The estate is flush with funds and supplies to weather the winter. The tenant houses are repaired, expanded and warmly decorated. Now, we must turn our attention to a more pressing problem,* Daisy thought, eyeing the three men who sat in leather armchairs perched at the four corners of a glorious red rug that beautifully complemented the warm wood of the floor. Her spot in the fourth chair felt strangely isolated, though her husband was only a short reach away.

"This is most irregular," the Right Reverend Cary said, examining each face in turn. He raked his fingers through his sparse, steel-gray hair. "I did as you asked, James." Here, he turned toward his nephew, who Daisy had learned was one of Colin's oldest friends. The younger man resembled his uncle: round-faced and handsome but with eyes that promised an unexpected strength. "I found no record whatsoever of the wedding having taken place. There is nothing in the civil registry, nor the records of your parish, Lady Gelroy."

Daisy inhaled sharply through her nose. "Oh, dear."

"I did ask some questions, however," the bishop added. "In fact, I had intended to stop by and check in on Reverend Williams after receiving several concerned messages throughout the summer about missed church services and erratic behavior. I learned that Reverend Williams's wife, Bertha, passed away in April. It seems he took her death so hard, it... it drove him mad."

"He was mad already," Daisy pointed out. "I always wondered about him, but his wife kept him on such a short leash, he didn't have a chance to act up. I'm not surprised he went berserk after her death."

"It would seem so," Colin agreed. "Last I heard, he was admitted to an asylum near his hometown. He is not expected to recover." He squeezed Daisy's hand.

"And Mrs. Farrell?" Daisy asked.

"She has been a bit daft for most of her life, as you know. It would seem that she met the mad vicar when he came to throw rocks at us from the woods. Their madness aligned in a way that made them worse together than either would have been alone. She's not likely to leave the asylum either. I fear we'll lose Farrell, as he's likely to want to remain close to his wife."

Daisy lowered her eyelids.

"But the vicar's mental break leaves us with a practical problem. When he attacked us last month, it occurred to me that… that we didn't know when he lost his wits… if it was before or after he… well, he… "

"Engaged in the commission of an illegal forced marriage against you both?" James Cary suggested.

Daisy frowned. "Yes, that."

"You know," James pointed out, "you should have told me this happened, Colin. I would have looked into it for you. There was no need for such drama."

Colin shrugged. "We decided to go along with it. My wife and I… we may not have chosen to wed how and when we did, but… we have no regrets."

"None except that we're not married at all. Right Reverend Cary, what can we do? I believed our marriage was legal so long as we didn't protest it. Grounds for annulment is not a requirement to annul, correct? I mean, we're not related to one another. The marriage being forced meant we *could* protest it, not that we must?"

The bishop nodded.

"So, we've been living as husband and wife for half a year because we decided we wanted to. We thought it was legal so long as neither of us objected."

"Yes, I understand the problem. I believe, under the circumstances, no one would blame you."

"They'd gossip enough," Daisy muttered.

"It's lucky then that you two are not often among high society enough to hear it. Listen, there's nothing I can do about that particular aspect except to say—to anyone who might ask—that you acted in good faith, not realizing your clergyman had lost his wits and failed to file your paperwork properly. The question is, children, what you want to do now."

Daisy looked at Colin, biting her lip. *This is his chance. He may have made peace with our union, given that I gave him no choice, but the fact remains that this is not what he wanted or planned. He could walk away and face nothing worse than a scowl. Meanwhile, my reputation will never recover.*

Colin stared at her face with an unreadable expression for a long, long moment and then turned back to the bishop. "While I have appreciated my marriage, more than I expected to..."

He paused, and Daisy's heart began to pound.

"The wedding itself was a frightening and unpleasant event, and what followed in the last half-year was nightmarish. I would like, if my wife should agree, to start over. Would you be willing to provide a special license? I'd like to marry Daisy, but because it's what we've chosen. What we want. No force. No gun. No crackpot minister messing about with the paperwork. I would like a proper wedding, at a church, with my friend officiating..." He turned to Cary. "Would you do that for us, James?"

"I'd be honored," Cary replied, "and I promise to file the paperwork properly."

Colin grinned.

"I'd like to invite my mother, stepfather and sisters. The elder and younger Bennetts. A wedding is a celebration, not a threat, and I'd like to create that memory this time around, surrounded by friends and loved ones." He turned to Daisy. "What do you say, love? Shall we try again? The right way this time?"

Daisy bit her lip as a tear streaked down her cheek. Words battered against her throat but could not escape, so she simply nodded.

"Would you like to invite your sisters?"

She nodded again.

"I assume your father will not be on the guest list."

A rusty laugh that had more than a hint of a sob about it escaped Daisy's chest.

"So, I'll take that as a no. Right Reverend Cary?"

"Why do you need a special license?" The bishop asked. "Read the banns. Do the whole thing properly?"

Colin raised one eyebrow. "I've been bedding this woman for half a year. Do you think I want to spend weeks or months apart while we wait? Besides, there's still the danger of her father and his idiot lapdog trying to intervene. We've undergone enough drama. I don't have any interest in inviting more."

Understanding dawned on Bishop Cary's face. "I agree to this entire course of action, and I'll be happy to do my part, provided I may attend the ceremony?" He raised dark, bushy eyebrows at the couple.

"Not only are you invited, but I'll buy you a pint afterward," Colin promised.

Daisy nodded again, squeezing Colin's hand.

Chapter 15

"HAT a lovely wedding," a blond woman in her mid-thirties cooed happily. Her dress, though attractive, was crumpled under the knees of a tiny girl with golden hair, who clung to her hip.

"Thank you, ma'am," Colin replied softly. Though he felt a bit overwhelmed, not only with having just completed the wedding they'd spent the last whirlwind week planning, organizing, sending telegrams and messengers... and sleeping apart from Daisy. He also felt the weight of his decision, of their vow, resting heavily on him. The weight was not one of pain or even discomfort but rather the solemn seriousness of the marriage vows. *Thank God for Daisy. No one else could have suited me so well, slipped under all my stings and shields, and taken up residence in my heart. She's a gift from heaven.*

The old melancholia tried to rise, tried to bring his sense of his own unworthiness up into his awareness, but Daisy's warm hand rested in his, and a broad smile spread across her face. Her radiant, joyous smile banished the shadows. They lurked there, not gone entirely, but greatly diminished in power. *I have to watch out for them. They lie so badly. I cannot let them play a role in my thoughts anymore.*

"Colin," Daisy said, breaking into his ruminations, "this is my sister, Rose Miller, and her daughter, Violet. Her husband, Jim, is over there." She gestured with their joined hands to a table where a tall, brooding man sat, clad in a wild, dandyish suit. "Jim is in shipping and imports." She turned to her sister. "I'm so glad you could make it! If only Iris could have come too."

"Your other sister?" Colin guessed.

Daisy nodded. "She lives in Scotland. It's too far to come on a whim."

181

"I know she'll send you a lovely card," Rose said. Turning to Colin, she added, "Iris is famous for her lovely, illustrated notes."

Daisy smiled. "I can't wait it add it to my treasures box. Rose, this is my husband, Colin."

"Pleased to meet you, sir," she said, shifting her daughter so she could extend a hand.

"My lord," Daisy corrected.

"I beg your pardon?"

"He's Colin Butler, Viscount Gelroy," Daisy informed her sister.

Rose's blue eyes bugged out. She dropped into and off-balance curtsey.

Colin compressed his lips. "Love, was that really necessary?"

Daisy smirked.

"How on earth did you bag a Viscount?" Rose blurted. Her graceless comment drew several eyes their direction from all around the overcrowded parlor of the elder Bennetts' home. Colin also paused to admire the hasty but attractive decorations: two small tables with skirts housed luscious arrangements of ribbons and summer flowers. The open doors admitted a waft of breeze, unfortunately scented with stale London street.

A sideboard groaned under the weight of meats, cheeses, fresh fruit, bread and glasses of champagne, along with several bouquets of pink flowers in crystal vases.

The gas-lit chandelier also hung with ribbons and flowers, a cheerful, pink knot over the central table. Daisy and Colin stood near the door in an impromptu receiving line, waiting for everyone who'd been at the church in celebration of their nuptials to arrive and greet them.

"Bagged, Mrs. Miller?" Colin asked, raising one eyebrow and ignoring Daisy's squeeze on his hand. "We were ill-met by moonlight."

Rose's face crumped in confusion.

"It's Shakespeare, Rose," Daisy pointed out drily, "and it's not true."

"Well, maybe not," Colin admitted, "but you, Titania, are most assuredly my fairy queen."

Daisy beamed. "Then you must be my lord," she paraphrased.

"I see you met your true match then," Rose said. "No one else could have as much Shakespeare memorized as you." Nodding to Colin and giving her sister an uncomfortable, one-armed hug, she crossed the room to join her husband.

He laid a hand on her back and scooped their daughter into his lap, his intense gaze affectionate as it fell on his family.

Colin, seeing no further guests were coming, urged Daisy to a seat, so the celebration of their wedding—their real, legal wedding—could begin.

Epilogue

 OME along, you two." Beth Turner stepped through the open doors onto the balcony, where she found Colin and Daisy in a passionate embrace. The winter chill meant nothing to them, not when they had generated such heat with their passion. "I'm delighted to see how you've turned your marriage into something beautiful, but you can snuggle any time. Right now, Katerina has settled her babies and she's offering to play Christmas carols on the harpsichord so we can all sing."

Daisy beamed. "That sounds lovely. Colin, shall we?"

Colin grinned. "One moment." He tugged Daisy back into his arms and laid a lush, wet kiss on her lips, unworried about his mother's presence.

Daisy blushed but offered no protest as he escorted her back through the open door into the parlor.

"My goodness, son, you're looking well!" Beth Turner exclaimed. "Have things gone so very right then?"

"So much righter than I would have believed possible," he replied. "The lambs and geese did wonderfully at market, and I've bred Pesadilla twice. He rather loves the ladies, silly horse. From my portion of the sales and from the stud fees, I have enough set aside for next year's taxes. We should have no trouble raising our payments as well. Though I'm down a man, we're managing. It will be so busy in the summer, though."

"Your eyes are sparkling at the prospect," his mother pointed out.

Colin just shrugged.

"I hope you're not too busy to hang some wallpaper this winter," Mrs. Turner added. "So many of my friends have admired the work you did in the parlor of my home, they all want to talk to you about custom designs."

Daisy beamed.

"Come on, you three!" Mrs. Bennett called from the other side of the room. "The babies won't sit with me forever, more's the pity, and I want to sing before they begin fussing for their mother."

" 'We will sing and bless this place,' " Daisy murmured, quoting their favorite play once again as they made their way to the seating area.

Colin winked at her. " 'Consecrate…and every chamber bless…with sweet peace.' "

The elder Bennetts, their sons, daughters-in-law and children perched on settees and sofas around the room. Their guests, the entire Turner family and Christopher's friend Vicar James Cary, with his wife Eliza and their seven-year-old son Ralph had joined them.

Hanging swags of greenery adorned with red bows decorated the room. A huge kissing bough of mistletoe and ribbons hung from the ceiling. A bushy evergreen, daintily dressed in glowing candles released its spicy fragrance into the evening air.

Julia Bennett, the benevolent matriarch of her family, looked radiant with her upswept red hair and vibrant green dress. She sat enthroned on an embroidered armchair, and Katerina's twins, now eight months old with drooly grins and wild wisps of dark hair, smiled on her lap.

Their mother, beaming despite the heavy fatigue crumpling her face, ran her fingers lightly over the harpsichord keys, playing a lilting tune to set the mood.

Her tension eased and a look of tired peace spread across her features.

Christopher and their daughter Sophia sat together on the sofa, with his brother Devin beside them. His dark-haired, olive-skinned wife, Harita—nicknamed Harry—sprawled on a chaise with their baby, who was closer to a year old, cuddled against her. The child squirmed wildly. As Daisy watched, the young mother released her toddler, setting her on the floor, where she stood clinging to the furniture and stroking her hand over the soft fabric. Harry ruffled her daughter's hair and smiled.

Mrs. Turner dropped into a seat beside her husband on the sofa. Their three daughters sat beside them; a tight fit, but they drew close without rancor, despite the youngest driving a teasing elbow into her sister's ribs.

Colin drew Daisy to the last unoccupied loveseat, and they perched there, indiscreetly close. She leaned her head against his shoulder.

"What carol shall we start with?" Katerina asked.

"I like 'Good Christian Men Rejoice,' " her husband suggested.

Katerina played a tricky prelude and then led into the hymn, starting the singing in her clear, sweet soprano. Christopher, his voice a husky, raspy bass, joined in, though most of his notes hit a bit south of expectations.

His brother joined in, more tuneful but higher, despite his towering size. His wife also sang, harmonizing in a minor key that Daisy had not expected. It sounded foreign and lovely. The three Turner girls joined in with practiced harmony, anchored by their parents who, while not professionals like Katerina, sounded good enough for the gathering.

Colin and Daisy also began to sing as well, and soon the entire room rang with music.

What a lovely family I've married into, Daisy reflected as one carol blended into another. *Both my husband's blood relations and his friends, who in their own way are no less our kin. So much nicer than my brute of a father and his stupid friend. I'm actually… happy, and I never knew I wasn't before. Life feels so vibrant. So bright. I have a home. Meaningful work. Friends. Family. This is real life.*

"Mother," Colin whispered, leaning over the arm of the seat, "I have to say…"

She turned to face him, pausing in her singing.

"I'm most disappointed. That tea you told Daisy to drink… it's failed already."

Mrs. Turner's eyebrows drew together. She looked confused for a moment, and then a stunned expression dropped her jaw and raised her eyes. "Do you mean… what? When?"

"I don't know when," he whispered back, "but Daisy's predicting a midsummer delivery. Will you be available?"

Mrs. Turner focused on Daisy.

She nodded, beaming.

"If Daisy wants me to attend, I will make time," she murmured. Then her face turned worried. "Are you… all right about this, son? It's a big change."

Colin's lips curled upwards. "Yes, Mother. We're quite happy. I've learned in the last half-year that change isn't necessarily a bad thing. When it involves Daisy, change might be surprising, but it's usually lovely."

Smiles all around, the three returning to their hymn singing just as Katerina launched into a majestic intro for "Hark, the Harald Angels Sing!" then "O Come, O Come Emmanuel" and last, "Silent Night."

Once the carol singing ended, and the group turned to confer.

"Dinner won't be for a couple more hours," Julia informed her guests. "Would anyone like to play a game?"

"I like hide and seek," Marjorie Turner girl offered.

Her sisters chorused agreement and little Sophia bounced to her feet, her black curls and the ribbons on her dress bouncing with excitement.

Katerina shuddered.

"Say it," her husband encouraged.

"Um, I've had a bad experience playing hide and seek and I've quite lost my taste for it, though you are all welcome to play if it's what you prefer. I'll stay here."

"I'll play!" Mrs. Cary offered. "In fact, I'll be 'it' this round. Off you dash!" She covered her eyes with her hands. "One, two, three."

The three adolescent Turners, Sophia and Ralph Cary raced for the door and disappeared into the Bennetts' spacious townhouse.

Devin Bennett and his wife glanced at each other.

"I'll watch over Maya," Mrs. Turner offered, "if you want to play."

That sufficed. Giggling like children, they ran for the door.

The two eldest couples regarded the remainder of the guests.

"I'll stay," Daisy said. "I'm not feeling all that well." She laid her hand on her belly, swallowing against the mild queasiness that overtook her from time to time. "Colin, you may go if you want. I won't feel neglected."

He shook his head. "I may not be as gloomy as I once was, but I lost my taste for childish frivolity long ago. I'll remain with you."

One of the twins began to fuss in his grandmother's lap. Katerina rose from the piano bench and retrieved the squalling boy, settling onto the settee and boosting him to her shoulder. He laid his head on her and settled instantly.

Daisy smiled at such a tender display of motherhood.

Christopher retrieved their other son and joined her, tugging her against his side.

"I'm so glad," Katerina said, turning to Colin, "that things have turned around for you."

"I'm certain your prayers played a role, Mrs. Bennett," he replied. "Thank you."

She smiled shyly.

Cary moved away from his spot and joined the new grouping of young adults. "How things have changed for us all. Remember when we all sat in my townhouse, drinking brandy and reading poetry, three single men with no thought of the future? Now, here we all are, married, fathers or soon-to-be fathers, and all our careers have fallen into place. We've been blessed, haven't we."

"That we have," Colin agreed.

In the Bennetts' comfortable home, surrounded by new friends and family, the man she loved, who had risked his life to protect her and who had pledged that life—willingly at last—to her, the tiny spark of life they'd created in love growing within her, Daisy couldn't wipe the smile from her face. *Sweet peace, to be sure. Heavenly peace.*

Author's note

Dear Readers,

Melancholia, called depression today, is one of the most insidious and prevalent of all mental illnesses. Characterized by sadness, loss of interest, insomnia or excessive sleep, appetite problems, intrusive thoughts and low self-esteem, depression can ruin lives. It's a major contributing factor to suicide. Depression can be chemical (caused by faulty 'wiring' if you will, in the brain) or it can be situational, caused by painful life events.

In Colin's case, he has mild hormonal depression, but the majority of his melancholia is caused by habitual sadness and stress. His father's abuse contributed to his intrusive thoughts, but just as Colin discovered, depression lies. To the sufferer, those lies feel absolutely true and real, and it's difficult to convince one's self that they're not. Replacing depression's lies with reality is one important step toward recovery for many people.

If you are suffering from depression, please know that your life is valuable. No, I don't know you personally (probably) but each and every human has intrinsic value. You are human; humans are valuable. Therefore, you are valuable. It's a simple syllogism. One that may sound completely foreign to you. But know that there can be help. Therapy. Journaling. Spending time with friends or in nature. Diet. Exercise and, yes, medication can all help a person with depression to create a new and meaningful life.

Need help? In the U.S. one place to start is the National Suicide Prevention Lifeline: 1-800-273-8255 or suicidepreventionlifeline.org. Or reach out to your doctor, therapist or emergency room. Call a friend or family member. Please don't hesitate to ask for help. Depression's lies are not worth your life.

Love Always, Simone Beaudelaire

Dear reader,

We hope you enjoyed reading Colin's Conundrum. Please take a moment to leave a review, even if it's a short one. Your opinion is important to us.

Discover more books by Simone Beaudelaire at https://www.nextchapter.pub/authors/simone-beaudelaire-romance-author

Want to know when one of our books is free or discounted? Join the newsletter at http://eepurl.com/bqqB3H

Best regards,

Simone Beaudelaire and the Next Chapter Team

You could also like:

Beautiful Rose by Simone Beaudelaire

To read the first chapter for free, please head to:
https://www.nextchapter.pub/books/beautiful-rose

About the Author

In the world of the written word, Simone Beaudelaire strives for technical excellence while advancing a worldview in which the sacred and the sensual blend into stories of people whose relationships are founded in faith, but are no less passionate for it. Unapologetically explicit, yet undeniably classy, Beaudelaire's 20+ novels aim to make readers think, cry, pray... and get a little hot and bothered.

In real life, the author's alter-ego teaches composition at a community college in a small western Kansas town, where she lives with her four children, three cats, and husband—fellow author Edwin Stark.

As both romance writer and academic, Beaudelaire devotes herself to promoting the rhetorical value of the romance in hopes of overcoming the stigma associated with literature's biggest female-centered genre.

Other Books by Simone Beaudelaire

When the Music Ends (The Hearts in Winter Chronicles Book 1)
When the Words are Spoken (The Hearts in Winter Chronicles Book 2)
Caroline's Choice (The Hearts in Winter Chronicles Book 3)
When the Heart Heals (The Hearts in Winter Chronicles Book 4)
The Naphil's Kiss
Blood Fever
Polar Heat
Xaman (with Edwin Stark)
Darkness Waits (with Edwin Stark)
Watching Over the Watcher
Baylee Breaking
Amor Maldito: Romantic Tragedies from Tejano Folklore
Keeping Katerina (The Victorians Book 1)
Devin's Dilemma (The Victorians Book 2)
Colin's Conundrum (The Victorians Book 3)
High Plains Promise (Love on the High Plains Book 2)
High Plains Heartbreak (Love on the High Plains Book 3)
High Plains Passion (Love on the High Plains Book 4)
Devilfire (American Hauntings Book 1)
Saving Sam (The Wounded Warriors Book 1 with J.M. Northup)
Justifying Jack (The Wounded Warriors Book 2 with J.M. Northup)
Making Mike (The Wounded Warriors Book 3 with J.M Northup)

Lightning Source UK Ltd.
Milton Keynes UK
UKHW041449030720
365951UK00007BA/255